Keri Arthur recently won the *Romantic Times* Career Achievement Award for Urban Fantasy and has been nominated in the Best Contemporary Paranormal category of the *Romantic Times* Reviewers' Choice Awards. She's a dessert and function cook by trade, and lives with her daughter in Melbourne, Australia.

Visit her website at www.keriarthur.com

D1142524

Destiny Kills

KERI ARTHUR

piatkus

PIATKUS

First published in the US in 2008 by Bantam Dell
A division of Random House Inc., New York
First published in Great Britain as a paperback original in 2011 by Piatkus

A CIP catalogue record for this book
is available from the British Library.

ISBN 978-0-7499-5302-7

Typeset in Garamond by M Rules
Printed in the UK by CPI Mackays, Chatham ME5 8TD

Piatkus
An imprint of
Little, Brown Book Group
100 Victoria Embankment
London EC4Y 0DY

An Hachette UK Company
www.hachette.co.uk

www.piatkus.co.uk

Acknowledgements

I'd like to thank:
Everyone at Bantam who helped make this book so good –
most especially my editor Anne, her assistant Josh, all the line
and copy editors who make sense of my Aussie English, and
finally Larry Rostant, the wonderful artist responsible for the
cover.

I'd also like to send a special thanks to:
My agent, Miriam, my wonderful crit buddies (the lulus),
Karenne (for all her hard work on the newsletter and the
forum), and last but not least, my ever-patient family.

Chapter One

S ome things I remembered.
    Some things I couldn't.

Like who I was.

Or why I was sitting naked on a beach next to a dead man.

And yet I knew why I was here. I was waiting for the dawn to give him a final kiss good-bye before she guided his soul on to its next life.

The breeze that curled around me was cold, as cold as the sand was harsh. And yet these sensations were a fleeting thing. Goose bumps might tremble across my skin, and sand might grate against my buttocks and thighs, but both failed to register on anything more than a flesh level. I felt no cold, no pain, no sorrow.

Nothing.

It was as if I were dead inside. As dead as the man lying beside me. Yet, for some reason, I was still breathing and he wasn't.

Why?

That was a question that haunted me, teasing the frozen edges of my thoughts and memories.

Why him and not me?

I didn't know, I just didn't know, and yet I knew it was a question that was important. I knew my life might well depend on the answer.

I drew my knees close to my chest and studied the distant horizon. Though dawn had yet to stain night's cover, it was coming. Already its warm power vibrated across the air, an eager humming that was both familiar and alien. I didn't understand the sensation, didn't know the reason behind it, and yet the mere fact that I could feel it had relief sweeping through me.

It was frustrating, this not knowing. Not remembering.

I let my gaze move across the ocean, watching the waves roll lazily toward the sand, seeing nothing out there in the vast expanse of white-capped blueness. No ship. No boat. No pursuit.

But I didn't bother questioning why I was expecting any of those things, because the past remained hidden under a blanket that was almost absolute.

Almost.

I rubbed a hand across eyes that felt like they'd cried a thousand tears, then glanced down at the body of my friend. I might not remember my own name, but I knew his. Egan Jamieson. Not only my friend, but also my guardian, my lover, and a man to whom I owed a debt more important than life itself.

He'd saved me.

He'd given me freedom at the cost of his own.

The need for revenge welled deep and fast and furious, until I was all but shaking with it. They would pay for this. Whoever they were, they would pay.

For Egan.

For all of us.

And it was a vow that was useless unless I could damn well remember who, exactly, I needed to take revenge upon.

I grimaced and returned my gaze to Egan. In the fading moonlight, his skin seemed to glow with a rich warmth, as if the sun itself still burned beneath his flesh. A birthmark marred his back, a snakelike stain that seemed to dive into his skin and out again, until it almost seemed coiled around his spine. In the night, it took on a reddish-gold appearance and contained a sheen oddly reminiscent of scales.

I shifted and ran a gentle finger down the mark. It was cool and leathery compared to his skin, as if it were indeed scales. Mine was all blues and greens and silvers, as if the brightness of a sunlit sea danced upon the surface of my skin. An inheritance from my mother, not my father.

I blinked at the thought, then grabbed it hard and tried to follow it back. But the fog of forgetfulness snapped in place, and all that was left were questions.

Yet more fucking questions.

I blew out a breath, then stretched out my left leg as the throb of pain finally began to impinge on my senses. There were scrapes across my kneecaps, and deeper cuts down my shins, accompanied by darkening patches that indicated bruising. But none of the wounds were currently bleeding, and there was no blood dried against my skin.

I glanced at the sea. No footprints marred the pristine sands. Not for as far as I could see. Nor were there any vehicle tracks of any kind. Though I guess with the tide coming in, none of that was really surprising.

But still, I had a feeling we'd come from the sea, that my skin bore no stain of blood because it had long since been washed away. That the wounds themselves were clean and healing rather than festering because of the saltwater.

I let my gaze follow the gentle curve of the beach until it reached the distance point. No lighthouse, no buildings of any kind, no indication of movement or life. Nothing to say where we were.

Maybe we were both dead. Maybe this was nothing more

than the dream of waiting that came before the soul moved on to the next life.

I glanced down at Egan. I knew if I rolled him off his stomach, I'd see the bloody stain in the sand. See what remained of his chest after those bastards shot him.

I closed my eyes and pushed the resulting images away. There were some things I didn't *want* to remember, and the way he'd struggled to survive and remain free was one of them.

And yet, while he might have fought them to the very end, he'd done it for my sake. He'd once said that for all intents and purposes, he was a dead man, so why did anything matter? I didn't understand it at the time he'd said it, and now I never would get the chance to do so.

The hum in the air intensified. Energy danced across my skin, a crazy tingling that warmed the chill from my soul. I studied the horizon, waiting, as the hum of power crescendoed and slivers of red and gold suddenly broke across the sky. Warmth began to flood through my body, as if the rising of the dawn was also a rebirth of my emotional and sensory centers. A stupid thought, really, when I was just at home in deep, dark waters that had never seen the sun, never known warmth . . .

God, it was so damn *frustrating* getting little snippets and hints here and there but never any real, definitive answers or memories.

I drew my knees close again, ignoring the slivers of pain and the blood that began to trickle down one leg, watching as the sunlight spread, smothering the stars and warming the night from the sky.

Watching as the growing light gradually flushed across Egan's unmoving body.

The warmth still radiating under his skin seemed to stir as the daylight caressed him, growing brighter as the day did, until the intensity made my eyes water and forced me to look away.

Still the heat and the brightness grew, until my own skin glowed under its radiance. But flesh was not designed to contain such heated iridescence for long, especially when that skin no longer belonged to a living, breathing soul. As the light broke free, reaching skyward with exuberant fingers, tears began to trickle down my cheeks.

'May the Gods of sun and sky and air guide you on your journey, my friend,' I whispered, my voice croaky, hinting at long disuse. 'And may you find in the next life what you could not in this.'

Then the radiance caressing my skin began to die, taking with it the underlying hum of energy. Day had broken. It was only those in-between times – first light or twilight – that held the moments of great power.

There was nothing left of Egan. Nothing except the stain of blood on the sand and an odd glint of silver. His ring.

I reached out and carefully plucked it free from its resting place. In the growing sunlight, the rubies shimmering in the coiled serpent's eyes glowed like fire. It had always sent a shiver down my spine, this ring, despite the obvious workmanship and beauty.

When I'd asked him about it, Egan's golden eyes had grown somber. 'It belongs to a man who once took something very precious from me,' he'd said, and in his normally calm tones there'd been an undercurrent that was an odd mix of anger and heartache. 'So I took something very precious from him.' And then he'd given me a cold, hard smile and added, 'But I will return it. When the time is right.'

I closed my fingers around the serpent, pressing the cold metal into my palm. I might not be able to do anything else for Egan, but I could do this. Find the ring's owner and return it. And perhaps along the way discover its history and the reasons why Egan had murder on his mind.

Because it was an odd desire for a man who claimed nothing mattered anymore.

I pushed upright. A dozen different aches came to life, and weakness trembled through my limbs, the sort of weakness that came from long hours of constant activity. My gaze went to the ocean, leaping across the waves to the distant horizon.

Somewhere out there lay the answers.

Somewhere out there lay my home.

But until the fog encasing my memories cleared, I could not blindly walk out into the sea and just start swimming. The ocean was a vast and often angry being, and I could not tempt her waters without a destination in mind.

It was a thought that raised my eyebrows. I might not be dead, but madness was surely a possibility. I mean, what sane, rational mind contemplated swimming *oceans?*

I did.

Because I could. Because I had.

I rubbed my forehead wearily, aware for the first time of the slight ache behind my eyes. Maybe when it went, my memories would fully return. Maybe then I'd know what sort of creature contemplated swimming the oceans as easily as a bird might fly.

Because whatever I was, it wasn't human. That was a belief I felt deep in my bones, deep in my soul.

But until memory resurfaced, one thing was certain. I couldn't stand here naked and exposed on a beach. The mere fact that someone had blown a hole through Egan's chest suggested that someone would rather see us dead than free. And that, in turn, meant they'd surely be looking for me.

I turned around. Rugged cliffs ranged high above the pristine sands, lining and isolating the long sweep of beach. There were trails – paths made by the passage of feet over time, meaning this place, wherever it was, was at least reachable. Which meant there surely had to be some sort of city or town or at least a dwelling nearby.

The first thing I needed was clothing – simply because the last thing I needed was to attract attention.

I glanced over my shoulder, studying the rolling waves for a moment, then resolutely made my way to the cliffs and the nearest trail.

No one but goddamn goats had been using *that* particular trail, let me tell you.

I was sweating, shaking, and wheezing by the time I finally got to the top. I leaned my hands on my aching knees, sucking in great gulps of air as I studied the surrounding countryside.

The slope rolled down to a small cottage. The area around the cottage wasn't fenced, and a blue car sat out front, indicating that someone was home. Beyond the house, the slope rose again, and the tops of pine trees were evident behind it.

I glanced back at the house. The cottage didn't look big enough to be a permanent residence, so maybe it was one of those places vacationers rented out short term. I hoped so, because vacationers were more likely to go out for the day, leaving their possessions – or, more particularly, their clothes – unprotected.

Of course, to steal their clothes, I first had to get there. Right now, collapsing in a heap seemed a much better option.

I blew out a breath and forced my feet down the grassy slope.

My legs protested the activity, and warmth began to trickle down not only my shin but the side of my face as well. I swiped at it with a hand, and it came away bloody.

Maybe Egan wasn't the only one who'd sustained serious injury. And a decent blow to the head would certainly explain the gaps in my memory.

I rubbed my hand down my thigh and kept on walking. What else could I do? I was in the middle of goddamn nowhere, with no idea who I was or how I'd gotten here. And no idea who I could trust. *If* I could trust.

As the slope flattened, the grass became long enough to brush my butt. Which in turn made me wonder if the grass was actually long, or if I was short. I *felt* long – long and rangy – but self-perception is an odd thing when the memory can give no references. I held my hands out and studied them critically.

Dirt-covered as they were from scrambling up the goat trail, they were still somewhat elegant – all long and slender. Neither my fingers nor my palms had calluses of any kind, so I obviously didn't do anything too strenuous for a living. A fact backed up by the length of my nails – or at least what remained of them after the climb.

I glanced down at my feet. There was nothing elegant about *those*. Given their length and width, they could be described only as paddles. Getting shoes had to be hell.

The thought intrigued me for some reason, and I stopped to

lift a foot. Thick, hardened soles. Obviously, I didn't wear shoes all that often, if *that* foot was anything to go by.

A door slammed, and laughter ran across the meadow. I dropped to my knees, my bruised left leg hitting a rock and making me wince. Two people emerged from the cottage, the woman still laughing and touching her companion. *Newlyweds*, I thought, for no particular reason.

They climbed into the blue car sitting in the driveway, the man opening and closing the door for the woman before getting into the driver's side and driving off.

On the right-hand side of the road. And though three quarters of the world drove on that side, I was suddenly sure that I was in America. Which in itself wasn't much help, because America was a damn big country, but at least it was a starting point.

I waited until they were out of sight, then rose and made my way quickly toward the house. The front door was locked, as was the back. But a window along the side was open enough to slide a hand in and push off the screen. After that, it was a simple matter of pushing up the window and sliding in.

Which I did. I hit the floor with an awkward thump and sat there listening, waiting to see if there was anyone else in the house. Which is something I should have done *before* I started breaking in.

Obviously, I could cross 'thief' off my list of possible past professions. Unless, of course, I was a very bad thief.

The only sound to be heard was the soft ticking of a clock. The air was still, and smelled faintly of age and lavender. This particular room had been made up as a bedroom, but the bed was a single and obviously unused. Which probably meant I wouldn't find anything in the wardrobe or small dresser. I checked them anyway. Nothing but mothballs.

I walked to the door, my footsteps echoing noisily on the polished floorboards. The room directly opposite was a bathroom, complete with an old claw-foot bath and a shower big enough for two. The main bedroom sat to my right, and the kitchen to my left down the end of the hall.

I glanced back at the bathroom, eyeing the shower and wondering how much time I had. Surely enough to get cleaned up. I could no more run around looking like something the sea had coughed up than I could run around naked. Not if I wanted to avoid detection.

Besides, I might not have noticed the bite of the sand when I was sitting on it, but I sure as hell did now, and it was *nasty*.

'Stop with the excuses,' I muttered, even as I wondered if dithering was a habit of mine.

I marched into the bathroom. After a quick, hot shower that seemed to uncover a dozen more cuts and bruises, I toweled myself dry, then moved across to the mirror.

It was an odd feeling, seeing a face I knew was mine and yet having no memories to correlate to the fact. The loss was so complete that part of me wondered if I'd *ever* been in front of a mirror.

My face was lean and angular, with a nose that was almost too big and a mouth that looked prone to dimples. My eyes were the green of a deep ocean, framed by long lashes that were as black as my hair. Under the bright bathroom light, highlights of dark green and blue seemed to play through the black, as if the sea itself had kissed it.

My gaze moved to the massive black-and-purple bruise smeared from my temple to my cheek. Someone had hit me *really* hard. Hard enough to split my skull open. The bruise, and the almost-healed three-inch gash on my head, proved that. It could also explain why my memory was working in fits and starts.

But what on earth had I done to deserve such treatment?

For the first time since waking on the beach beside Egan, I felt scared. Scared of the past I couldn't remember, scared of where the future might lead.

Scared of the fury that lay waiting deep inside me.

I rubbed my arms. In the mirror, Egan's ring gleamed, the rubies afire with life as my hands moved up and down. A shiver ran down my spine. I didn't like this ring, didn't like its touch against my skin. It never seemed to warm up, as if its metal soul was as cold and as unforgiving as the waters underneath the arctic ice.

I frowned at the thought, then pushed it away as I headed into the main bedroom. A quick search through the woman's clothes revealed an inclination toward skimpy and revealing. She was also several inches shorter than me, and the skirts that would have been minuscule on her were positively indecent on me.

I tried several combinations of track pants and tops, but they all clung too tight, making me feel oddly restricted. Eventually, I settled on a loose pair of black pants that fit me more like three-quarter-length shorts, and a blue sweatshirt that showed off plenty of midriff, and left my thieving at that. Anything else she might miss.

I padded down the hall to the kitchen, which turned out to be a combined kitchen-living area. After peering through a curtained window to see if I was still safe and alone, I flicked on the TV, changing the channel until I found the news, then walked across to the fridge. Opening the door revealed a nice selection of drinks, including Coke with lime. Very cool. I grabbed a bottle of that, as well as enough stuff to make a hefty sandwich, then dumped it all on the kitchen counter and began putting it together. I might be able to live for several weeks without food, but I'd grown used to eating every day . . .

The thought trailed off into nothingness, and I swore softly. With a little more force than necessary, I thumped the top slice of bread onto the sandwich, then squashed it down and cut it.

After finding a plate, I grabbed my Coke and walked across to a chair to watch the news. Hell, maybe I'd get lucky and find out what part of the damned country I was in.

'And in overseas news this week,' the anchorman said, his tone one of false charm anchormen the world over seemed trained to use, 'scientists from the Loch Ness Research Foundation are today refuting the many monster sightings that have been reported over the last week. Dr. James Marsten had this to say . . .'

The picture flicked to a craggy-faced, gray-haired man, and something within me stirred. It was something more than recognition. Something stronger.

Hate.

The type of hate built on a foundation of fear. Years and years of fear.

'As much as I might wish otherwise,' he said, 'our findings do not reflect or confirm these so-called sightings. Quite the opposite, in fact. Our sonars and sensors have picked up no unusual movements in the loch. If anything bigger than an eel had swam through these waters, believe me, we would have recorded it.'

The anchor came back, but I didn't hear anything he said because I was too busy staring at the picture of the scientist frozen on the screen behind him. Fury rose, until my hand was shaking so hard I had to put the bottle of Coke down. *He* was the cause of all this. And I wished he were dead so badly I could practically taste it.

The sheer depth of what I was feeling was scary, but at least it gave me some sort of starting point. You had to know someone pretty well to hate *and* fear them that much, and that meant Marsten was someone I had better find out more about.

Other news reports came on, and the anger began to fade. I munched on my sandwich, watching but not learning anything more than the fact that I was definitely in America.

I sighed and took a final swig of Coke to empty the bottle. Watching the news for information had been a long shot, at best, but at least it *had* given me someplace to start. Though how I was going to find out more information about Marsten without him finding me again ...

The thought faded. Frustration swirled through me as I picked up my plate and headed back to the kitchen.

Outside, a door slammed, and my heart just about crashed through my chest. I dumped the plate and Coke bottle in the sink, then ran to the nearest window and peered out.

The newlyweds were home.

And a cop had come back with them.

Chapter Two

Fear froze me to the spot for too many valuable seconds. But the sound of the key scraping in the lock got my big feet moving, and I ran like hell for the second bedroom.

'Del, did you leave the TV on?' The voice was male, and he spoke in a slow drawl that had me visualizing a cowboy.

'Jack, you saw me turn it off,' a woman answered. 'Why?'

'Because it's now on and there's a mess all over the kitchen counter.' The man known as Jack paused. 'It looks like someone has been in here. You want to call the officer back? He wouldn't be that far along the beach path yet.'

The bedroom door creaked as I swung it closed. My breath caught in my throat, but I didn't dare stop to find out if anyone else had heard it. With my heart pounding like a jackhammer,

I ran to the window, shimmied my way out, then reached back in to grab the screen.

'You folks got trouble?' a new voice said.

I swore softly and abandoned my attempt to get the screen back in place, scooting instead along the side of the house and around the corner.

Not a moment too soon.

'Window's open in the second bedroom, and the screen has been pushed out,' the gruff voice said.

'Couldn't have been the wind,' came the other man's comment. 'I checked them when we first arrived. It was on solid.'

'You want to see if anything has been taken? I'll look outside.'

Oh, crap.

I looked about frantically for somewhere close to hide, but there didn't seem to be much about. I sucked in a breath, then ran like hell for the long grass and the not-so-distant hillside. If I could get over the crest, I'd at least be out of sight. Of course, plowing through the long grass would leave a trail for all to see, but right now, that couldn't be helped. The last thing I needed was to be caught by a small-town cop.

And I had no idea why I needed to avoid the cops or capture. It was just a feeling. A certainty that capture, in any form, was a very bad thing.

Because of the past. Because of that scientist.

I bit down frustration and tried to concentrate on the here and now. Footsteps began to echo on the wooden patio, so I threw myself down behind the hill and prayed like hell that the grass hid my body.

For too many seconds I didn't move, hardly even dared to breathe, as I listened to the gentle sounds of the day, waiting for the footsteps that would mean my doom.

When they didn't immediately come, I carefully shifted and peeked up over the hill. I might not have heard the footsteps, but the damn cop was coming up the hill anyway.

I swore under my breath and wriggled back down the hill. When I'd moved far enough down, I rose and ran. But there was nowhere to go, nowhere to hide. The thick, regimented strands of pines would have provided excellent cover, but they were just too far away. And the only thing between them and me was a small dam.

It would have to do.

I ran toward it as fast as I could. Quite a few yards out I found a cattle track and followed that thankfully. At least the soil was hard and compacted, and wouldn't show any footprints. Hopefully, the cop would think I'd simply disappeared rather than suspect I'd hidden in the water.

As I neared the dam, I risked a look over my shoulder at the hilltop. Still no cop. I had time yet, but probably not a whole lot. I shucked off my stolen sweatshirt as I sprinted around the water, throwing it behind the dam's erosion-rutted shoulder, then did the same with the pants. If luck was on my side, I'd at least have dry clothes to climb into once the cop had left. If not, well, I'd have to find something else to steal.

I dove into the water. It was so damn cold it snatched a gasp from my throat, and the sound seemed to echo across the softer sounds of the day. I swam to the far edge and peered through the reeds and grass at the hillside. The cop had breached the top of the hill and was following my trail down toward the dam.

I took a deep breath and slid under the water. An odd sensation ran across my eyes – it felt for all the world as if some sort of film was being drawn over them. It made me blink, and in that moment I realized I could *see* under the water. It might have appeared muddy as hell from the surface, but I could see the bottom through the muck, see the water beetles and insect larvae swimming through it. Hell, even the banks and the sky were as clear as could be.

It was probably a pointer to what I was, but it was one I didn't understand. Nor did I have time to contemplate it, because the cop suddenly walked into sight.

I floated under the water, watching the cop and hoping like hell that being able to see him so plainly was just a weird aberration, and not any sort of indication that the water had magically gone clear.

The cop was a big man – big in an overweight sort of way –

but even so, he reminded me a little of a boxer. He moved light, like a man ready for action. His face was on the paunchy side, too, his cheeks veined and nose red. But his blue eyes were sharp and clear, and however out of shape his body might appear, those eyes suggested there was nothing flabby about his mind.

He stood on the bank and stared at the water, then the surrounds. His expression was dour, unhappy, his gaze continually returning to the water. Meaning he probably suspected I was here, and was waiting for me to surface.

How long could I hold my breath? I guess I was about to find out.

He waited, and I waited. After a while, he unclipped the small radio from his belt, pressed a button, and said, 'Frank to base.'

The answer was little more than a buzz of sound to my ears. He said, 'No, I haven't had a chance to look for bodies on the beach yet. We've got another break-in, this time over at the Doughertys' cabin.' He paused briefly, listening, then added, 'Yeah, it's the newlyweds. You want to get Mike to bring the dogs out? We got a trail, but it ends at the old dam.'

Great. Someone had not only seen us on the beach, but they'd reported it to the cops. And it was just plain bad luck that I'd been in the cabin when the newlyweds and the cop had arrived back.

21

'I'm not sure what's been stolen. The cocky bastard helped himself to a sandwich and some Coca-Cola, though.' He paused, listening. 'Yeah, they're both fine. I'll write up a list of what's missing, and wait for Mike. You might want to get young Aaron out here to check out the beach, though. It's going to be a while before I get the chance.'

He paused again, then grinned. 'Yeah, I know the old coot was drinking, but we still gotta check it out.'

He snapped the radio back onto his belt, then glanced at his watch. Seconds passed into minutes. He didn't move, I didn't move, and somewhere deep inside, curiosity grew.

Regular people couldn't hold their breath for *this* long. I might not be 'regular' as humans defined the word, but my lungs weren't even burning and yet I had to have been under the water for a good five minutes. Even free divers couldn't stay under water that long, could they?

But I guess that for someone who contemplated swimming oceans, someone who could compare the coldness of a ring to the waters under the arctic ice, floating in dam water like it was a second home might well be easy.

God, why wouldn't my memories just damn well *return*? Tell me who I was? *What* I was?

And why wouldn't the cop *leave*?

He stood there for another minute or so, then finally turned around and made his way up the hill. I waited until he'd disappeared from my watery sight, then slowly rose up until my head was free of the murk. I blinked, and that odd sensation happened again. It definitely felt like something was being drawn across my eyes.

A tremor ran through me. I licked my lips, tasting the muck in the water, knowing that if I wanted to, I could name the minute particles that ran across my tongue. Part of me was desperate to remember the reason behind the skill. The rest of me just wanted to get the hell out of here.

When the cop had finally disappeared, I got out of the water, scooped up my clothes, and ran for trees. I had no idea where I was going, but the property's road seemed to head in the same direction as the line of firs, so maybe the main road was up that way. There had to be a town somewhere close by, because the newlyweds hadn't been gone all that long before they'd come back.

With a cop who'd actually come to investigate the report of a body on the beach. Which they wouldn't find, because Egan was long gone, but they would probably discover the blood-soaked sand where he'd lain, and that in itself might be enough to bring out more hunters.

I *had* to get to Maine.

Had to see my dad before it was too late, and tell him . . .

The thought faded, and I resisted the urge to scream. What was so important that I'd crossed continents and risked the life of a rare friend to tell my dad?

I blinked at the thought, then kicked the soil savagely. And only succeeded in stubbing my toe hard enough to feel like I'd broken it. I cursed and hobbled on.

By the time I hit the trees, my body was a little drier and I was able to dress. I wrung out the remaining water from my hair, and half-wished I had something to tie it back with. It was only just over shoulder length, but that was long enough to be bothersome when running.

I twisted it into a knot instead, knowing it wouldn't hold long, then continued on my way. Twigs and leaves rustled under my bare feet, and in the shadows of the pines, the day was cool. Insects buzzed lightly, but little else stirred. After a while, the drone of traffic began to invade the peacefulness, and I slowed cautiously.

Ahead, the tree line came to a sudden halt. Beyond that was a short run of grass to a fence, then what had to be a main road, given the traffic that passed by regularly.

I had no money, no identity, and no clue as to where I was. And no way of getting out of this area quickly. Which meant my best option for the moment was hitching. I could worry about finding a way to Maine once I knew where the hell my starting point was.

Of course, getting someone to pick me up when I was barefoot, wild of hair, and looking a little worse for the wear was easier said than done.

After half an hour of less than stellar results, I was getting more than a little frustrated, so when the red Ford crested the distant rise and zoomed down toward me, I marched into the middle of the road and held out a hand.

I swear to the Gods of sea and sand, the driver gunned the engine rather than slowing, and the car rocketed toward me. The roar of the motor seemed to fill the air, and my stomach began to churn. I licked my lips, but stood my ground. Damn it, I needed help, and the bastard in *that* car was at least going to stop and listen. Or rather, listen to a rather creative lie, because who actually knew the truth?

As I stood there staring at the car, silently demanding it stop, another sound edged through to my consciousness. The baying of dogs.

The cop had called for tracker dogs at the dam. While I hadn't seen any police cars go by, that didn't mean anything. There could be a hundred different roads into that property that I didn't know about. And while those dogs might *not* actually be hunting me, I really couldn't take that chance. Which meant it was more important than ever that this car stop.

As the vehicle grew closer, the blur that was the driver gradually clarified into a broad-shouldered man with sun-kissed brown hair. I could see his strong hands on the wheel, see the almost insolent grin twisting his lips.

And realized I was facing a man playing chicken.

I might not want to get caught by the cops, but I sure as hell didn't want to die, and that's what faced me if I stood my ground any longer. I threw myself sideways, hitting the side of the road hard, skinning my palms and the tops of my feet as I slid to a long stop in the dirt and stones. Heard the screech of brakes and twisted around to see the car slew to a stop only feet away.

The idiot could have *killed* me. If I had stood there a moment longer, he probably would have. He'd only missed me by inches as it was.

I closed my eyes and took several deep breaths to try to calm myself down. A hard task when I was shaking like a leaf. My hands and feet were stinging, and my heart was beating like crazy.

Behind me, a car door opened, then footsteps approached. 'What the fuck are you playing at, lady?'

Even with the anger so evident in his rich, deep tones, the stranger's voice was as sexy as all get out.

Not the sort of thoughts any *sane* person would be having about the man who'd just tried to run them over.

'Me?' I said, voice little more than a squeak thanks to a mix of annoyance and pain. 'You're the idiot who apparently forgot where the brake pedal was.'

I tried pushing upright, but that forced more stones into my already scraped hands, and I yelped.

He muttered something under his breath, then stepped closer. 'Here, let me help you.'

Before I could even open my mouth to say don't bother, a rather large pair of feet appeared on either side of me, then hands grabbed me under the armpits and he unceremoniously hauled me upright.

Only his touch had my senses exploding, and suddenly, dizzyingly, I was hyperaware of everything about him – the warm lean strength of his body, his spicy scent, his aura of confidence and sheer masculinity. It all swirled around me, filling every breath, caressing every pore, setting my skin afire, and making my blood burn.

I didn't even *know* this man. Hadn't even turned around to look at him. And yet my body was reacting to him in a way it had *never* reacted to Egan.

Maybe I'd hit my head on the road, as well, and just didn't realize it.

He dumped me on my feet, then quickly stepped back, making me wonder if he'd had a reaction similar to mine.

'You okay?' he asked, voice gruff and still as sexy as hell.

'No thanks to you,' I muttered, picking out the larger stones from my hands before turning around. A gaze as blue as the summer sky met mine, and something deep inside quivered.

Partly because no matter how pretty those eyes were, there was only cold calculation beyond the surface depths. These were the eyes of a man who knew what he wanted and exactly how to get it. But more than that, there was a wildness in them that was both familiar and yet alien. A wildness that spoke of sun and sky and air, and had absolutely nothing to do with humanity.

Egan had that look, I thought. Now, if I could just remember what Egan actually was, that would be handy.

But recognizing a similar wildness didn't actually mean I could trust this man. After all, many of our hunters had shared that same untamed look.

Of course, *that* thought came and went with no further clarification.

'Why the hell didn't you slow down when you first saw me?'

He waved a hand in the general direction of the still-idling car, his voice incredulous as he said, 'I was doing sixty. Why in the hell would you just stand there? That's insane.'

Yep, it was. But this day had gone to hell anyway, so what did one more act of madness matter? Besides, he did stop, so at least I'd achieved part of my aim.

'I needed a lift, and no one was stopping.'

'Considering the less than appealing way you look, I'm not entirely surprised.'

'That's no damn reason to try and run me over,' I muttered, tucking thick strands of matted hair behind my ear.

A smile tugged at his lips, and it transformed his face, lending his aristocratic features a brief moment of warmth and compassion.

Then the warmth faded and he considered me, his gaze lingering on the bruise marring my forehead before moving down. It was deliberate, that gaze, designed to tease, to arouse. To scare, even. Like he was testing me. Testing my seriousness. Only it stopped abruptly when his gaze reached my hands. 'Nice ring.'

The sexiness had fled his voice, replaced by a flatness that made my toes itch with the need to run. I resisted the urge to tuck my hand behind my back, and said, 'It's a friend's.'

His gaze went past me, searching the trees. 'And where is the friend?'

I hesitated. 'Elsewhere.'

The baying of a hound ran across the brief silence, and I glanced over my shoulder. I couldn't see any movement, but those barks – and obviously my hunters – were getting closer.

His gaze came back to mine. 'Then why don't we go find him?'

Wariness swirled through me. *Don't trust, don't trust.* The mantra ran through my brain, words from a past I had yet to remember. 'And why would you want to do that?'

'Because if you're willing to risk your life standing in front of a speeding car to get help, your friend obviously needs a lot of it.'

I studied him, not entirely sure what to do. True, I needed help, but did I need it badly enough to trust a stranger who suddenly seemed overly eager to help out two people he didn't even know?

Of course, Egan was beyond anyone's help – and I might just suffer the same fate if I wasn't careful. They were out there, and they were hunting me.

And this stranger could be one of them, for all I knew.

Suddenly my idea of stopping a car to get help didn't seem so bright after all.

'I don't think—'

He laughed, a sound so soft, and yet so cold. 'You have no idea who I am, do you?'

Meaning I should? 'Other than the man who just tried to run me down, you mean?'

He snorted softly. 'Yeah.'

I frowned and tried to force a memory through the fog. He *did* remind me a whole lot of Egan – he had the same broad-shouldered, athletic build and shaggy, sun-kissed hair. But this man's face was more aristocratic and a whole lot handsomer. And there was an odd sort of grace and elegance to his movements. Egan, for all his gentleness, had often resembled a bull in a china shop.

But then, in all the time I'd known him, he hadn't really seemed to care about anything at all.

Except for me.

And the kids.

Tears touched my eyes again, but with them came anger. And I had no idea why, because the answers to all my questions were still locked behind the walls of forgetfulness.

I glanced down at my somewhat bloodied feet and blinked the tears away. Whatever the reasons behind the anger, it was an undeniable fact that I hadn't deserved Egan's caring. I'd liked him, I'd enjoyed being with him, and I'd slept with him – but it had never been anything more than that. Not for me.

And not for him.

Yet he'd still given his life for me.

Nothing could ever repay such selflessness.

Nothing except stopping this. Stopping Marsten.

I looked back at the stranger. 'No. Who are you?'

'Egan's brother.'

I blinked. Of all the answers I'd been expecting, *that* certainly wasn't one of them. And it made me even more wary. 'Egan hasn't got a brother.'

'Egan has three brothers, two sisters, and one half brother. That last one's me.' His gaze went past me again as the hound barked, closer than before. 'That dog seems to have found the scent of whatever it's chasing. You want to stay, or do you want to go?'

I hesitated, but really, what choice did I have? It was either stay here and confront the police – try to explain why I wore stolen clothes, and had no ID and no memory – or go with this man who could be spinning me more lies than a used-car salesman desperate to close a deal.

'They're almost on us,' he prompted.

'Let's go. Please.'

'Good decision. Come on.' He grabbed my arm and pulled me forward, the heat of his fingers seeming to burn through the sleeve of my sweatshirt and brand my skin. He opened the car door, then ran around to the driver's side.

A prickle of awareness ran down my spine, and without turning around, I knew we were no longer alone on the road.

'Oh, fuck,' the stranger said, about the same time as another voice said, 'Hey, you two, stop right there.'

'Get in,' the stranger said. 'Quickly.'

I wasn't about to argue. I got in as fast as I could, then slammed the door.

'Police. Stop,' the other voice called.

I looked around, saw the big cop accompanied by another man wearing a checkered shirt and holding two dogs in check. Then the stranger gunned the big car's engine, and we were speeding off.

'Thank you,' I said, after a few moments.

'Forget it,' he said, his voice holding an edge. 'But why are they chasing you?'

'I broke into a house to get some clothes.'

'And that outfit was the best you could come up with? Lady, you make a pretty poor thief.'

'It wasn't as if I had a whole lot of choice,' I muttered. 'And what would you know about thieving, anyway?'

'A whole lot more than you, apparently.'

He glanced in the rearview mirror and swore softly. I twisted around. The cop had the radio to his mouth. He was either calling in the troops or calling in the registration. Either way, too much heat would soon be swarming around my hard-won ride.

'Look, I don't want to get you into trouble—'

'Well, good, because I can manage that quite well by myself.'

'If you'd just drop me off at the nearest town—'

'And you'll what?' He glanced at me briefly. 'You appear to have no clothes, no money, not even shoes, for God's sake. Besides, you're not the only thief in the car.'

I raised my eyebrows, not entirely sure whether he was being serious or not. 'Really?'

'Yes.'

He glanced at the mirror again and his expression grew grimmer. I took another look behind us. The cop was climbing into a squad car – obviously, *that's* what he'd been calling. The stranger's car seemed to leap forward, the engine a howl that filled the interior with ear-splitting noise. Either he really *was* a madman, or he was speaking the truth about being a thief.

'You're not the man who's been breaking into various houses around these parts, are you?'

He snorted softly. 'No.' He glanced briefly at the rearview. 'Where's Egan, Destiny?'

Shock rolled through me and, for a moment, all I could do was stare at him. *Destiny.* It felt right, that name, felt comfortable.

Question was, how did he know it? Had I stepped into an even worse situation than being chased by the cops? God, *was* he one of the hunters?

I licked my lips, and repeated, 'Elsewhere.'

'Where? Damn it, tell me where my brother is!'

'Why should I?' The retort came out before I could really think about it, but I was growing more and more convinced that I'd made the biggest mistake yet by getting into this car. 'How do I know you're really even his brother?'

'I haven't exactly got time right now to stop and show you my credentials,' he said coldly.

'Well, until you do, you get nothing from me.' I crossed my arms and stared out the windshield. The trees were zipping past way too fast, making my stomach feel queasy. Looking at him seemed a better option. 'How did you even know he was back in the country?' And how did he know we'd be here? That was just too weird a coincidence, and another reason to be wary.

'He contacted me last night.'

He had? How, when he'd died last night? 'Why did he contact you?'

His gaze met mine. The cold depths were assessing. Distrusting. 'We were supposed to meet in Florence. So what happened?'

'Florence? Where the hell is that?'

'Oregon.'

So I was in Oregon? God, that was a country away from Maine. And if I needed to get *there* so urgently, why would I have even agreed to come here?

And how did he know about me? Even if he *had* somehow talked to Egan before he'd died, I doubted Egan would have told him much about me. We were both too aware of the need for secrecy.

'How did he contact you?'

'If you knew anything at all about Egan, then you'd know how he contacted me.' He gave me another one of those cold glances. 'Unless, of course, you really are a thief, and the police are after you because you stole Egan's ring.'

Again the shock rolled through me, but this time it was accompanied by a sick churning in my stomach. 'What makes you think this is Egan's ring?'

35

He smiled, and this time it was a cold, harsh thing to behold. 'Egan had that ring on his hand the last time I saw him.'

'You know, I find it very strange that Egan never mentioned having siblings, let alone a half brother, in the ten years I was with him.'

Even as I said the words, sadness washed through me. Ten years was a long time to be with someone you could never love. But it wasn't as if we'd had any other choice. We'd been locked up, caged like animals. The two of us, my mom, and the little ones – some of them barely more than toddlers who had never really known the freedom of the skies . . .

The memories faded yet again. I flexed my fingers and resisted the urge to scream.

'That's the second time you've used past tense,' he said softly. 'Why?'

I briefly closed my eyes. God, I was an idiot. Yet now that he'd picked up on the mistake, part of me desperately wanted to blurt it all out – all the confusion, all the pain. I needed someone to talk to, someone to confide in. Someone to be what Egan had been to me.

Someone to end up dead just like him?

Besides, no matter how good it would feel to confide in someone – anyone – about the stuff I could remember and the stuff I couldn't, the truth was that I didn't know if I could even trust this man. His sudden appearance seemed a little too convenient. And hell, trusting a stranger was what had landed me in this whole mess in the first place. I'd lost eleven years of my life thanks to that mistake, and I wasn't about to repeat it.

Maybe I was being a little paranoid, but without the benefit of memories, I was working blind, and the urge for caution was humming through my bloodstream.

I couldn't end up caged again.

I *wouldn't* end up caged again.

'Slip of the tongue,' I said, twisting around to look behind us rather than facing the stranger's knowing gaze. 'The cop car is getting closer.'

'I'll worry about it when it's ramming our tail.'

'Worrying about it before it sends us flying into the trees might be a better idea.'

'They won't ram. They're probably arranging a roadblock up ahead as we speak.'

I studied him for a minute. 'What do they really want *you* for?'

He raised an eyebrow. 'What do they want you for? I doubt they'd be so intent on chasing someone over a pair of sweatpants.'

'Well, apparently you're wrong.' I hesitated, but had to ask the question that came instantly to mind. 'Have you killed anyone?'

'Have you?' he shot back.

'No,' I said, but somewhere in the back of my mind, screams mingled with the splatter of blood and white matter across stark white walls. No, I thought. *No.*

But the memories would not be denied.

It wasn't Egan's death. The responsibility for that might be mine – if only because he'd died trying to protect me – but he'd been shot through the heart, not the head. The death I remembered was another one entirely.

I *had* killed. I just didn't know how or why. And that was a scary thought.

Maybe the stranger should be scared of *me*, and what *I* might do, not the other way around.

He didn't say anything and I looked behind us again. The cop car was catching up. No matter how powerful the engine in this car sounded, we weren't gaining any ground. I glanced back at the stranger and studied his profile. His lips were like Egan's – same shape, same lush kissability. I pushed the annoying thought away, and said, 'Do you have a name?'

'Trae Wilson.' He glanced at me. 'And I find it hard to believe that Egan never talked about any of us.'

'The only thing he ever said was that the past no longer mattered.'

'So he never talked about his clique and what they did?'

Clique? What the hell did he mean by that? His family?

'No, he didn't.' I hesitated, my fingers clenching around the cold metal ring as the decision I'd made to return the ring to its owner reverberated briefly through my thoughts. 'What did they do?'

'What didn't they do might be a better question.' His gaze went back to the rearview mirror.

I twisted around again. The cops were closing in fast. The big man who'd tracked me to the dam was talking into the radio, meaning that Trae was probably right in his earlier assessment that they were setting up a roadblock.

'If I was the betting kind,' I said, 'I'd reckon they're working up a trap.'

'Looks like it.'

He didn't sound in the least concerned, and I studied his face for several seconds before letting my gaze slide downward. Was it his similarity to Egan that had the flick of attraction racing through my veins, or was something else going on?

'Have you actually got a plan to get us away from them, or are you just playing it by ear?'

'I always have a plan.' His gaze met mine, the sky-blue depths holding an intensity and an awareness that sent a warm shiver across my skin. 'Always.'

I rubbed my arms and pulled my gaze from his. I didn't understand what was going on, but for once my lack of memory had absolutely nothing to do with it. This man seemed to be working on a whole different level.

The car swept around another bend, revealing a long straight stretch of road. Two cars sat across the road at the far end, completely blocking it.

'Well, there's our roadblock,' I said, pointing out the obvious. 'What are you going to do?'

He didn't answer, just wrenched the wheel sideways. The car slewed around, the tires screaming in protest. The unexpected motion threw me against him, hard. And that odd awareness rose again, thick and strong, until all I could feel, all I wanted, was him.

And then the car was straightening again, and I was thrown back, this time against the door, hitting my head so hard against the glass it was amazing one or the other didn't crack.

'Seat belt,' he snapped, voice little more than a heat-filled growl.

Or maybe it was my imagination, a leftover of the weird awareness our brief touch had caused.

I took a deep, shuddery breath and tried to concentrate on the matter at hand – escape.

We were currently gunning down a dirt track that barely looked wide enough to fit a motorcycle, let alone a car the size of this one. Tree branches and God knows what else slapped across the windshield and scraped the sides, but somehow we were getting through. But a look behind soon revealed the cop still followed.

'Have you any idea where we're going?'

'Not really.'

I looked at him. 'I thought you said you always had a plan?'

'Maybe I lied. Maybe I just like winging it.'

Amusement played about his lush lips, and I frowned. 'Is that meant to be comforting?'

'Sweetheart, it's not meant to be anything more than the truth.'

'I'm *not* your sweetheart.'

His amusement bubbled, stretching his lips into a devilish grin that had my pulse doing happy little cartwheels.

Why? That was the question that still echoed through me, even as another part of me bathed in the sexiness of that grin. What the hell was happening to me? Why on earth was I reacting like this to a stranger? A man who might yet prove more dangerous than the cops chasing us?

'You may not be my sweetheart,' he said, blue eyes twinkling as he glanced my way, 'but you could be, if you play your cards right.'

'In your dreams, my friend.'

'You don't *want* to know about my dreams. Trust me on that.'

I pulled my gaze away from his, unsure whether the sudden erratic beat of my heart was excitement or fear. A whole lot of me was praying for fear, because that was the sensible reaction in this situation.

Unfortunately, there didn't seem to be a whole lot of sensible around at the moment.

The car hit a bump and jumped into the air. I did the same, yelping as my head hit the roof before the car and I crashed back down.

'You really might want to put on your seat belt,' he said. 'This is going to get a lot rougher before it's over.'

I looked out the windshield, saw that we were approaching a forest where the trees were all big and sturdy and impassable looking, and quickly pulled on the belt, as advised. 'I really need to know that you have a plan right now.'

Especially seeing that the gap between those trunks didn't seem to be getting a whole lot wider. I braced myself against the car and resisted the urge to squeeze my eyes shut.

'I do have a plan,' he said, voice calm and still touched by warm amusement. 'Which is not to say you're going to like it.'

'What the hell is that supposed to mean?'

He didn't answer, and I couldn't really be unhappy about that. The tiniest loss in concentration on his part could easily send us splattering across the trunks we were approaching way too fast.

One thing was becoming obvious, though. This man and sanity weren't exactly chummy.

He was driving us full bore at a forest. My heart began beating so hard I swore it was going to leap out of my chest, and the sweat trickling down my spine almost became a torrent. Part of me wanted to grab the wheel, the hand brake, do *something* that might divert or stop the car. Truth was, though, we were going far too fast and were far too close now to prevent the inevitable. I gave in to the desire to squeeze my eyes shut and hoped like hell I lived long enough to beat the crap out of the crazy man behind the wheel.

Only the crash didn't happen. Instead, the surrounding light grew dim, as if someone had suddenly swallowed the sun. I forced an eyelid open, saw the trunks and shadows and branches slashing past, impossibly close, and promptly shut it again.

Better not to know.

'How far behind us is that cop car?' he asked.

The sudden sound of his voice had me jumping. I sucked in a breath that did nothing to ease the pounding of my heart, then twisted around. Through the green shadows and trees, lights flashed. They didn't seem to be going as fast as us, because they were certainly a lot farther behind than they had been before we entered this forest. But then, I guess not everyone became a crazy person behind the wheel like Trae apparently did.

'They'd have to be a good ten or so car lengths behind.'

'It'll have to be enough,' he muttered.

'Enough for what?' I asked, more than a little alarmed.

'Escape.' He glanced at me briefly. 'What else would I be talking about?'

Who knew? With this man, it could have been *anything*.

I looked ahead. Though we were still surrounded by shadows and trees that zipped by at gut-wrenching speed, up ahead sunlight danced. It lifted my spirits a little, even though I suspected Trae's surprises were not done with yet.

A point he proved by slamming a foot on the brake. I screamed as the car slewed sideways and shut my eyes, waiting for the inevitable crash. Which didn't happen. The car came to a halt, rocking gently from side to side.

'Out,' Trae ordered. 'Quickly.'

He flung his own door open, grabbed a backpack from the backseat, then ran around the front of the car.

I hadn't moved. Fear – and disbelief – had me glued to the spot.

'Out, Destiny, unless you want to be caught by the cops.'

He grabbed my hand, half pulling, half assisting me out of the car.

'You're a maniac,' I said, as he kept hold of my hand and forced me into a run.

'But I'm a free maniac, and I have every intention of remaining that way. Come on, faster.'

I obeyed. One good thing about having long legs and big feet was speed and surety of step.

We came out of the trees and into sunshine. Up ahead there was no land. Only ocean. Deep blue ocean, far, far down.

'What kind of escape plan is this?' I cried, trying to stop, trying to slow him down. To no avail. He ran on toward those cliffs regardless, pulling me with him. 'You've managed to trap us, you idiot!'

He tossed me a grin that was all wildness and dangerous excitement. 'You're never trapped when you have wings, sweetheart.'

And suddenly a golden haze was sweeping across his body, and he was shifting, changing, *growing*. Becoming something more than just a man.

Becoming a beast with scales of molten gold and wings that swept me off my feet and out over the ocean.

Then I was *in* the ocean, and the sudden shock of cold water had my body shifting, changing, just as Trae's had. Except he was the sun to my darkness – he was born to fire, and a brother to the wind. I was of the sea and the tides and the great ocean depths.

And suddenly the past was crowding close, filled with pain. Filled with bloodshed. Mine, Egan's, and others'. It hurt, remembering. Hurt because there was so much I'd done, so much I'd yet to do. In so many different ways, I now realized, *not* remembering had been a blessing. A brief respite in the twisted bloody mess that my life had become.

But at least I knew who I was.

Knew what I was.

And most important of all, I knew what I had to do, and how many lives I had yet to save.

Chapter Three

I swam to the wild surface of the sea, blowing water out of my snout as I looked around for Trae. He swooped low, powerful and beautiful against the brilliant blue of the skies, then flew on, heading down the coast.

I followed. I could have easily escaped had I wished to, because the sea was my home and my sanctuary, but even with my memories retrieved, there were answers I still needed.

Like why Egan might have called Trae to help us. He *must* have had a reason – a good reason. He wouldn't have risked either of our lives otherwise.

But at least I knew now *how* he'd contacted Trae. Air dragons, like sea dragons, share a form of telepathy between loved ones. It is often restrained by distance – at least it is with sea dragons – but dire circumstances can sometimes shatter that restriction. And Egan getting shot could certainly be classed as a dire circumstance. I closed my eyes against the images that rose. I didn't want to think about Egan just yet. Didn't want to deal with the pain and the guilt.

Instead, I concentrated on the shoreline, wondering where we were going, wondering if Trae even knew.

Eventually the trees and wildness of the shore began to give way to houses. Trae dipped one wing low, turning lazily and heading toward the sand line. Then the golden haze swept across his form again, so that what strode onto the beach was human rather than beast. Only there was blood all over his back.

I shifted shape and followed. The magic that allowed us to change took care of the clothes we were wearing – although anything we were carrying as humans we would be carrying as dragons – but it didn't actually keep them dry, so I was rather bedraggled by the time I joined him on the beach.

'Why are you bleeding?' I asked.

His eyebrows rose, as if surprised by the question. 'I'm a draman.'

Like *that* was supposed to explain it all. 'Which is?'

'Half human, half dragon.'

'And this is important because?'

'Because the magic that allows dragons to change is muted

in we draman, and when the wings tear out of our flesh, we bleed.'

'Does it hurt?'

He shrugged, which could have meant anything, then looked me up and down. 'You look cold.'

'That would be because it's fucking freezing standing here in wet clothes.' I might be a sea dragon, and I might be able to stand the coldest of waters even in my human skin, but that didn't mean I had to *like* it. 'That was a bit dangerous, wasn't it? The cops could have easily seen you in dragon form.' Or anyone else who happened to be walking along the cliffs at the time.

He shrugged. 'They may see me, but who's actually going to believe them?'

'People may if there's enough evidence to back up the sighting. And air dragons are big enough to be tracked by radar, you know.'

'Yeah, but humans are decidedly dumb when it comes to what is walking – or flying – around them. They wouldn't say anything if they did spot me because they don't want to be taken for idiots. It's that whole UFO effect. Besides, I doubt the cops would have seen us. We were well gone before they got to the cliff.'

'Humans are not *that* dumb, trust me,' I muttered. Otherwise I would not be in this pickle, and Egan would not be dead. 'And that was still a stupid risk to take.'

He shrugged again, his gaze moving past me and his expression still remote. 'I think the first thing we should do is find somewhere to rest for the night.'

'Good idea.' Once I was warm, I might be able to think coherently and ask some questions.

'Come on, then.' He grabbed my hand again, his fingers hot against my own. That was the good thing about air dragons – they were nice to snuggle up to, even on the coldest of nights.

Not that I'd be snuggling up to *this* dragon any time soon – no matter how strong the weird awareness zinging between us might be.

We managed to catch a cab, then Trae directed the driver to a hotel several miles inland. It wasn't the Hilton – I doubt it was two-star let alone five – but the beds looked clean and the water was hot, and that's basically all that mattered.

While Trae took his turn in the shower, I hung up my clothes to let them dry, and then snuggled into the bed. And even though I had no real intentions of sleeping, that's exactly what I did.

It was dark when I woke. Blue light flashed intermittently through the shadows, revealing glimpses of the still-neatly-made second double bed. Trae hadn't slept, though his tangy, spicy aroma still rode the air.

I shifted some more and saw him. He was a shadow in the darkness, untouched by the flickering light coming in through the window to my right. He sat at the end of my bed, his pose seemingly casual, and yet there was something about his very stillness that seemed both unnatural and deadly. The predator watching his prey.

What I had to work out now was whether that predator was friend or foe. Marsten and his scientists had used our kind to capture most of the dragons currently being held in their Loch Ness research facility. Of course, most of those dragons were youngsters ranging in age from seven to fifteen and, as such, had put up little fight. My mother, Egan, and myself had been the only adults, and while I had no idea how they'd captured Mom, I knew it had taken three hunters to bring Egan down. My own capture was due more to my own foolhardiness – and willingness to trust – than any form of skill on their part.

Which was why I had to be so careful now. I might *want* to trust Trae, I might want to believe he was Egan's brother, but that didn't mean I could actually do either of those things.

My gaze slid down Trae's shadowed front, coming to a halt on one extended arm. He seemed to be pointing something at me. Tension crawled through my limbs, and the sense of danger leapt into sharp focus.

I reached to my left and turned on the bedside lamp. Pale yellow light washed across the room, revealing the cracked walls, worn-looking paint, and the gun in Trae's hand.

'Well, well,' I said, glad my voice was steady because my

pulse rate sure as hell wasn't. And I wasn't entirely sure whether it was fear or attraction or maybe a bit of both, because there was something dangerously attractive about the heated anger in his bright eyes. 'The thief has a sting.'

'The thief wants answers.'

I pushed myself into a sitting position, and hugged my knees close to my chest. My skin was cool, infused with the chill of the night, and glowed with an odd luminescence – the result of taking after my mom more than my dad. It was only the day and the sun that warmed me.

The sheet that had been covering me slid down my legs as I moved, probably revealing a whole lot more than was wise. But after eleven years of being kept naked by the scientists, it no longer particularly worried me.

Trae's gaze didn't waver, and neither did his aim. 'Where's Egan?'

'I'm not telling you anything about Egan until I know whether you're telling the truth about who you are and what you're doing here.' My gaze flickered to the gun and a tremor ran through my limbs. His hand was too steady, too still. That spoke of familiarity, and practice. 'Go ahead and shoot me if you want. I'm sure the scientists will give you a handsome reward for my dead body.'

The confusion that flitted briefly across his face eased a little of my tension. If he didn't understand what I meant, then he

52

probably wasn't a hunter. A small mercy, perhaps, given that he still had a gun on me, but the long years of captivity had taught me to be grateful for such things.

'I have no idea what you're talking about,' he said, his voice still cold, his eyes still filled with anger, 'but I can assure you, I'm not working with any scientists, and I don't want a reward for your dead body.'

Even as he said the words, his gaze slid down my length ever so briefly. He mightn't want my dead body, but he sure did want my live one. His desire filled the cool air, heating it, heating me. And while I wasn't entirely sure whether my own reaction was merely lust or something far stronger, I *did* know it was damned inconvenient timing. Even so, I couldn't help dragging in a breath, drawing in the scent and heat of him, letting it briefly chase away the chill and set my soul alight with a deep-seated hunger that I'd never known with Egan.

Part of me wanted to feel guilty about that, but honestly, I just couldn't. Egan and I had been lovers because we'd been lonely, and because we'd had little other choice. Had we met in the outside world, I doubted if we would have even shared a hello. Which would have been a shame, because Egan was a good man who deserved a whole lot more than what he'd gotten out of life and me.

'So if you're not intending to hand me over to anyone, why are you pointing a gun at me?'

'Because I have no idea what, exactly, the powers of a sea dragon are, and I certainly don't trust you.'

'A sea dragon can't do much away from the sea.' Which wasn't entirely true. We could control any sort of water we wanted – and if it was a lake, often the land that surrounded it – but it was the sea that held our true strength, the sea where we had full control. 'And you holding a gun on me isn't doing a whole lot to make me want to answer your damn questions.'

He stared at me for a moment longer, then shook his head and lowered the weapon. 'I sit here with a loaded gun and a mean look, and you sit there completely naked and totally unfazed. You're crazy.'

'If that's the best mean look you have, you really need to go to acting school.' I rested my chin on my knees and watched him carefully. Just because he'd lowered the weapon didn't mean he had no further intention of using it. This man was a dragon, and air was his element. He could move faster than I could blink. 'Are you really Egan's brother?'

He didn't answer immediately, just reached into the back pocket of his jeans and pulled out a wallet. 'Look inside,' he said, tossing it onto the bed in front of me.

Opening it, I saw that he was indeed Trae Wilson, and that he was thirty-five. The same age as Egan, and six years older than me. Then my gaze was drawn to the picture sitting inside the small photograph window. It was of two almost identical boys. Same age, same cheeky smile, same golden skin and sun-shot hair. The only thing that was different were the eye colors – one pair golden, one sky blue. Egan and Trae as boys.

Behind that were a couple of other photos – Trae with two women, one older, one younger, but all three sharing the same blue eyes, and another shot of him and Egan, this time as teenagers. Both of them were goofing around with surfboards, and the laughter and friendship – love even – between the two seemed to have been caught in that single photo.

There could be no doubt that they were, indeed, brothers. God, how was I going to tell him that Egan was dead?

I tossed the wallet back on the bed, then said, 'Have you been searching for him the whole time he was gone?'

'No, because he told me he was disappearing for a while. I just didn't expect it to be for ten years.' He raised the gun again, and anger sparked in the depths of his blue gaze. 'Now stop avoiding the question. Where is he?'

I blew out a breath. There was no easy way to do this. No gentle words that could make the hearing of it any easier. 'He was shot in the chest last night. We escaped, but I couldn't get him to a hospital and he died.'

Pain, deep and haunting, flashed briefly through his eyes. He'd known, I thought. Had felt something was wrong, which is why he'd been so angry with my refusal to talk about Egan's whereabouts.

'Where is his body, then?'

I hesitated, closing my eyes briefly against the sudden sting of tears. 'I waited with his body until dawn's final death, and prayed to the Gods of sun and sky and air to guide his soul onto his next journey.'

He didn't get angry. Didn't react in any of the ways I'd half expected – which only confirmed the thought that, deep down, he'd known his brother was dead. He stared at me for a moment, his gaze moving up to the scar on my head then back again to my lips, and then he lowered the gun. 'Thank you for doing that much.'

I nodded, a little thankful that he hadn't asked *why* Egan had been shot. But then, maybe he already knew – after all, he'd been in contact with his brother before his death.

'Egan was a good man. I couldn't just leave him there alone. It wouldn't have been right.'

'No, it wouldn't have.' He stood up abruptly. 'Would you like a cup of black coffee? We haven't got any milk.'

'I can live without milk. I can't live without three sugars.'

'Three sugars? It's a wonder your teeth aren't rotten.'

I stretched out a foot and toed open the wallet. 'Who said they aren't?'

'Sweetheart, those teeth of yours look in fine biting order.'

'Well, they aren't going to be biting you any time soon.'

He flung me a grin that briefly lit the room with its bright cheekiness. 'What a shame. I might have enjoyed it.'

I snorted softly. 'Your license says you live in San Francisco, but that's not where Egan came from.'

'No, we were both born and raised in Stewarts Point, and our clique still lives there. I was there visiting my mother when he contacted me.'

A clique, I remembered from the few talks I'd had with my dad about my air cousins, was generations of air dragon families living together in a community. Unlike sea dragons, who tended to live in single-family units.

I had no idea how many cliques of air dragons there were, but I knew there were more of them than there were of us sea dragons. The sea might be a vast and mighty mistress, but she was also full of predators, and the ancient safe havens where we could birth and raise our young were few and far between. And getting more crowded with humans every day.

'What did he want?' I asked. 'Why did he contact you?'

'He wanted help.' He hesitated. 'And he wanted protection.'

He had to have meant from Marsten. And I guess the help of a thief would be valuable, given our plans to break into Marsten's mother's place and steal the backup security codes apparently kept there. But protection? 'What can you do that Egan couldn't?'

57

'Nothing.' He hesitated, then added, 'He didn't really explain what was going on, he just said he needed an extra pair of hands to protect you.'

That was Egan all over, I thought, blinking back tears. He was always more worried about everyone else than himself. Which was probably why the younger kids at the research center had taken to him so quickly – he was their protector. Or as much as anyone could protect them in that place.

He'd been my protector, too. Only now he was gone, and I was left with his brother.

'Carrying a gun doesn't make you capable of protecting me.'

'No. But my willingness to use it does.'

I supposed that was true. I looked out the window, studying the cold night. Moonlight washed across the small parking lot beyond the room, highlighting several cars and the twisted shapes of the trees lining the boundary. They spoke of sea and sand and wind, those trees, even though we weren't anywhere near them.

The small coffeemaker began to splutter. Trae clicked it off and poured two mugs. The sharp smell of coffee touched the air, mixing with the tangy scent of man, tantalizing my senses and stirring my desire to greater heights.

Which was annoying, to say the least.

I hitched the sheet up over my knees. Maybe covering up would offer some sense of control. He walked across the room and offered me a cheap white mug. 'Black coffee, sickeningly sweet.'

'Thanks.' I took the offered mug, my fingers touching his briefly and sending little shocks of electricity up my arm. 'Where, exactly, are we?'

He stepped back and sat down on the other bed. Though his moves were casual, I could taste the sudden tension in him. See the flare of desire in his bright eyes. 'We're in Newport.'

'Where's that? Besides in Oregon?' I hadn't swum that far, but I had no idea where he'd actually picked me up from, and therefore no idea where in relation to Florence that was.

'About fifty miles north of Florence.'

'So we actually went past it? Why, when that's where we wanted to go?'

'Because when you're being chased, it's always safer to go past a target, then come back to it.' He took a drink, his gaze holding mine over the rim. Those blue depths were still watchful, still distrusting, despite the deep burn of desire. 'Are you going to explain what you were doing, and how Egan got shot?'

I blew out a breath. As much as I'd wanted to avoid remembering, he deserved an answer. 'We'd gone to Mexico—'

'Mexico?' he interrupted. 'Why there?'

'He had this place near San Lucas—'

Recognition sparked in his eyes. So did surprise. 'Villa Costa Brava?'

59

I nodded. 'You know it?'

'Yes.' He shook his head, amusement and old pain evident in his expression. 'It's a long story, but let's just say it was our escape house when we were teenagers. Go on.'

'He'd wanted to check that the villa was okay. He said something about it being the home of his heart, if not his soul.' The pain that had been evident earlier came to the fore, accompanied by a sadness that tore at my heart.

'It was indeed. Sila is buried there.'

I raised my eyebrows. 'Sila?'

'The black dragon he loved.'

'What happened to her?'

'As I said, it's a long story.' Trae's voice held a bitterness so cold, so deep, that my soul quaked. 'Go on.'

I didn't want to. I wanted to hear about Egan – the man I'd spent ten years sharing a bed with, and yet who I so obviously knew so little about. But Trae's commanding tone suggested he wasn't about to be derailed from getting his answers.

'They were waiting for him at Costa Brava. Waiting for us.'

'Who?'

'The scientists. The hunters.'

Pain rose and I closed my eyes. But the memories would not be denied this time, and images flashed – sharp stills of a past part of me didn't want to remember or relive. The crystal-white sharpness of the glorious building, juxtaposed against the blue of the sky and the pool that from a distance seemed to meld right into the ocean itself. The smoky gray of the stone surrounding the pool, the coldness of it under my bare feet. The fingers of dread that ran down my spine as shadows moved and became our hunters. Fighting and fear and flames – hot, yellow-white flames – flung from Egan's fingertips, which surrounded those who threatened us, consuming them. My hand, encased in the warm security of Egan's grasp as we ran for the ocean and the safety it offered. The sharp echo of gunshots. The burn of a bullet tearing past my scalp. The man who'd jumped out of seemingly nowhere, right in front of us. Then blood – thick and crimson – splattering across the crystal walls, flooding across the gray stone.

And panic, sheer panic, as I tried to save a dying man and myself from recapture . . .

I gulped for air, fighting the tears, fighting not to remember – to see – anything more. I scrubbed an arm across my eyes, and said, 'They were waiting for us. I don't know how or why, but they were waiting for us.'

He leaned forward and touched a finger to my cheek, catching a tear I missed. 'Why were the scientists even hunting you? How would they even know either of you existed?'

'Because we'd been their captives for the last ten years. Well, eleven in my case.'

'*What?*'

My gaze searched his, surprised. 'Egan didn't tell you?'

'Egan didn't have a whole lot of time to tell me anything.' He hesitated. 'I thought he'd sounded strange – distant. I guess now I know why. He was dying.'

And even in dying, he'd thought about others. Had contacted Trae to look after me.

More tears tracked down my cheeks. God, he'd deserved more – so much more – than what life had dished up to him these last ten years.

I sniffed, and continued. 'They were shooting at him more than me. I didn't think they'd want either of us dead, but I was wrong. Egan fought back. He . . .' I stopped again, trying not to think of those burning figures, trying not to remember the smell of their flesh or the way they'd screamed. Trying to remember that in many ways, they'd done far worse to both Egan and me.

'Burned them?' Trae said softly.

I nodded. 'We broke free, but one of them jumped out in front of us and shot Egan in the chest.'

'How did you escape?'

I closed my eyes. 'I called for help. I called the sea.'

And she had answered, rushing up over the white walls, crushing the vibrant red hibiscus, sweeping away the man who threatened us even as she left Egan and me untouched.

'You called the *sea*?'

'She is ours to call, much like flame is at your command. A large wave came in and over, sweeping away the man who'd shot Egan.'

Swept him away, and swept him deep. Because I had asked it, because I had called. The scientists hadn't known about that power. They'd never suspected that we were the water to an air dragon's flame. That same energy had helped us get far away from San Lucas. But in the end, it had not saved Egan.

Of course, the scientists now knew of the power. And they would want it, want me, even more fiercely. Maybe that was why I was still alive and Egan was dead.

They only had two sea dragons. They had six other fire dragons to examine and play with.

'Egan should have been able to survive a gunshot if it didn't kill him straightaway,' Trae said.

I smiled bitterly. 'Except that no man – no matter how gifted, how strong, or how magical – can survive having his heart shot to smithereens.'

Trae reached out to touch me, but I jerked away. 'Don't,' I said. 'Just don't.'

I don't know why I said it when I actually hungered for his touch. Maybe it was just the sympathy in his eyes. The feeling that if I did give in to the need to be held, it wouldn't end there.

That I would come to depend on him, just as much as I had come to depend on Egan.

I couldn't let that happen. Couldn't let anyone else get captured or killed. I had more than enough blood on my hands already.

He let his hand drop. 'You don't trust me.'

I met his gaze squarely. 'It's not a matter of trust. It's a matter of believing that your help probably isn't the best option right now.'

'Egan believed otherwise.'

'Egan's dead. And the people who killed him are still out there.'

He considered me for a moment, then leaned back. Cool air swirled in between us, sending a chill across my already cold skin. 'So are you telling me to walk away? That you don't need my help at all?'

I hesitated and looked down at my coffee. I might not want to lean on him, or involve him any more than necessary, but the fact was, I had no money, no clothes, and no mode of transport. I might be able to swim oceans, but the scientists would probably be looking for me in the sea.

Of course, his wallet was still sitting on the bed, and it was stuffed with cash. He probably wouldn't miss a few bills. Maybe not even a credit card. But if I did steal them and run, that would leave me alone. And no matter what, I needed help to break into the safe and get the security codes.

I let my gaze rise to his again. 'What I'm worried about is the cost of your help.'

I meant death-wise, but the sudden twinkle in his eyes suggested his mind had gone in a completely different direction.

'Ah, well,' he said, his gaze sliding down my body, burning where it lingered. 'Perhaps that is something we can discuss when we have a little more time.'

'I doubt it,' I said, even as I drank in the awareness that seared us both, letting it wash through me and chase away the night chill. 'Because I have no intention of bedding my lover's brother.'

I owed Egan that much. I might not have loved him, I might not have been even attracted to him as much as I was to his brother, but we'd spent ten long years together, and I'd cared for him. And caring did not mean hopping into the sack of another when the warmth of his touch still lingered in my mind.

Trae's warm expression died a little at the mention of Egan. He stood abruptly and glanced at his watch. 'Actually, we need to get moving. I want to be out of here before dawn.'

'Dawn is ninety-five minutes off yet.'

He raised his eyebrows. 'To the second?'

'Ninety-five minutes, forty-three seconds, if you want to be precise.' I knew, because I could feel it. Feel the distant hum beginning to touch the air. Dawn was coming, bringing with it warmth and power. I frowned at him. 'Air dragons are as attuned to the dawn and dusk as we are, so what's with the disbelief?'

'I think it's safe to say that I'm not your average dragon—'

'You got that right,' I muttered, then added, 'Is it because you're a draman that you can't feel the dawn?'

'Yes.' Amusement toyed with the corners of his lush mouth. 'And the woman who plays chicken with cars has no right to consider me strange.'

'I was just trying to get help. You were the one who couldn't find the brake pedal.'

The amusement finally reached his eyes, and the bright sparkle did stranger things to my breathing. 'I was never going to hit you.'

'That's not the point.'

'Yes, it is.' He picked up his wallet from the end of the bed, dumped it on top of the bag sitting in the chair in the corner. 'I'm going for a shower.'

'Another one?'

His grin flashed over his shoulder. 'This one will be a lot colder.'

I smiled. I might be resisting him, but it was still nice to know the heat and desire I was feeling was mutual.

I watched him retreat into the bathroom, then my gaze was drawn back to the wallet. I might need his help, but I also needed a backup plan in case things went wrong – because things always *did* go wrong. And what I needed most besides help was cash. Without it, I had no way of getting around by myself.

I waited until I heard the sound of water running and the shower door close, then scrambled across to the chair and grabbed the wallet. There were four credit cards, and at least five hundred bucks in there, if not more. I slipped out a credit card and two hundred bucks, and only felt a little bit guilty. If things went ass up with Trae, at least I'd be able to look after myself for a day or so. As I threw the wallet back on top of the bag, my fingers brushed the nylon exterior and a familiar, cold sensation ran through my fingertips.

Frowning slightly, I undid the bag's zipper and looked inside. Sitting to one side of the roughly packed clothes was Egan's ring.

Anger ran through me. The *bastard.*

I grabbed the ring and took a step toward the bathroom, then stopped. Wouldn't it be better – safer – if he didn't know I'd discovered the theft? Neither he nor I had mentioned the ring since waking, so maybe he was hoping I'd forgotten about it. Which meant that maybe he wouldn't check his bag for it. Not while I was around, anyway.

I zipped it back up, then spun and walked back to the bed. After a moment's hesitation, I hid my stolen prizes inside the second pillowcase. It might not be the safest place, but at least I could get to them there in a less obvious way than hiding them anywhere else.

With that done, I sat back on the bed and slowly sipped my

coffee, listening to the shower and imagining all that water running over lean, hard flesh. It was a nice way to spend the next five minutes.

He walked in a few minutes later, his clean, male scent filling the room. 'You having another shower?' he asked, vigorously toweling his hair dry.

I finished off the last of my coffee, then rose. His gaze swept down me, sending little prickles of desire skating across skin already overheated from my earlier imaginings.

'That's like asking a dog if it wants to roll in something disgusting.'

'I know I alluded to you being scruffy earlier,' he said, voice wry, 'but even I don't think the analogy fits.'

'Of course it does. Think about it – a dog doesn't *have* to roll in the muck, but it always *wants* to.'

Amusement touched the corners of his mouth again. 'You're right.'

'I usually am.' I brushed past him, teasing us both. I swear his toweling got a whole lot more forceful. Grinning slightly, I turned on the faucet and ran the water over my hands, stepping in once the water was tepid.

For several minutes, I did nothing more than simply stand there, allowing the water to wash over my skin. The sea might be my home, but we could survive in freshwater for quite a while. Which is why there were so many myths of monsters in lakes and lochs. In times of sickness, as well as times such as birth or death, the gentler waters of the ancient lakes were a far safer refuge than the wildness of the seas.

Of course, I had no idea just how long we could go without seawater. Or whether, after a certain time, it began to have ill effects. Certainly I'd been locked up for eleven years in the research center without going near it, and I was basically fine, but that wasn't to say that there couldn't have been problems further down the line.

Mom would have known, but aside from the brief moment of contact when she'd told me that I needed to get out for my dad's sake, I hadn't managed to talk to her.

After washing my face and hair with the little bar of soap the hotel had so generously provided, I got out and dried myself. There was no toothpaste in the bathroom, let alone a clean toothbrush, so I used my finger to give my teeth a rough clean, then rinsed my mouth out with water.

'So where do we need to rush off so early to?' I said, as I walked back into the main room.

Only to stop in surprise.

Trae – and his bag – were gone.

Chapter Four

My gaze immediately went to the bed, and the two pillows sitting there. Had they been disturbed? Was the ring and the money still safe? With Trae gone, I'd need my stolen goodies more than ever.

Heart accelerating, I walked across and quickly lifted the second pillow. My fingers touched cold metal and plastic, and relief swam through me. The thief had been in such a hurry to get out, he hadn't noticed his own pockets had been picked.

But there was no guarantee he wouldn't notice soon, and that he wouldn't come back. His need for the ring was obviously greater than his need to fulfill any promise made to Egan, which meant I couldn't trust him any more than I could those who hunted me. He might mean me no harm, but he definitely had an agenda of his own, and it didn't seem that my needs were high on it. I had to get out of here.

I dropped the pillow onto the bed and walked across to the window. The hotel's sign flickered intermittently, washing blue light across the moonlit parking lot. There'd been three cars in the lot when I'd looked out before. Now there were only two. The thief had obviously stolen himself a new one.

Annoyance ran through me, though it wasn't really caused by him running. I might not have any idea how I was going to break into the safe, but at least now I wouldn't have the worry about him being caught or killed by the scientists. What pissed me off was the fact he'd obviously intended to run all along. And while the ring would technically probably belong to him now anyway, he still shouldn't have taken it without telling me. For all he knew, Egan had gifted me that ring, which meant he certainly had no right to it.

But then, when did a thief ever ask for permission to steal?

And if Trae had asked for the ring rather than simply trying to take it, would I have given it to him?

Probably not, I thought ruefully. Not before he'd explained what was going on with the thing, anyway.

At least I'd discovered the theft before it was too late. At least I could still return the ring and uncover its secrets myself.

Question was, how was I going to protect the ring, and make damn sure Trae didn't get anywhere near it a second time? He was bigger, stronger, faster. If it came to force, he'd overpower me in a second. I didn't think he would do something like that, but who really knew? I hadn't actually thought he'd run out on me the minute my back was turned, either.

I blew out a breath. First things first. I needed to get out of this room.

Now.

I grabbed the room keys, then headed out the door. The night was clear and cool, the breeze lazy but smelling ever so faintly of the sea. I breathed deep, and again felt that flick of longing run through me. After eleven years away from the power and beauty of the deep, cold oceans, it seemed my soul just couldn't get enough.

I walked across to reception and slid the keys under the door, then turned and studied the street. The desire to get to Maine was a slow, strong beat in the back of my mind. I needed to get there soon, because my dad was dying and I had no idea how much longer he had left.

Which is part of the reason why we'd taken the awful risk of attempting a breakout in the first place. It could have gone so wrong – more than it had, anyway – and we could have been killed, leaving the kids with no one at all to guide and protect them.

But I'd had no choice. Dad was a fire dragon. His death would come near dawn, as Egan's had, but unless someone was there to pray for him – to guide him – his spirit might get lost between this world and the forever lands.

Dad had no one else but me and Mom. I couldn't ever remember him mentioning his family or having photos of them. It was as if something big had happened in his past, something that he didn't want to – or rather, refused to – acknowledge or remember. I knew he was American, that he'd grown up near Las Vegas somewhere, and that he had scars – terrible, criss-crossed scars down his left arm and leg, like someone had tried chopping him up with a large knife – but that was about the extent of my knowledge.

Which is why Mom had demanded I go to Maine rather than attempt any immediate release of herself and the others. She didn't want him to die alone.

And yet, she might well have been condemning herself to a lonely death and an eternity drifting lost between two worlds. Because she was dying, too.

I blinked back the sting of tears, and tried not to think about the unfairness of it all. There was nothing I could do to alter the fact that I was going to lose both parents. What I could change was the way it happened. The way they went.

But as much as I wanted to get to Maine, it just wasn't practical when Florence was so close. We – I – needed those codes. I'd promised little Carli and the others that I'd come back, that I'd get them out of there, no matter what. They only had Jace to protect them now, and a fifteen-year-old shouldn't have that sort of responsibility on his shoulders for too long.

I had no idea where in Florence Marsten's mother actually lived. All we'd really known was that she and his brother were investment partners in the foundation, as well as members of the board. It was no certainty that she actually held backups of everything that was going on at the facility, but Marsten was a careful man. He would have made sure that if anything went wrong at the foundation, he could still get to the years and years of data he'd collected. And we were also hoping that he'd included the security information in that backup plan.

But with any sort of luck, Marsten's mom would be in the phone directory. If not, I'd have to go to plan B. When I could figure out what plan B was, anyway.

My gaze went to the dark horizon. My first priority, though, was taking care of this ring. And really, there was only one place where I could be totally sure it would be safe.

The sea.

I glanced up the street at the sound of an approaching car. I doubted it was Trae, but I broke into a run anyway, heading across the parking lot and into a side street. Trees lined the curb, blocking many of the streetlights, casting shadows across the pavement that swayed gently to the tune of the soft breeze.

Headlights swept across the night behind me. I jumped the nearest fence and dropped behind a spiky-looking shrub. The lights, and the car, got closer, and my breath caught somewhere in my throat. But the car didn't stop.

The sudden surge of relief had me shaking my head in amusement. Here I was, having a near heart attack at the thought of being caught by a thief when far worse people were out there hunting me. It was them I should be frightened of, not some damn thief who had no intentions of looking after anything but himself.

I shoved the cash and card into the zippered pocket of my pants, then climbed back over the fence and broke into a run again, heading down the street toward the sea.

If I wanted to ask my favor, I had to be there by dawn.

I kept on jogging. I was reasonably fit despite all those years of being caged, but by the time the long blue line of ocean became visible on the horizon, I was beginning to pant. I slowed to a walk as the houses gave way to more historic-look-ing buildings and shops. I crossed another street paved in what looked like cobblestones, and under an arch that said Nye Beach. Old-fashioned streetlights washed brightness across the cobbles, sloping down toward the beach. I followed their lead, walking in and out of shadows, listening to the sigh of the wind and hearing nothing beyond the mournful cry of gulls and the hiss of foam across sand. My pulse rate quickened, as did my steps.

There weren't any cars parked in the turnaround and not a

soul on the beach. Of course, dawn had yet to break free. I had no doubt that when she did, I would not be alone on this beach.

I jumped the fence lining the turnaround, and dropped down onto the sand. It was cool under my toes, gritty and sharp. I took a moment to wriggle my toes in delight, but the sea, and the task I was about to ask of it, pulled me on.

The hum of dawn touched the air. Energy began to dance lightly across my skin – a crazy tingling that once again chased the chill from my flesh. My gaze rose to the horizon. Night still held court, but that would soon change. I had to be in the water by then.

I quickly stripped, dropping my clothes well out of the water's reach before continuing on. My feet slapped across the wet sand, barely leaving an imprint as sea foam rushed up and caressed my toes. I strode on, into the water.

The hum of power filled the air with its forceful beat, flaying my skin with its rawness. The sea washed across my thighs, the chill water a sharp contrast to the warmth of the air and yet welcoming in its own way. When the gentle waves began to wash across my butt, I stopped and waited. On the horizon, slivers of gold began to breach the curtain of darkness. The energy grew frenetic, reaching a crescendo as the slivers became a river of red and yellow, flooding across the sky. As the beat of energy came to a peak, and the air came alive with the hum and power of a new day, I raised my left hand, the ring sitting in the middle of my palm and my fingers clenched around it.

'To the Gods of the sea, I call on thee.'

The words rode across the energy, held by it, shaped by it, becoming things of power and beauty and command. The waters around me began to stir, the rush of waves momentarily lost to the gathering whirl of energy. Droplets of water shot into the sky, sparkling like diamonds in the gathering brightness.

'To my brothers of deep, dark waters, and my sisters of the quick shallows, I call on thee.'

More energy touched the air – a deep bass thrum that spoke of vast, cold places. It flooded through me, filling me, completing me, in a way the warmth of the day never would.

The droplets became a water spout that glittered, spun, and danced on the rich, dark waters. I unclenched my fingers, offering the ring. In the gathering light, the dragon's jeweled eyes gleamed like blood dripping from a wound.

'Keep this ring safe. Keep this ring unfound. Take it to the dark and secret places and let no man nor animal nor fish near it until I command otherwise.'

There was a flash of silver, the warm kiss of water across my palm, and then the ring was gone.

'Thank you.' My words were little more than a whisper, but they seemed to linger, riding the disappearing night and the thrum of power, accepted and acknowledged by the deeper energy of the sea and the sparkling, spinning spout of water. I lowered my hand. The water spout gave a final whirl, then fell away.

Dawn broke fully across the night. The hum of energy faded, as did the rich resonance of the sea. The waves were just waves, buffering my legs and butt, chilling my skin.

It left me feeling oddly empty.

I sniffed, then turned around and walked back to the beach. When I reached the water's edge, I stopped, letting the sea foam tickle my toes as I looked left and right. How did I get to Florence from here?

I could hire a car, but that would take ID, and all I had was Trae's credit card. Stealing a car was also an option, but only if some fool left their keys in the ignition. Unlike Trae, I wasn't a thief. Except when it came to clothes and some much-needed cash.

Which left me with some form of public transport. A bus, maybe?

I studied the buildings lining the beachfront. Given I didn't know this area, the logical thing to do was ask the locals which was the best way to get to Florence. Shops lined the bottom of the turnaround, near the street, and at least one of them was a café or restaurant of some kind, if the packing and crates out back were anything to go by. I had no idea when any of the shops would be open, no idea if they would even *be* open today, because somewhere along the line, the days and nights of constant running had merged into a blur, and I actually had no idea what day it was. Still, asking a storekeeper for directions was a good option. It was either that or stop a local in the street. And shop and café workers, especially in a tourist area like this, were far more used to people asking for directions.

Frowning slightly, I got dressed, then made my way up the last bit of sand and back onto the turnaround, only to discover that the parking lot was no longer empty. A dark car stood in the middle of it. Leaning against it, arms crossed and looking decidedly sexy, was Trae.

I stopped. 'What day is it?'

He raised an eyebrow. 'What, no accusations? No tantrums or histrionics?'

'Would they get me the truth?'

'Probably not. And it's Thursday.'

'Ah.' At least I'd have more chance of catching a bus if I needed it. 'Why are you back?'

'Because I discovered my wallet had been picked.'

'How?'

'Pulled into a gas station to get some gas, and discovered I was missing a credit card and some cash. Further investigation revealed a ring was also missing.'

'Is that the only reason you're back? For the ring?'

'Yes.' He gave me a twisted little smile that had my pulse rate leaping. 'Sweetheart, as much as I'd love to stay and explore your—' He paused, and his gaze did a slow, heated tour of my torso, sending pinpricks of heat skating across my body and a shiver that was all delight running through my soul. ' – "problems," I have business that negates that.'

'But what about the promises you made to Egan?'

His gaze met mine, the pretty blue depths still so cold, yet showing hints of regret and determination combined. 'I made no promises to Egan. I agreed to meet him in Florence, but that's all.'

'So why ask me before if I wanted your help, if you had no intention of giving it?'

'Just playing the game, sweetheart. Nothing more. You want to tell me where the ring is now?'

I studied him for a moment, believing his words and yet sensing something more behind them. Something deeper, darker. 'No, because I have no idea where the ring actually is right now.'

'What were you doing out in the Pacific, then?'

'Talking to the sea. It, at least, doesn't lie.'

Amusement gleamed briefly in his eyes. 'Whether you believe it or not, I haven't told you any lies, either.'

Maybe he hadn't, but that wasn't the point. Egan had believed he *would* help, and Trae had not disabused him of the notion. That, in my book, was just as bad as lying and stealing.

Of course, I shouldn't talk, considering I'd stolen a stranger's clothes and *his* cash.

'After Egan's death, I made myself a promise to return the ring to its rightful owner. That's not you, is it?'

He snorted. 'No, we half breeds certainly have no right to *that* particular ring. But I need it anyway.'

'Why?'

He hesitated. 'I made a deal with my father. If I give him the ring, he gives me some information I need.'

'It must be some pretty heavy information if you're exchanging a ring your brother valued for it.'

'Egan didn't value the ring,' he said, voice edged with annoyance. 'He valued what taking it meant.'

'And that makes total sense.' Not.

He waved a hand dismissively. 'It involves clique politics and history, and I'm not about to go into that here. Give me the ring, Destiny.'

'Sorry. No can do.'

He uncrossed his arms and took a step toward me. In that instant, the little warmth that had been evident in his eyes fled completely, and the dragon came to the fore. It was like facing a stranger – a complete and utterly dangerous stranger.

This was not just a dangerous thief, nor even the man who'd

held the gun at me. This was someone totally new. Someone who didn't care who or what he hurt as long as he got what he wanted.

And I could see why Egan might have called him in for protection.

'Give me the ring, Destiny,' he repeated.

I lifted my chin, a small defiance that made me feel better even if it had no perceivable effect on the man standing opposite me. 'I can't.'

'Why can't you? What have you done to it?'

'I sent it somewhere safe. Somewhere where no one can get to it.'

'You gave it to one of your people in the sea?'

I *had* no people in the sea. Mom's relatives had become virtual strangers the day we'd left Scotland. But I wasn't about to disabuse him of the notion that I'd given the ring to someone else. The control we sea dragons had over the sea – indeed, any sort of water – was something of a well-kept secret. Well, until Costa Brava, anyway.

Hell, legends had us physically attacking boats of old, and while I'm sure there were some old sea dragons who loved to smash and crash before they looted, most had no need to take it that far. Not when the sea could smash and crash for us.

Trae took another step forward. The ice in his eyes, the

tension knotting his limbs spoke of anger and violence bubbling under the surface. I should have been afraid. Very afraid.

Part of me – most of me – definitely was. Yet that last step brought him within a couple of arm lengths, and the raw, spicy aroma of his masculinity washed over me, heating my senses and making my body burn.

I crossed my arms and fought the desire to traverse the distance between us, to fling myself into his arms and taste those uncompromising, yet undoubtedly lush, lips. Think of Egan, I told myself sternly. He deserves the respect of a decent mourning period, at the very least.

Trouble was, the part of me that hungered just wasn't listening.

I wished I knew whether it was simply lust or something more. I'd never really had a chance to talk to my mom about life and love, and I had no idea what it actually felt like when you finally met the one man destined to be your mate. I *had* talked to my dad, of course, but he could only bring his experiences and his knowledge as a man and an air dragon to the table.

And there were greater differences between sea dragons and our air cousins than just the elements we dominated. Our society was more matriarchal than patriarchal, and it was the women who decided when and if the men could impregnate them. I had no idea, however, if females generally remained virginal before they met their mate, or whether they were able to enjoy the company of others. No idea if me being a half breed had any effect on my sexuality and the restrictions that might have been patterned into my DNA. Certainly I hadn't fallen pregnant in the ten years I was with Egan, so that again suggested I was more my mom's daughter than my dad's, but did the mere fact that I *hadn't* remained a virgin mean that the restrictions were muted in me?

Was I even capable of breeding? Of having that one true mate?

I didn't know.

And if I didn't get my mother out of that place, I might never know.

'Destiny, did you give the ring to someone else?'

I stared at him for a moment longer, then nodded. It was close enough to the truth, and he couldn't do anything about it anyway. The dawn had gone, and my ability to recall the ring had fled with it. There was always another dawn, of course, but if he didn't know the truth of the ring's disappearance, then he couldn't force the issue.

'It's out of my reach – and out of my control – for at least a couple of days.'

He swore softly and thrust a hand through his hair. 'Damn it, you had no right to do that.'

'I had *every* right to protect what is mine. That ring was left to me by Egan' – a lie, but he wasn't to know that – 'and I have no intention of giving it to anyone until I'm good and ready.'

He made a hissing sound and spun around, his hands on his hips and his head raised. As if he'd rather look at the brightening skies than me.

My gaze traveled down his leather-coated back. He had good shoulders, good shape, and a butt that filled jeans the way the Gods meant them to be filled. But from the back, he looked more like Egan than ever, and though sorrow stirred through me, it was mixed with guilt.

I owed his brother more than just half truths.

'How about we do a deal?'

He turned back around. The wild, dangerous remoteness had left his eyes, leaving them icy and yet human. If you could ever call a dragon 'human,' that is.

'What sort of deal?'

'You help me get the security codes—'

'What security codes?' he asked, frowning.

'The codes are for the Loch Ness Research Foundation, where we were held captive for so long.'

His frown deepened. 'Why would you want those?'

'Because my mom's still there, as are the kids, and because I promised I'd go back and free them. And I intend to keep that promise, no matter what it takes.'

He considered me for a moment, then said, 'That's pretty brave.'

'Or pretty stupid,' I muttered, and knew which one would win my vote. 'Once we get the codes, if you can then get me to Maine, enough time will have passed for me to be able to recall the ring and give it to you. That way, you can have the ring within days, and I get the protection and help Egan wanted me to have.'

'What's in Maine that's so important?'

'My dad. He's dying.'

'Oh. Sorry.'

'So am I.' But I was also angry – at the scientists for keeping me away for so long, and at myself for so stupidly leaving him in the first place. 'Do we have a deal?'

'I think I could live with a deal like that.' His gaze rested on mine and played havoc with my heart rate. And I wasn't entirely sure if the cause was the heat that surged between us or the dragon spark that seemed to glow deep in his eyes. 'But be warned – if you're playing me for a fool, or if you betray me in any way, you will regret it.'

'I've got too many regrets in my life already, Trae. I don't intend to add any more.'

'Good. Where do you want to go first, then?'

'Florence,' I said, and walked around to the passenger side of the car. The car beeped as I approached the door and lights flashed. I wondered where he'd gotten the keys from, decided I didn't want to know, then opened the door and climbed in.

'So who are we going to steal the codes from?'

'From a Louise Marsten, mother of Doctor James Marsten, who is the founder of the Loch Ness Research Foundation and chief tormentor of all things dragon.'

He started the car and drove out of the turnaround, then asked, 'How many of you were there in this place?'

'Three adults and six kids, the youngest of which is only seven.'

'Seven? Bastards. What the hell were they doing to you all?'

I snorted. 'What do scientists the world over do with the new species of animals they've discovered?'

'We can hardly be classed as animals—'

'In their minds we can, because we turn into monsters that shouldn't exist.' I rubbed my arms, but it didn't do a lot to ward off the sudden chill. 'They prod, they poke, they examine, and they cut. They put us through hoops and they expect us to be happy about it.'

'But, as you pointed out, we can turn into monsters. Why didn't you, and just get the hell out of there?'

'Because for many years, we didn't realize they were drugging us.'

'You should have destroyed them while you had the chance.'

'We couldn't. We barely escaped as it was.' And only because the scientists had been too busy fighting the fire that had taken the life of one of their own, and had almost claimed ours.

I looked away, watching the buildings, shops, and houses coming to life as people began waking to the new day. Longing flicked through me. For too many years, my life had been one of white walls and bright lights. And air so cold it could turn the skin blue – which wasn't such a problem for me and my mother, but it had certainly been one for the air dragons. The scientists had discovered fairly early that cold limited their movements, restricting their fire and making them extremely sluggish. Which of course, had proved a big problem for Egan. But it had been an even bigger one for the kids – especially Carli. The small brown dragon had been the first of the young ones snatched and she was still the youngest of them all – she'd barely been three when she was taken, and she was only seven now.

It was Egan who had realized that the cold was killing her, and he who had insisted that they turn the heat up in both her room and in the common rooms. For some reason I'll never understand, the scientists had actually listened. Maybe they just didn't want to lose their only female air dragon. But it was around that time they must have begun increasing the dosage of the drugs they'd been giving us – so much so that we actually started tasting them.

It was a realization that had begun our plot to escape.

But those plans had taken a very long time to come to fruition, I thought, my gaze lingering on the warmly lit homes zooming by. God, the luxury of waking in a home, surrounded by family, was not something any of us had experienced for a very long time. My capture might have been my own stupid fault, and Egan's had apparently been due to carelessness, but most of the kids had been netted in those magical, mystical hours of dawn and dusk, when young air dragons rode the energy in the air, trusting the still-flaring skies to hide their forms as they attempted to master the wind. They'd been easy pickings for the older hunters who'd been high above, waiting for that one who strayed a little farther from flock than they should have.

And to take a *three*-year-old? Hunters who would do such a thing – who would not only betray their own but tear families apart for the sake of money – disgusted me. I think I hated them more than I hated the scientists.

At least we'd taken one of them out in San Lucas, which meant there would be one, maybe two, hunters left on my trail. That I knew of, anyway.

I tore my gaze away from the roadside and looked at Trae. The golden light of dawn shone through the windshield, washing across his features, making the spiky bristles lining his chin gleam like molten gold.

I have to say, twenty-four-hour whisker growth on *this* man was incredibly sexy.

'Tell me about the ring,' I said, as much to keep my mind off desire as to find out the history behind the ring.

He shrugged. 'It's basically the king stone, and it was Egan's by birthright.'

'Why?'

He looked in the rearview mirror, then said, 'Our father is the king of our clique, and Egan was the firstborn pure-dragon son. As such, he was heir to the family fortune.'

'And throne?'

'Possibly.' He glanced at me. 'I'm surprised that he didn't talk to you about all this.'

'As I said, he wouldn't. All he'd say was that the past no longer mattered.' I studied him for a minute. 'Was that because of this Sila you mentioned earlier?'

'Undoubtedly.' Though his voice was flat, without emotion, the heat of his anger swirled around me, scorching my skin.

'What happened to her?'

'My father happened.'

'He tore them apart?'

'He killed her.'

'*What?*' I stared at him, horrified. 'Why?'

'Because my father's eye was always on the greater prize. Sila was a black dragon with no family links that would enhance the clique's position and standing in the dragon community, and therefore useless in his eyes.'

'He killed her because she didn't have the right *connections*?'

'Afraid so.'

My God . . . 'Your father sounds like a murdering bastard.'

He snorted softly. 'That's the understatement of the year.'

No wonder Egan hadn't wanted to talk about the past. No wonder nothing had really mattered to him anymore – at least until the kids had come along. He'd lost the woman he'd loved and, as a result, had simply closed up and retreated emotionally.

Everything about him made so much more sense now. I blew out a breath, then asked, 'So where do you fit into all this?'

'Me? I'm the unwanted get of the maid.' His tone was lightly mocking.

I raised my eyebrows and said, 'You don't have the attitude of someone unwanted.'

He glanced at me, amusement bright in his blue eyes. 'And just what sort of attitude would that be?'

'Sullen. Angry.'

'Oh, I'm angry. Trust me on that.'

'Yeah, but it's a different kind of anger. More vengeful than the-world-owes-me-a-living.'

A smile teased his lips and my hormones again. 'You're quick to judge someone you've only just met.' He glanced briefly at the rearview again. 'Tell me how you and Egan met.'

'I told you how we met. In a cage, in the research center.'

'And the scientists forced you together?'

'Well, it wasn't force, but we weren't given a whole lot of choice, either.' It was either mate, or have them force the issue by in vitro fertilization. Something they'd ended up trying anyway after so many years of nothing happening.

And it still hadn't worked, simply because they had no understanding of a sea dragon's nature. They might well implant me with a fertilized egg, but it wouldn't stay that way nor grow in my womb.

'I'm gathering they wanted you to reproduce?'

'Yeah.'

'Egan wasn't your mate, so that wasn't going to happen.'

I raised an eyebrow. 'You seem very certain of that.'

He smiled. 'You wouldn't be responding to me so fiercely if he *had* been. Besides, Sila was his mate.'

'God, it's a wonder he didn't kill his father.' I would have, had I been in his shoes. 'So can female air dragons dictate when they get pregnant, like we sea dragons can?'

He looked surprised at the thought. 'No, that's the male's prerogative.'

'And when air dragons finally meet their destined mates, do the males remain faithful?'

He glanced at me, amusement touching his lips. 'Why the questions? Sourcing out a potential mate, are we?'

Heat touched my cheeks and I looked away from his knowing

gaze. 'No. But Egan wouldn't talk about this stuff, and I have no one else to ask.'

'Ah.' He contemplated the road for a second, then said, 'It depends on whether they actually commit to their mates or not. If they do, then they remain faithful. If they don't, then no. My father is one of the latter – he has no regard whatsoever for his soul mate, and beds whomever he can at will.' He glanced at me, one eyebrow raised. 'What about you sea dragons?'

'I don't know. Mom was captured when I was very young, and there was only ever me and Dad. I love my dad to death, but he wasn't very forthcoming about that sort of stuff.' And he certainly hadn't encouraged exploration as I'd gotten older. Not that I would have, anyway. I'd spent most of my life hiding what I was from the world, pretending to be human when I was anything but. I had friends, but never close ones. Male friends, but never boyfriends.

'So what is the story behind your birth?' I continued. 'Did your dad deliberately get a human pregnant?'

'Not deliberately. He was drunk, apparently, and she was just a warm body when he needed one.' He shrugged, a seemingly casual gesture that belied the deeper anger I could feel in him. 'Human and dragon matings almost always result in a pregnancy, even if the male doesn't wish it. No one really knows why.'

'So why mate with humans in the first place?'

'Because they can. It's as simple as that.' He glanced in the rearview. 'In times past, we draman were killed on birth.'

'*What?*'

'To keep the purity of the master race, you understand.' Again his voice was mocking. 'It's only in the last fifty years or so that the practice has been outlawed by the council.'

I raised my eyebrows. 'There's a council of dragons?'

He nodded. 'It consists of the kings from the thirteen major cliques. They make the rules and clean up the problems.'

'So basically, they make sure the cliques continue to operate under the human radar?'

'Basically.'

'How come no one did anything about Marsten?'

'They might not even know about him. The council only concerns itself with problems on our continent, as far as I know.'

Well, if there was a European council, they were fucking falling down on the job.

He looked in the rearview mirror once again, and something in the way he did it sent unease prickling across my spine. 'What's wrong?'

'I think we're being followed. Don't look,' he added, just as I was about to.

'Cop?'

'Nope.'

The unease gave way to fear. 'Do they look official?'

'Hard to say.'

I flipped down the sun visor and slid open the vanity mirror's cover. It took several seconds to position the mirror so that I could see the traffic following, but then the big black car leapt into focus.

And though I couldn't see the faces of the driver and the passenger, I knew what they were all the same.

Hunters.

Chapter Five

Fear ran through me, stifling in its power, sucking away my breath and my strength. All I could do was stare at the car behind us – the car that held the men who had helped kill Egan, and who would probably kill me if I gave them too much trouble.

And all I could think of was getting away. Even though I couldn't move, couldn't even talk. I was frozen to the seat in fear of the men behind us. Men who had snatched away so much of my life.

I *couldn't* let them catch me. Not again. Not when there was still so much to do.

'Destiny?' Trae said, his voice seeming a long way away.

I gulped down air and tried to rein in the tide of panic.

'Floor it,' I said, my voice a low tremor. 'Get us out of here.'

'The minute I floor it, the people in that car will know we've spotted them. The situation could end up being a whole lot worse than it already is.'

'The situation will end up a whole lot worse anyway.' I had to grip the door to stop the urge to slide down the seat and keep out of their sight. They obviously knew I was here or they wouldn't be following us. It was pointless, trying to hide.

Trae shot me a sharp look. 'You know the people in the car?'

'Personally? No. But I know what they are, and I know just how far they're willing to go. We need to get away from them. *Now.*'

That last word held an edge of panic, which Trae seemed to ignore as he said, 'So who are they?'

'They're the people who shot Egan. They're dragon hunters.' And the scientists would be close by somewhere. If not in the car behind us, then somewhere near. They were *always* near.

He swore softly.

'Look, we need to get out of here,' I insisted. 'We need to lose them.'

'I will, I will.'

'*Before* we get out of the built-up areas and onto open road. They hunt in packs. They always hunt in packs. There'll be another car around – somewhere close.'

'You make them sound like animals,' he muttered. But nevertheless, he pressed the accelerator and the car gathered speed.

Not sharply, not enough to notice immediately, but enough to ease the clamoring of my nerves.

I looked in the vanity mirror. The big black car was still very much behind us. 'Their car looks faster than ours.'

'It is.'

'Then what are we going to do if we can't outrun them?'

'Outsmart them. You feel like breakfast?'

I blinked. 'You can't stop and eat breakfast at a time like this!'

'You tell me where in the rule book it says I can't, and I'll obey.'

'But—'

'I'm not a free-roaming thief for no reason, you know, so just trust the fact that I know a thing or two about getting away from people.'

His expression and voice might have been bland, but there was nothing bland about the look he cast my way. It was all dangerous, hungry male. Heat sizzled across my skin, followed by a rush of desire.

'What?' I said, voice suddenly breathless.

'Time to use the charms God and your parents gifted you with.'

'What charms in particular are we talking about?'

'That sexy body, of course.' Even as he said the words, his gaze skated downward, causing my pulse to flutter.

It sure as hell was a fine way to banish fear.

'To do what?'

The question came out breathy, and amusement crinkled the corners of his eyes.

'Make out.'

'I'm not making out with you.' Though I wanted to. Lord how I wanted to.

'Not me. The cook.'

'What?' Why did this man always leave me feeling I was three steps behind?

'Of the burger joint we're going to stop at up ahead.'

'How do you know there's a burger joint up ahead?'

'Because I've been this way before, and I always scout out localities.'

'When you're planning a job, you mean?'

He shot me an amused look, neither confirming nor denying my accusation. 'The place is open twenty-four hours. The early morning shift is one man, and he's both the cook and waiter. You're going to charm the pants off him.'

'No, I'm not.'

'Yes, you *are*. You're going to make that man want you bad enough to take you out to his truck.'

'Where you'll deck him and snatch said truck?'

'Precisely.'

'I'm not happy with this plan, I have to tell you.'

'Well, unless you got a better plan, this is the one we're stuck with.'

'The car behind us will spot us leaving in the truck.'

'The car behind us will unfortunately have two flat tires by that time.'

'Why not do all four?'

'Four is trickier, and the chance of getting caught increases dramatically.'

I stared at him for a minute, then crossed my arms. But one glance in the mirror at our black shadow and the men within left me little in the way of options.

I blew out a breath. 'What's this cook look like?'

'Like a cook?'

'I'm not making out with a lecherous old man.'

'So you'd rather be caught by those behind us?'

No. I'd just rather come up with something else.

The burger joint turned out to be attached to a gas station, though the cobwebs draped over the pumps suggested they hadn't been used in some time. The building itself was brick, and it was hard to say what color they were thanks to the years of grime coating them. The large windows that lined the front were decorated with Christmas lights that cheerfully flashed in the early morning sun, and a huge burger sign sat above the weather-worn entrance, flashing on and off intermittently.

The burger on that sign looked no more appealing than the place itself.

I sniffed. 'I still don't like this plan.'

'Sweetheart, we have no choice. They're right up our asses.'

My gaze flickered to the mirror. The black car had stopped on the side of the road.

Great. Just great. I unbuckled the belt and gave in to the inevitable. 'Okay, let's get this over with.'

We climbed out of the car and walked over to the door. All the time the back of my neck prickled, and it was all I could do not to run.

They were watching.

They were *always* watching.

No matter what Egan or I or the kids did, they were there. Them and Marsten.

I shivered, and jumped a little when Trae touched a hand to my back. 'In you go,' he said, guiding me through the door.

A little bell chimed as Trae closed the door, and a voice from the rear of the building called out, 'Won't be a moment, loves.'

I raised my eyebrows and looked at Trae. 'Now, that's the most feminine-sounding male voice I've heard in a long time.'

He frowned. 'That it was.'

'Could it be the great planner got this one wrong?'

'I don't get things wrong, sweetheart.'

'Call me that one more time and I'm going to stomp on your toes.'

He looked down. 'Bare feet versus boots. Not so worried.'

'You obviously haven't spent enough time looking at my feet.'

His gaze twinkled. 'Most certainly not. There's nicer things to look at than toes.'

Footsteps echoed as someone marched smartly up the hall to our right. Seconds later, a matronly looking woman with gray hair and a merry smile appeared behind the counter.

'Now, what can I get you young people?'

'Is old Harry here?' Trae asked.

'Nope. That bastard got sacked a month ago for pilfering the till. Me and Frank run the place now.'

'There goes the seduction plan,' I murmured cheerfully.

'Don't suppose you do a traditional breakfast?' Trae said, cupping his hand under my elbow and leading me over to a table near the window.

'Depends what you mean by traditional,' she replied. 'We do pancakes, waffles, and bacon and eggs.'

'One pancakes, one bacon and eggs, and two coffees, thanks.'

'The pancakes had better be for you, buddy boy,' I said, as the woman headed back out to the kitchen. 'Otherwise there's going to be words said.'

'You don't have a sweet tooth?'

'Not when it comes to breakfast.' I slid into a booth seat and kept my back to the black car.

'How about we share the plates?' He slid in the booth opposite and crossed his arms on the table as he casually looked out the window. 'There's three men in that car.'

'Three?' A shiver ran through me. 'There's probably two hunters. The driver would be one of the scientists.'

He looked at me, eyebrow raised. 'You make them sound like cowboys intent on drugging cattle.'

'They are. And we're the cattle.'

He studied me for a moment, then shook his head. 'I wish I'd known. I would have done something to try and get Egan out. And, in the process, the rest of you.'

I smiled. 'I had the same thought when I was eighteen. I got caught.'

'I'm not eighteen, and I'm also a very good thief.'

'It wouldn't have mattered.'

'So little confidence in my abilities,' he said, voice bland. 'And yet here you are, trusting them.'

Because I had no other choice. I needed those codes, and I knew nothing about breaking into houses, let alone safes. I crossed my arms and stared out the window, watching the tufted grasses that lined the parking lot sway lightly in the breeze. Remembered wind of a different kind – a wind that howled and moaned through long, dark nights. A wind so cold it could kill if it touched bare skin. We'd gone to the Arctic to avoid them when we'd first escaped, but hadn't stayed long. It had been far too cold for an air dragon to survive, despite Egan's protestations that he was fine. So we'd looped around Iceland, and had come back through the North Atlantic, making our way down and around South America before swimming – or in Egan's case, flying – back up to Mexico.

It had all been for naught, because they'd been waiting for us. And yet Egan had been so sure that they wouldn't know about the villa. So how had they found us so quickly and easily?

Trae snapped his fingers in front of my face, and I jumped. 'What?' I said, scowling at him.

'You were off in your thoughts again.' His gaze went from me to the car and back again. 'Tell me, why do you think they killed Egan? If he was the only full-grown male, it makes no sense for them to get rid of him.'

'I think they considered him to be more dangerous than Mom or me, and he did start the fire that allowed us to escape.' Even if the fire wasn't *his*. I shrugged. 'I'm sure they were intending to keep his body and study him that way, but I foiled that by snatching him away.'

'I would have thought being able to control water was a greater threat than fire. Especially when you're all being kept beside a loch containing a huge amount of freshwater.' He leaned back in the seat as the old woman walked over with two coffees.

'There you go, loves. Breakfast will be another five minutes or so.'

'Thanks,' I said, giving her a smile.

Trae waited until she'd walked back to the kitchen, then added, 'If a sea dragon *can* control any sort of water, why did you never call the loch?'

I grimaced. 'I can't tell you why my mother never did, because I just don't know. In my case—' I blew out a breath. 'I did *try*, but the loch didn't answer. I thought at first it was because I was a half breed, that maybe I simply didn't have the strength to make the water obey over any distance. When we finally realized they were giving us a drug that restricted our abilities and we managed to wean ourselves off it, I could have tried, but then there were the kids to worry about.'

He frowned. 'Why would they be a worry?'

'Because while I might have been able to call freshwater, I can't control its fury or its path like I can with seawater. Carli and a couple of the others couldn't swim – I asked them. If I'd called the loch, they would have drowned.'

'Ah. A nasty situation, then.'

'To put it mildly,' I agreed. 'What are we going to do about the car and the people within it?'

He picked up his coffee and took a sip. 'First priority is to deflate the tires. Then we can ditch our car once we're free and get a new one.'

I wrapped my hands around my coffee mug, but it did little to warm them. 'You're pretty free and easy with other people's cars, aren't you?'

He shrugged. 'Part of the joy of being a thief is an easy contempt for other people's belongings.'

'Does that include the girlfriends of other men?'

His sudden grin was so sexy, so filled with heat, that an answering flame rose from deep within me.

'I am *not* my father's son. Not in that regard, anyway.'

'So you're a one-woman man?'

'I will be, when I find the right woman.'

I raised an eyebrow. 'So you're totally unattached right now?'

His gaze met mine, and something in those bright depths sent a shiver through my soul. This man was hunting, too.

'Currently, I'm single,' he said softly. 'But you never know when that might change.'

Another tremor ran through me, and I wasn't sure whether it was anticipation or fear. I pulled my gaze from his and tried to calm the idiotic racing of my pulse. 'How do you intend to get out of the diner without being seen?'

'Simple. I'll go to the bathroom.'

I took a sip of coffee, and raised my gaze to his again. The heat of hunting had faded from his eyes, but not the amusement. It leant a warmth to the cold, bright depths. 'So there's a window in the bathroom?'

'A small one, but I should be able to get through it.'

'I don't know,' I said, skimming my gaze down his body and keeping my voice dry. 'Your ego is pretty damn large.'

He laughed. It was such a warm and carefree sound that it dragged a smile to my lips and made my heart do an odd little dance.

'You could be right about that,' he said. 'Maybe I should send you through it instead.'

'Sorry, I know squat about sneaking.'

'Considering you've escaped from what I presume is a very secure research center, I find that extremely hard to believe.'

'That was a mix of luck and good planning more than any ability to sneak, believe me.'

The old woman brought in the plates of food. Trae gave her a smile and waited until she'd recovered from the power of it enough to head back into the kitchen before he asked, 'Luck how?'

I snagged a piece of bacon from the nearest plate and munched on it meditatively. 'Part of the research center was destroyed by fire. That took down the security system, as well as distracted a lot of the guards, which enabled us to get out.'

Of course, there was a whole lot more to it than that. More

violence, more pain, more death. Escape hadn't been easy, just like remaining free hadn't been.

'Am I right to assume the fires were dragon-lit?' Trae asked.

'Actually, they weren't. They kept the facility so cold that the air dragons couldn't use their fires.'

He raised his eyebrows. 'That sort of cold can be a killer.'

'So they discovered.' I hesitated, and grinned. 'Of course, when it comes to kids and temper tantrums, the cold isn't really a restriction. Trust me, a few things got singed over the years.'

'But never by Egan?'

I shook my head. 'But we were being drugged. The kids weren't.'

'So when you and Egan escaped, why didn't you take the kids with you?'

'We couldn't.' But I'd wanted to. Oh, how I'd wanted to. I'd fought with Egan for days about it – until Jace had stepped in. Jace – the fifteen-year-old who was so much older and wiser than his years would suggest – had calmly told me that it just wasn't practical, and that he'd look after everyone until we got back with help. 'The kids were in a separate section than us, and there were common rooms and research rooms between us. We couldn't get to them without going through a whole lot of sci-entists and guards.'

'So how did you and Egan escape?'

'We attacked one of the feeders as he was coming into the

cell, then ran for the kitchen area. Egan didn't have his flame, thanks to the cold, but there were plenty of lighters laying about. We put them to good use to blow up the kitchens.'

'Wasn't that a little risky?'

Brief memories of flames and heat, combined with the metal ping of bullets against walls, rose like ghosts through my mind.

I closed my eyes against them, but there was no fighting it. The flames meant to free us had almost killed us both. It was Egan who had saved us – saved me. Despite the cold, he'd tamed the flames the same way I could tame the sea. In the end, we'd come out singed but alive.

The same could not be said about sections of the research center. Or the scientists within it.

'Destiny?'

I blinked, then tore off a chunk of toast to dip into the egg yolk. 'The kitchen was a fair distance from where the kids were being held. It wasn't that much of a risk.'

'I meant for you and Egan.'

'Well, yeah, but we had to do something to divert enough attention so that we could escape.'

He considered me for a moment, his blue eyes somber, as if guessing there was more to my glib statement. 'How did they find you in San Lucas? How did they track us here?'

'I don't know.'

'Why didn't they kill you when they killed Egan?'

109

'Some of them were definitely trying.' And I had the scar on my head to prove it. 'But I think I'm still alive because I'm the only female of breeding age they have. Mom's too old, and Carli's too young.'

He didn't say anything, just studied me for a minute before flicking his gaze to the black car. 'Looks like those men are getting antsy.'

Trepidation ran down my spine, but I resisted the temptation to turn around. It would only let them know I knew about them, and that could prove dangerous. 'Meaning they're likely to come in here?'

'I don't know. Maybe.' His gaze met mine. Distant. Fiery. The dragon was getting ready to fight. 'You know these people, not me.'

'I might know them, but that doesn't mean I can predict everything they might do.' I picked up my coffee again to warm suddenly cold fingers. 'All I know is that they prefer not to have witnesses, so we may be safe in here for a while. But the threat of witnesses won't stop them for long.'

He didn't say anything, just picked up his coffee and stared out the window for several minutes. Tension crackled through the air – evidence that he was not as calm as he appeared.

'Okay, one of them is on the phone,' he said, as he put his coffee down. His blue gaze came to mine, sharp with excitement. 'I'll head to the bathroom now. If you see any of them walking past the gas pumps, get up and head to the counter to pay our bill, then get into the bathroom. I'll get you out from there.' He hesitated, and a grin twitched his lips. 'Feel free to use some of the cash you stole to pay the bill, too.'

I raised my eyebrow. 'I never said I stole the cash. I only admitted to stealing back the ring. Maybe you're a thief who loses track of what he has in his pocket.'

'Sweetheart, I never lose track of *anything* that's mine.' He rose, drawing my gaze up the long, lean length of him. 'Remember that, if you intend on stealing anything more important than cash or credit cards.'

I raised an eyebrow. 'And what else have you got that I'd be interested in?'

He grinned. 'I'm sure we could think of something.'

'I'm sure you could,' I said, voice dry. Just as I was sure I'd love it. Whatever 'it' was.

He left the booth. I sipped my coffee and watched his retreat. Egan and I had never shared easy banter like that. Had never teased or touched or done any of those fun things most lovers do. He'd been too uncomfortable with the whole situation, too aware of the white coats and the cameras. Thank God they'd never installed microphones, otherwise he'd have never come near me. As it was, we'd only ever made love at night, with the lights off, when he had the illusion of some degree of privacy.

It wasn't exactly the most normal introduction to sex and sensuality a girl could have had.

The old woman wandered over with the coffeepot. 'Want a top-up, love?'

'Thanks.' I held out my cup, and pushed Trae's forward. He might not get to drink it, because we'd probably have to run once he deflated the tires, but it was better to keep up appearances for our watchers.

'You two down here for a vacation?' the woman asked, as she poured coffee into Trae's cup.

'Just passing through.' I shrugged. 'Wish we could stay longer, though. It's pretty.'

'Well, not so much around these parts. It's pretty old and dumpy here.'

I smiled, remembering my distaste as we'd approached the old building. And yet, once inside, it had proved to be warm, homey, and friendly. Just went to show, the old saying about the book and its cover was correct.

'But the food is as good as any of those uptown places.'

She beamed. 'Can I get you anything else?'

A life. Or maybe a leash for my hormones. I smiled and shook my head. 'Just the bill. We'll have to go once my partner gets out of the bathroom.'

'If he wanted to sneak out to let the air out of the tires of that car, he could have just asked to slip out the back. Has to be uncomfortable, a man his size squeezing through the bathroom window.'

I just about choked on my coffee. I coughed as the hot liquid slid down the wrong way, but somehow managed to say, 'What?'

There was a mischievous twinkle in the old girl's eyes. 'Frank saw him sneaking around. Pretty good, he reckons, and Frank would know. He had a bit of a wayward past, when we were kids.' She paused. 'So is it husband trouble, or the law?'

'Husband,' I said, probably much too quickly. Not that she was likely to believe the truth, anyway. 'We've been separated for over a year, but he just won't accept it. Has me followed everywhere.'

She nodded. 'Some men are like that. What you need to do is give him a little of his own medicine.'

'Who can be bothered?'

She grimaced, and patted me on the shoulder. 'If you feel the need to slip out, just come through the kitchen and pay. Frank will let you out the back door.'

'I appreciate it.'

She nodded and walked back to the counter. I sipped my coffee and watched the wind roll an empty Coke bottle across the road. Part of me longed to turn around and see just what those men in the black car were doing, but I dared not let them know anything might be wrong. So I drank, and ate the pancakes, and generally tried to ignore the tension creeping through my limbs.

After a while, the woman came back with the check. 'He's just slipping back in now, in case you're wondering.'

'Thanks,' I said, with a smile.

As she walked back toward the kitchen, I glanced at the check and got out the money, adding an extremely generous tip in the process. Hell, it wasn't my money anyway, and maybe she'd be more inclined to think kindly about us if things got nasty.

Trae slipped into the booth a few seconds later, and wrapped his hands around his coffee. 'You know, for a woman who doesn't like pancakes, you sure as hell made a good job of finishing them off.'

'And for a thief, you sure as hell did a lousy job of sneaking about.'

He frowned. 'And why would you think that? Those men didn't spot me.'

'No, but the old girl and her cook did. I told them we were sneaking away from my hubby's trackers.'

'Not very original.'

'When lying, it pays to stick to the classics. They tend to be more believable.'

'And you know this from experience?'

'Hey, *you* were caught.'

He grimaced. 'I misjudged the size of my shoulders and that window, but I was hoping they wouldn't notice above the usual kitchen noise.'

'Frank apparently has a past and eagle eyes. The old girl said we could slip out the back if we wanted to.'

'As long as they're watching us, they're not noticing the tires. That's what we want right now. You ready to go?'

I gulped down the rest of my coffee and rose. The itching at the back of my neck got stronger, and as we made our way to the door, I stole a glance at the car.

One man was out and leaning on the door, and his expression, even from this distance, looked somewhat agitated.

'Act normal,' Trae repeated, as if reading my thoughts. 'And keep hoping they won't do anything here, out in the open.'

He pushed the diner's front door wide and ushered me through. The wind swirled around us, lifting the hair from the nape of my neck and running cold fingers down my spine. I shivered and crossed my arms, trying to keep warm against the sudden chill.

Trae touched my back as he moved up beside me, placing his body between me and those men. His light touch sent warmth skittering across my skin, and though it did little to battle the internal chill, I felt a tad more secure.

But not safe. Not with those men so close.

'Has he gotten back into the car yet?' I murmured, my gaze on Trae's stolen black car.

'No. He's still standing behind the open door. The driver is still on the phone.'

'Something is going on.'

'It won't matter in a couple of seconds.'

In a couple of seconds I'd be a nervous wreck. God, how I wanted to run to his car and get the hell away from them. The urge to do just that was so great my muscles were practically twitching.

As we neared Trae's car, his touch left me, and the chill returned twofold. He pressed the auto unlock. The lights flashed, and orange light skittered across the road, looking almost bloody against the dark asphalt.

A tremor ran down my spine. I grasped the handle, eager to get out of here.

But even as I began opening the car door, movement caught my eye. I turned and saw the man standing behind the open door of the scientist's car raise his arms and rest them on the top of the door frame.

Saw the glint of metal in his hands.

Realized I'd been wrong, so wrong, in my earlier estimation of how far they might go out in the open, in front of witnesses.

I heard the incongruous popping sound.

I swore and flung open the door. Something slammed into my shoulder, spinning me around, smashing my head against the top of the car.

Then I was falling . . .

Chapter Six

I hit the roadside with a grunt, and for a moment, everything went black. But I could hear voices, and shouting. I could feel anger. Thick, thick anger. Then there was this weird whooshing sound, and heat filled the morning, burning bright. The taint of burning rubber and paint began to touch the air.

I forced my eyes open. Saw flames, leaping high. Flames that were coming from Trae, who stood behind our car, and flames that roared from the fingers of the dark-haired man standing in front of the other car. The two fiery lances met in the middle of the parking lot and erupted upward.

Then the car behind the hunter exploded, sending him and the men who were cowering behind it flying. Trae appeared and dragged me upright, shoving me hastily into his car. Pain swirled, and I made a sound that was half groan, half curse.

'I'm sorry, I'm sorry.' Trae's voice was raw, and filled with the anger I'd felt moments ago. 'But we have to get out of here before they come back. How's that shoulder?'

'Hurts,' I said, voice sounding distant even to my own ears. Something pressed against it. 'Hold that. Don't let go.'

When I didn't move, he grabbed my good hand and pressed it against the cloth. 'Hold it, Des. Hold it tight, and just stay awake.'

'I'll try.'

I did try. I just didn't succeed.

I have no idea how long I was out, but waking was a long, painful process.

My shoulder felt like a throbbing furnace, and there were a thousand tiny gnomes armed with sharp little axes working away at the inside of my head.

I shifted, trying to ease both the aches, but that only managed to make them both worse. A groan escaped my lips, and the sound seemed to echo.

The hollowness reminded me of the cells that had been a part of my life for so many years, and my heart began to race. Part of me wanted to open my eyes and find out where the hell I was. But the cowardly part was afraid of what might be revealed. Of what it might mean.

Because there was no sound of the car. No feeling that there was anyone or anything near. Just an unearthly, unending hush that had the hairs along my arms standing on end.

I breathed deep. Dustiness filled the air, along with a sense of age and regret – as if wherever I lay had once been cared for but now lay abandoned.

At least the air wasn't filled with the scent of antiseptic cleanliness, which surely had to mean I wasn't caught. Wasn't with *them* again.

Reluctantly, I forced my eyes open. Afternoon sunlight streamed into the room from the ceiling-high windows that lined the end wall directly opposite. The brightness sliced through the middle of the room but left the corners to shadows and imagination. But not even the shadows could hide the neglected state of the room. Ornate wallpaper hung in fading strips down the walls, and what paint remained on the high ceilings and fancy cornices was so cracked and yellowed that it was hard to say what color it might have been originally. I shifted to get a better view of the rest of the room, and discovered the hard way that my skin had decided to cling to whatever it was that I lay on. It peeled away with an odd sort of sucking sound and almost immediately began to sting and itch.

The reason, I discovered, as I looked around at the high back of the old sofa on which I lay, was plastic. The whole sofa was covered in it. And the T-shirt I was wearing had ridden up at the back, exposing my butt and spine.

There was another plastic-covered chair stuck in the far corner but little else in the way of furniture. Just a tired-looking fireplace that added to the cold and forlorn air.

'Trae?' My voice came out a croak. I cleared my throat, and the sound echoed softly. 'Trae?'

No answer came. I wondered if I were alone. Wondered if he'd run out on me again.

I forced myself upright – too fast, I quickly discovered, as the ax-wielding gnomes got to work with a vengeance. Sweat popped out across my forehead and a hiss escaped my lips. I closed my eyes, waiting until everything stopped spinning, then slowly, carefully, got to my feet.

My arm and shoulder throbbed in protest, and suddenly felt heavy. I looked down. Bandages were poking out from the frayed end of an old gray T-shirt. And though I doubted that Trae had actually abandoned me again, at least if he had, he'd patched me up first and given me a clean shirt.

I scratched my back with my good hand and glanced around the room again, spotting a door at the far end. I took a deep breath, then began a careful walk toward the door. The caution paid off, because the ax-wielding gnomes made no further protest.

A wide, marble tile floor lay beyond the grand old room in

which I'd woken. Stairs curved upward about halfway down the hall to my left, and an ornate entrance foyer and doorway lay to my right. Beyond the stairs there were more doors, and the smell of coffee was suddenly, tantalizingly close.

I followed my nose and eventually found a kitchen that seemed big enough to fit a regular-sized house in. Trae wasn't there, but he had been. His tangy scent clung to the air, as tempting and rich as the aroma of the coffee.

A timeworn percolator sat on a bench at the far end of the kitchen, and beside it, a sheet of paper held down by a coffee cup.

I walked across and poured myself a drink, then tore open the sugar packets Trae had left near the percolator. Once I'd fortified myself with a sip of the strong, sweet liquid, I finally read the note.

Gone to get some supplies, it said. *Be careful and stay put.* Trae's elegant – almost extravagant – signature followed, as well as the time. I looked around for a clock, but there was none to be found. Still, given the way the sun streamed in through the kitchen window, it couldn't be much past four. Which meant he hadn't been gone long when I'd woken.

But how long had I been out? I had no idea, but that wasn't exactly an unusual state for me lately. I absently scratched my leg as I glanced at the kitchen window and studied the long sweep of wildness that had obviously once been a lovingly manicured garden. Was this another of his previously scouted locations? Or had my getting shot forced him to find suitable accommodations fast?

If it was the latter, he certainly had a knack for finding high-class, abandoned properties. There can't have been many places around like this. Good land was getting scarcer and scarcer these days – especially prized plots near lakes or the sea.

Places like my mother's ancestral home in Loch Ness. Her family had lived there for hundreds of years, using the loch's deep, dark waters as not only a safe place to give birth, but a sort of 'winter home' when the storms made the sea a danger-ous place to be.

Not all sea dragons did this, of course. Most simply migrated to calmer, warmer waters during the winter months. But Mom's lands on the loch had been her pride and joy – a place where she and her family could be themselves without worry or con-cern. And the good thing was, even if a dragon form was occasionally spotted, the legend of the monster covered it amply enough.

But then the scientists had come. Taking her and taking her lands, all without a quibble from the uncles and aunts I could barely remember now. Even Dad didn't discuss them, though I have vague memories of him arguing with a man whose hair was as blue as the rich Pacific waters. Dad hadn't been happy with him, and I think it was because they refused to help Mom.

Sea dragons didn't live in large family groups, as air dragons seemed to, but that didn't mean there was no contact, no closeness. I'd seen my uncles and my aunts many times in the brief few years that we had lived in peace on the loch's shore. But then Mom was taken, Dad had fled with me – at Mom's insistence, apparently – and the visits had stopped. Except for that one visit from the man with the blue hair.

I drank my coffee and stared blindly out the window, seeing nothing, and trying not to think about anything, just letting the coffee and the sunshine work its magic on my cold, itchy body. By the time I reached the bottom of the cup, I felt a little more 'human' and a lot less shaky. I poured myself another, and decided to undertake a little exploration.

The remaining rooms on the first floor consisted of a huge butler's pantry, a dining room, what looked to be a study, and, off that, a library. There was also a huge bathroom that looked to have become home to generations of seabirds, thanks to several smashed windows. A fresh wind trailed in, whisking away the clinging, musty aroma of bird. I moved on. The sweeping stairs – which I took extremely slowly because the gnomes with the axes weren't finished with me yet, no matter what I might have thought – led up to another living area, a huge bathroom and five large bedrooms. From the master bedroom, the sea was visible, a broad sweep of white-capped blue that had my soul singing. I could live here, I thought, as I opened the window and breathed the sharp, salty scent. It rushed deep into my lungs, and flushed both strength and longing through my body.

My gaze ran back from the sea, following a barely visible path from the cliff tops to the property's fence line. I could get there if I wanted to. If I needed to.

And I would need to, soon.

The sound of a car drawing closer had me leaning farther out the window. But I couldn't see the driveway or the property's main gate, so I walked as quickly as my aching head would allow into the living room and peered out the windows there. An old gray car had stopped near the gate, and a figure in a black shirt and dark jeans was hunkered down near one gate post, doing God knows what. After a moment, he rose, and the sunlight ran through his hair, making it gleam like finely spun gold.

He walked back to the car, but paused before getting in, his gaze sweeping the house and coming to rest on my window. He smiled and gave a half wave, then got back into the car. I checked my own wave, and tried to stop grinning.

For God's sake, I didn't even *know* this man. I should be acting with a bit of decorum – *and* caution – not like some giddy schoolgirl in the flush of a first teenage crush.

Not that I'd actually *had* any teenage crushes. I'd been far too aware of my differences – and the need for caution – to ever get too attracted to anyone at my school. Especially when I was the only dragon – sea or air – among them.

I turned away from the window and headed back downstairs. Yet the minute Trae walked in the back door carrying a fistful of plastic bags in one hand and a laptop in the other, my silly grin broke loose and my pulse rate went into overdrive.

'Hey, darlin', nice to see you up and about so soon.' He dumped everything on the counter, then looked me up and down somewhat critically. 'You're still looking a bit peaked, though.'

The concern in his voice and eyes sent a delicious tingle scampering across my skin. 'Getting shot will do that to a girl. Where are we?'

'In a big old abandoned house that I just happen to own.'

I raised an eyebrow. 'And how would a thief be able to afford this place? It must be worth a fortune, even in its current condition.'

'I told you, I'm a very good thief.' There was a glint in his eyes that was all cheek. 'And it's just perfect for the brood I intend to have one day.'

'If you can find a woman to put up with you long enough to produce a brood,' I said wryly.

'Oh, I'll find her.' His gaze caught mine, holding it, and suddenly there was something very serious deep in those bright depths. Something that made me want to dance. 'And when I do, she won't *want* to get away from me. Trust me on that.'

That had almost sounded like a warning. 'I think the over-inflated ego I mentioned earlier is rearing its ugly head again.'

He didn't bother denying it, simply shoved several plastic bags my way. 'These are for you.'

'Ooh, presents.' I peeked inside. Jeans, T-shirts, sweaters, and underclothing. I raised my eyebrows and met his bright gaze. 'That's very generous of you.'

His sudden smile was so warm, so mischievous, heat sparked low down and my legs started trembling. Damn, but that was one sexy smile.

'I'm sure we can figure out a way for you to pay me back.'

'I'm sure you could,' I said dryly, trying to ignore hormones that were up for repaying in kind right here and now. 'But I'm not sure I'm up to that sort of payment just yet.'

'One of the drawbacks of being shot, I suppose,' he said, and began pulling food and bottles of drink out of the bags. 'You hungry?'

'I'd better be,' I said, watching the growing mountain of cakes, sandwich stuff, and nibbles. 'You've got enough here to feed an army.'

'The thrill of a close escape always makes me hungry.' He shrugged. 'And we can take whatever is left over with us when we leave.'

His words had a sobering effect. 'Just how close was our escape?'

'Very.' He walked over to the percolator and poured himself a coffee. 'It's only thanks to the fact that their car blew up that we weren't caught.'

'I remember you and the other dragon having a flame battle. That'll give the old couple in the diner something to talk about for weeks.'

'Undoubtedly.' He didn't look all that concerned, and I suppose he had no reason to. After all, who in their right mind would actually believe the old couple's tale? The scientist and the other man wouldn't back it up, after all. Not when they wanted to keep their project a secret.

'The car blowing up was a fortunate piece of timing,' he added. 'It killed one of the men, and sent the dragon flying. Though I have to say, I'm finding it hard to believe our kind would work with these people.'

I ferreted out a box of Twinkies from the food pile. 'Some people will do anything for money.'

'True.' He pointed with his mug to the bench. 'I brought my laptop in. I found Louise Marsten's address in the phone book, and thought we could do a little Internet search. See if we can find some house plans to make it easier for ourselves.'

'Good idea.' I opened the box, dug out some Twinkies, then opened one of them and bit into the squishy, overly sweet cake.

I couldn't help a sigh of delight. Around the mouthful of cake and cream, I added, 'God, I missed these things.'

'Twinkies?' He shuddered. 'I was a Pop-Tart kid myself.'

'I almost burned the house down with one of those. Got stuck in the toaster.' I picked up the second Twinkie. 'Those suckers sure do burn for a long time.'

'Which is why you don't toast them.'

'They are designed to be toasted,' I said dryly. 'That's the whole point.'

'But they taste better untoasted.'

I shook my head sorrowfully. 'We obviously have incompatible tastes. What hope is there of a future together?'

'If incompatible tastes in snack food is the worst problem we ever face, then I think I'll live a happy man.' He sipped his coffee, his blue eyes twinkling and filled with a heat that caused all sorts of havoc to my pulse rate. 'I take it, then, that as soon as you and Egan got the codes, you were planning to go back to Scotland?'

'Not immediately. As I said before, I have to see my Dad first.'

'Is it just age, or something more?'

'It's diabetes.' And while it might be a common and somewhat controllable disease for the majority of the world's population, for dragons it was deadly. The insulin produced for humans didn't work on the different body chemistry of a dragon, and research was nonexistent simply because few knew dragons – let alone the many other mythical races that haunted this earth – actually existed. Dad was lucky to some extent – we'd found a dragon-born doctor who'd been willing to drive to our place to treat Dad privately. Between the doc's herbal medicines and diet management, they'd been able to slow the advance of the disease for many years, and had given Dad a pretty good quality of life. He might have lost an arm to it – and therefore his ability to fly – but otherwise there wasn't much he couldn't do.

But the fact that Dad was now dying suggested any containment had well and truly gone. Which only made the guilt I felt for leaving him that much sharper.

Surprise flitted across Trae's face. 'I know a lot of human diseases and medicines can be deadly for us, but I didn't realize diabetes was one of them.'

'We were lucky, because we found a dragon-born doctor who knew a lot of traditional herbal medicines. It helped for years.'

'My mom's into the herbal stuff. You wouldn't believe the concoctions she used to give us as kids.'

My ears pricked up. 'Us?'

He hesitated, then nodded. 'Me and my sister, Mercy.'

'So she's a draman, like you?'

'Yes, but not kin to Egan. Her father is one of the lesser males.'

I raised my eyebrows. 'Lesser males?'

He nodded. 'Air dragons have a hierarchy system that's based on both color and bloodline. The strong color lines – like blacks, reds, and golds – tend to raise more kings than the browns and the blues.' He shrugged. 'There are some bloodlines that have never raised a king, and are considered "lesser" families.'

'Much like British royalty.' I paused, and opened up a packet of chips. 'What about the ring? You said it's the king's ring, but I get the feeling that it's more than a bit of fancy jewelry.'

'It's basically the succession ring. Without it, a new leader cannot be chosen.'

I raised my eyebrows. 'I wouldn't have thought that would be a problem. I mean, assholes like your father generally don't want to lose the top job.'

His smile was grim. 'Perhaps not. But without the power of the ring behind him, my father has become weaker and weaker, and will eventually die.'

'What? Why?'

He shrugged, yet the glimmer in his eyes hinted at malicious pleasure. The thief was enjoying his father's predicament. 'Apparently, the life of the king dragon is tied into the stone. Don't ask me how, because I don't know.'

'So by taking the ring, Egan found a way to kill your dad without actually getting his hands bloody?'

'Egan would never have won a fight with my father. Not

only is our father older and cannier when it comes to fighting but, thanks to the ring, he's all but invincible.'

'The ring is magic?'

'Only in the hands of the rightful king.'

How cool. And it also explained why the thing always felt cold and icy – certain magics could never hold warmth or life, according to my dad. Though how he got *that* knowledge, I don't know. 'So do all king dragons have the aid of such a ring?'

'As far as I know, yes.' He raised an eyebrow. 'I'm gathering sea dragons don't?'

'Not that I know of. We don't even live in groups like you lot do.'

'That's probably a good thing, trust me.' He hesitated. 'So where precisely is this research center? Loch Ness is a fairly big place from what I recall.'

Obviously, he was through talking about his family, hence the sudden change of topic. 'Where else would it be? Drumnadrochit.'

He blinked. 'Where?'

'Drumnadrochit. The home of Nessie and the Loch Ness Monster industry.'

He smiled. 'So there really is a Loch Ness Monster?'

'Hell, yeah. Only she's generations of sexy, slinky sea dragons, not that god-awful dinosaur-looking thing you see in so many pictures.'

The laptop beeped as he started it up. He glanced down at it, quickly typed something in, then looked up again. 'So why do you think that Marsten's mother will have these plans?'

'Because the mother supports the son.'

'Ah. The supplier of money.'

'Yes. We learned a few months ago that Marsten's mother was a major investor, and that Marsten often uses her house as an office when he's here in the States. We figured that maybe he'd have a set of backup plans there.' I shrugged. 'We thought it might be safer coming here than to try and get into his quarters in Scotland.'

Trae considered me for a moment, then said, 'So you went to San Lucas, a place they supposedly didn't know about, and yet they were waiting. And then they found us today.'

I met his gaze steadily. Saw the wariness sharpening into suspicion. 'What are you implying?'

But even as I asked the question, I knew. It was the only logical explanation for them constantly finding us.

'You probably have a bug in you somewhere,' he said, saying aloud what was going through my brain. 'Do you have any odd scars on your body? Scars you have no memory of getting?'

'Everywhere. They used to knock us out and take little – or not so little – samples.'

'Bastards.' He shook his head, and anger swirled around me, heating my skin as sharply as flame. 'Is there any particular scar that strikes you as odd?'

'In what way?'

'I don't know – slightly darker, more raised than others.' He shrugged. 'Anything like that could be a clue to location.'

'I haven't noticed anything, but then, we've pretty much been on the run since we escaped. There hasn't been much time to scratch, let alone notice, strange scars.' I ate some chips, then said, 'Trackers are a reasonable size, aren't they? Why wouldn't I be feeling one if I have it in my body?'

He grinned. 'Micro- and nanotechnology are now the in-thing. It could be something the size of a pinhead, and you'd never guess it was there.'

'Then how are we going to find it?'

'Simple. We look.' He hesitated, and the grin that split his lips went way beyond sexy. 'Which means, of course, that you have to strip.'

'I'm only wearing a T-shirt, so that's hardly a hassle.' I grabbed the thing and pulled it over my head. My shoulder twinged, a sharp reminder that it wasn't as healed as I thought it was. 'Now what?'

'You really don't have a modesty problem, do you?' he said, his grin stretching as his gaze skated down my body.

'No, because we were all kept naked at the foundation, and

modesty tends to die after a while.' I raised an eyebrow, amusement teasing my lips. 'Is the lack of it a problem for you?'

'I don't think it could be a problem for *any* man with hormones and common sense.' He turned on the kitchen light. 'Come over here, where I can see better.'

I grabbed a few more chips, then walked across to the kitchen counter. Trae took my left arm, moving it into the light as his fingers gently probed and caressed my flesh. My skin tingled in response, and heat flushed through my body. If he noticed my reaction, he didn't respond, his gaze narrowed and concentration almost fierce. He dropped my left arm, then grabbed my right and repeated the process. I closed my eyes, delighting in the soft sensation of his touch, enjoying his closeness and the warm spicy scent emanating from him.

'Nothing there,' he said, after a while. 'Turn around and I'll check your back.'

I did, and he did, his soft caress inching over my shoulders then down my spine, the warmth of his fingers searing past the leathery skin of my dragon stain and sending little waves of pleasure racing through the rest of me. *This,* I decided, was nothing short of torture. I mean, it was one thing to have a delicious man run his warm fingertips all over my flesh, but to have it go no further than that? To have him concentrating on finding something other than the ultimate pleasure for us both? Torture of the highest degree.

'Still nothing,' he said, his voice sounding completely normal. Like he was watching some totally boring TV program rather than standing in front of the naked woman he professed to desire.

Either the man had abnormal control over his hormones, or he was all talk and no action.

'Lift a foot, so I can check it.'

'My feet?' I held up one hoof for inspection. 'Wouldn't I feel something imbedded in my feet?'

'Not if it's tiny.' His fingers began to probe my heel and arch. 'Man, you were right about the thickness of your feet. I gather they didn't give you shoes, either.'

'It was all part of their keeping us cold and uncomfortable philosophy.'

His fingers had stopped roaming, and he was pinching a small section of flesh in the center of my arch.

I twisted around to look at him. His face was a picture of concentration, and part of me was disappointed. I mean, the man could at least look a little distracted, for heaven's sake. 'You found something?'

'I think so.' He released my foot for a moment and reached into his pocket to retrieve his Swiss Army knife. 'Tell me about the kids to distract yourself.'

Yeah, like that was going to work when he was sticking a bit of metal into my flesh. Now, had it been flesh sliding into flesh . . . I gave a mental sigh, and tried to remember what his question had been.

'There were six of them, as I said. Carli was the youngest, and she's the sweetest little girl you could ever meet.'

'Sounds like you cared for her a lot.'

'It wasn't hard. I think Egan and I became surrogate parents for them all.'

'Which would have made leaving them there even harder.'

I flinched slightly as the knife pressed into my skin, but it didn't really hurt as much as I'd expected it to.

'Yeah.' I tried not to remember Carli's tears or the fear in the other little ones' faces when we'd finally told them what we planned. 'Sanat is eight, Tate and Marco are nine, Cooper is thirteen, and Jace is fifteen.'

'And how long have they all been in there?'

'Carli's been there the longest – four years.'

He grunted. 'Did you ever see your mother?'

I shook my head. 'They kept us separated at all times.'

The knife dug deeper. I winced and clenched my fist against the need to jerk my foot away.

'Then how did you know your mother was a captive like you?'

'Because I could feel her. And she was able to contact me twice.'

'If sea dragons share kin telepathy—'

'And they do.'

'Then why weren't you able to contact her more than that?'

The knife twisted in my flesh. 'Ow!' I said, then added, 'I tried, trust me. Whether it was the drugs that stopped me for so long, or something else entirely, I don't know.'

'But she was the one who warned you about your dad, wasn't she?'

'Yes. But that was the first contact we'd had for years.' And her mind had been a jumbled mess of confusion and distance. Only her fear for Dad had been sharp and true.

'Got it,' Trae said, and held out his hand for inspection.

Sitting in the middle of his palm was a small disk little bigger than a freckle. Only it was metallic and shiny looking.

'You sure that's it?'

There was doubt in my voice and he smiled. 'Well, unless it's part of your unique body makeup to have circuitry in your flesh, then yeah, I'm sure.'

I studied it dubiously. 'So what are we going to do with it?'

'This.' He dropped it on the floor and smashed it with his heel. 'Hopefully, that'll end the problem.'

I frowned at the metal bits on the floor. 'Not necessarily. They might be on their way here right now, for all we know.'

'Which is why I've set up perimeter alarms. We'll have plenty of time to sneak away should they come.'

'Air dragons can fly over alarms.'

'But the scientists can't, and any attempt to disconnect them will set them off anyway.' He reached out and caressed my cheek with his thumb, his touch so soft, so warm and somehow so caring, as if he were touching something very precious.

It made me feel good, and yet in some ways, it scared me. I didn't need another reason to be afraid, and those damn scientists had already snatched away too many people I'd cared about.

'How's the shoulder?' he said softly.

'Fine, for the moment.' I deliberately stepped away from his touch and moved back to the other side of the counter, even though it was the last thing I wanted to do. I grabbed some more chips, then waved my free hand toward the laptop. 'Are you going to use that thing, or did you just bring it in for show?'

'Nothing I own is merely for show, sweetheart.'

'Will you stop calling me that?'

Amusement crinkled the corners of his eyes. 'Why should I, when it's nothing but the truth?'

That was a loaded gun I wasn't about to touch.

He continued, 'Why do you think Marsten's mom holds copies of all the plans and security codes for the research center in Scotland?'

'Because it makes sense to have backups.' I leaned across the bench and watched as he Googled Marsten's name. 'And because he did a lot of groundwork here in the States before he ever shifted operations to Loch Ness, and he was working out of his mom's house for a long while.'

Hell, he and his family might still have facilities here in the States. Just because we never heard them mentioned didn't mean they couldn't exist.

'How big is the research center in Drumnadrochit?'

'Huge.' I hesitated. 'Though the center is actually between Drumnadrochit and Abriachan.'

'Oh, I know the area intimately.'

His voice was dry and I smiled. 'It's a very pretty area.'

'And your birthplace?'

I nodded. 'Marsten is using my mother's ancestral lands as his base.'

'He couldn't have just walked in and claimed it.'

'He didn't. He caught Mom first, and threatened me.'

He looked at me. 'Which is why your dad ran?'

I nodded, rubbing my arms. 'Mom gave him no real choice. She made him swear at my birth that if anything should ever happen to her, he'd take me far away.'

'Sounds like she had a premonition.'

'She might have. She was canny like that.'

'Maybe it's a mom thing. Mine's like that, too.' He pressed a finger to the screen and added, 'Look, there's an article on Marsten's old lady in *Oregon Home* magazine.'

'I don't suppose it comes complete with pics?'

'Let's have a look and see, shall we?' He clicked the link. 'When did your mother disappear?'

I hesitated. Memories rose, ghosts of a past part of me didn't *want* to remember. Not because it was unhappy – it wasn't, even when we'd left Mom far behind to come to America – but because darkness had overshadowed it. My life after childhood had been very dark indeed.

'I was only five or six when I came here.'

'Explains why there's only the barest trace of an accent.'

I nodded. 'My dad's American.'

He looked at me, one eyebrow raised. 'So how did you get caught if you were basically raised here?'

'I hit eighteen and decided that Mom needed rescuing.' I grimaced. 'What a bad move *that* turned out to be.'

'Because the scientists grabbed you?'

'Yes.'

'But why?'

'Because I am a sea dragon, and female, and they consider us extremely rare.' Which we weren't, but thankfully, they didn't seem to know that. I pointed at the screen. 'Nice interior shots, but is there anything that can help us get in?'

'One or two shots are useful.' He grabbed some chips and munched on a couple meditatively before asking, 'So if your dad knew she was alive, why didn't he call in her kin to protect you while he tried to free her? I have to say, if it had been my mate who was captured, I'd have battled hell itself to get her out.'

'Mom's kin disappeared about the same time she was captured.'

'Why didn't they try and get her out?'

I shrugged. 'I don't know. Maybe they didn't want to get caught themselves.'

'And she never tried to free herself?'

'She might have. They kept us well separated, so I couldn't physically talk to her, and the telepathy thing was a wash, as I said.'

Trae clicked one of the photos, enlarging it, then pointed to the ceiling area above the ornately curtained French doors in the picture. 'See that disk mounted onto the ceiling?' I nodded, and he continued, 'It's an infrared motion detector. Probably has a glass-break detector installed, too, seeing as it's positioned near the French doors.'

'Well, breaking in through a window wouldn't have been advisable anyway. I really don't want them knowing we were there, if we can help it.'

'Which means you can't actually steal the plans and codes.'

'No.' I hesitated, and yawned. 'Sorry. Egan was going to buy a digital camera and photograph them.'

Trae glanced at me, concern suddenly bright in his eyes. 'You look tired. Why don't you go get some rest? I'll search the Net and see what else I can find about our Mrs Marsten.'

I nodded, grabbed my T-shirt, then headed for the living room and the sofa in which I'd woken. I was sleepier than I thought, because I could barely even remember my head hitting the padded arm rest.

When I finally woke, wisps of moonlight were filtering in through the windows, not only washing the room with its pale light, but highlighting the footprints in the dust-covered floorboards. Trae had been in here more than once to check on me.

I smiled and pushed upright. Like before, waking on the plastic-covered sofa was painful, only this time my whole body was itchy. Infuriately so. I scratched at my side, my legs, my arms, then got up with a semi-growl. Moving didn't help any. In fact, it only seemed to make the itching worse.

I walked into the hallway, then stopped. There was a light in the kitchen, but it was faded, like a flashlight that was rapidly losing battery power.

Part of me wanted to go down there, see what Trae had uncovered, and grab something to eat.

But as tempting as that might be, the reality was, I needed to get to water.

Fast.

Chapter Seven

I swung around, walked back into the living room and over to the French doors. The moonlight flooding in through the dusty glass was as cold and as distant as I felt deep inside.

But through the hush of the night came the call of the sea.

It was a call I could not disobey.

I unlatched the French doors and walked out into the cold night. Paving gave way to grass, then grass to sand as I made my way though the overgrown gardens and onto the path I'd spotted earlier.

The wind swirled around me, sharp with the scent of the sea, tugging at my hair and at the hem of my T-shirt, as if trying to hurry me along. I all but ran down the path, my speed making my shoulder ache, and yet the ache getting lost in a growing sense of urgency. Fear even.

I had to get down to the sea. *Had* to.

I scrambled down the old steps that lined the cliff face, the occasional loose stone digging into my feet but causing no pain. The night had once again stolen such sensory details, leaving my skin cold and, for the moment, unfeeling. Leaving me the same.

I strode out across the sand. Waves rushed toward me, reaching with foamy fingers for my toes. When those fingers raced up and over my feet, a shudder that was part pleasure, part relief, ran through me. I stopped and stripped off the T-shirt, then the bandages, tossing them both back up on the beach. The wind caught them, flinging them backward, well out of the reach of the sea.

The waves roared as they rolled toward the pristine sands, the sound seeming to hit the cliffs and spin back, until the night was filled with the cry of the ocean. I flung my arms wide, breathing deep, filling my lungs with the cold, salty air, feeling it wash through every muscle, every cell, invigorating, renewing. There was power in the sharpness of the night and in the chill of the water, and my sudden laugh swirled across the waves, mingling joyously.

I was home. Maybe not my *actual* home, but the home of heart. My soul.

I continued on into the water and, when I was deep enough, dove under the waves. The icy water caressed my skin, a lover's touch that soothed and healed. The itching vanished, replaced by a feeling of wholeness. The sea replenishing what the day had taken away.

I played in the waves, diving under and over, a fish who had no fins or tail. I have no idea how long I stayed there, but it must have been hours, because the moon was losing its strength by the time I began to make my way back to the shore.

Only then did I realize I was not alone in the cold, starry night.

I hesitated, but a wave hit my butt, forcing me on. I smiled, half wondering if the ocean was sick of my presence, but took the hint and kept moving.

Trae rose as I approached the sand, his eyes sparkling in the moonlight, filled with heat, filled with desire. His gaze slid down my body as I left the grip of the waves, and my skin prickled and warmed.

I knew in that moment that no matter how much I wanted to honor Egan's death by showing a little bit of restraint, I wouldn't. Not if the opportunity now arose. The night and the sea were filled with magic, and the longing to share it all with another was very much a part of who I was, what I was.

His gaze rose, annoyance warring with desire in those rich blue depths. 'Why didn't you tell me you had to come down here? I just about had a heart attack when I walked into the living room and found you gone.'

I stopped several feet away from him. 'I'm sorry. It didn't even cross my mind, and it should have.'

He contemplated me for a few moments, his spicy, masculine scent swirling around me, teasing my senses, stirring desire.

'That water is icy, and yet you come out of it glowing with warmth rather than cold. A gift of your heritage, I gather?'

I nodded. 'We don't have to change in the water – except if we want to go deep or stay under for longer periods. And my skin is always cold at night.'

'I noticed.'

A smile teased my lips. 'So the thief has stolen a caress or two?'

His own smile emerged. 'The thief has. And he has no regrets.' He took several steps, closing the distance between us before raising a hand, lightly brushing strands of hair away from my cheek, his fingers so warm, so tender against my skin.

'Why is the water so important to you? Besides the fact that you're a sea dragon, of course.'

I raised an eyebrow. 'Did no one teach you about your undersea cousins?'

'*My* family barely even taught us about the other cliques. Draman may not be killed, but they don't get the same sort of education as full bloods.'

'Ah. Well, it's because if I do not immerse myself under some form of water every twenty-four hours, I will die.'

'So it doesn't have to be seawater?'

'I survived eleven years in that facility without seawater, so it doesn't seem like it.'

But even as I said the words, doubt crowded my mind. What if there *were* side effects, and I just didn't know about them? After all, my mom had been insistent that I get away from that place quickly. So what if it wasn't *just* because of Dad, but because I was reaching the end of my limits, sea-wise?

I shivered and rubbed my arms. Trae immediately took off his coat. 'Here, take this.'

I didn't want to. I wanted to stay naked and cold and a part of the night and the magic, but there was something in his eyes — a steel that would brook no arguments. And why stand here and argue when there were many more interesting things we could be doing? So I slipped my arms into the sleeves, breathing deep the dual scent of leather and man, then let him slide up the zipper. His hands lingered near the top, his fingers brushing oh-so casually across my breasts.

'I notice the bullet wound is almost healed.'

I nodded. 'The sea always heals. It is her gift to us.'

His hands slid down my arms, lightly rubbing, sending little shocks of electricity through the leather and across my skin. 'I think we'd better get you inside.'

148

His voice was edged with a huskiness that had my hormones dancing. 'Or we could stay here, and talk about whatever pops up.'

'Sweetheart, you may not feel the cold, but I'm fucking freezing. Trust me, nothing worthwhile is going to pop up on a night like this.'

'Really?' I skimmed my gaze downward. 'That seems pretty worthwhile to me.'

He grinned. 'Trust me, it's only a halfhearted effort.'

If it was, it had to be pretty damn impressive when he was serious. I stepped closer, pressing myself against the warm, enticing hardness of his entire body. His hands slid around my waist, holding me closer still. It felt good, felt *right*. And that made the fear swirl again, because I really didn't want to find someone else for the scientists to threaten and maybe even kill.

And yet the part of me that burned made me say, 'Are you sure you want to go inside?'

'Yes,' he said, then lowered his head and kissed me.

Not sweetly, not tenderly, but forcefully, desperately, like a man in the desert who'd been deprived of water for too long. I returned it in kind, wrapping my arms around his neck and holding on tight as I tasted and explored and enjoyed. It was a kiss that seemed to go on forever, a kiss that I *wanted* to go on forever, until a dizziness that I wasn't sure was due to his closeness or lack of air crept over me. It was only then that he pulled away and stared down at me. I was breathless, burning – and not just from the force of our kiss, but also the intentness of his gaze, from the resolve and determination so evident in the rich depths.

Whatever it was I was feeling, he was feeling it, too. And that made me even more frightened.

There was too much at stake already. I couldn't – wouldn't – put someone else in danger. Especially someone who might just be important to my future.

If I had a future.

I forced myself to step back, away from his warm body and marvelous kisses. 'Maybe we'd better get inside.'

He ran one hand down my arm and clasped his fingers around mine. 'Let's go.'

I resisted the urge to wrap my fingers tightly around his, and just let my grip remain loose. 'Don't forget my T-shirt.'

He leaned down and scooped it up, then tugged me lightly toward the cliff and the old, worn steps.

The wind was stronger on the top of the cliff, tugging at my hair and freezing my exposed butt and nether regions. Which only served as a pointed reminder that next time I went for a night swim, I'd damn well better make sure to bring some decent clothes to wear afterward.

I huddled a little closer to Trae, and his scent spun around me, warming me almost as much as the heat emanating from his body. He released my hand, then wrapped his arm around my shoulder, drawing me closer still.

'The fish is suddenly feeling the cold, huh?' Amusement ran through the huskiness of his voice.

'It's the wind.' I crossed my arms against a shiver. 'There's a storm blowing in, I think.'

He glanced upward. 'Not a cloud in the sky.'

'Not yet. It'll be here by mid-morning, though.'

'And how would you know that?'

'I can taste it in the air.'

'Of course you can.'

I shot him a sideways glance. 'That wouldn't be sarcasm I can hear in your voice, would it?'

'Why would I be sarcastic when the woman making the statement predicted – to the second – the time the sun would rise?' He slid his hand down my shoulder and lightly rubbed my arm. Warmth trembled across my limbs, and my fingers and toes began to tingle. As if this man was forcing life into extremities long used to being cold at night. 'Another gift of your heritage, I gather?'

'Much like your fire,' I said, voice a little breathless.

He glanced at me, blue eyes gleaming with hunger. He might have said no on the beach, but that didn't mean he didn't want me.

'An air dragon's fire is linked with daylight. Or rather, sunlight.'

'So Dad told me. He never did explain why, though.'

He shrugged. 'It's not a phenomenon that's really been studied. It just is.'

'But why just sunlight? I mean, sea dragons can control water night or day, though the greatest power comes during the twilight times between day and night. It always struck me as odd that air dragons had much greater restrictions on their skills.'

'We're creatures of air and the sun. We can shift shape at night, but when the darkness sweeps in, it puts out the flames. Literally.'

I raised an eyebrow. 'So no one in your family has ever been curious enough to question why there seems to be a link between the sun and this flame-throwing skill? I mean, you can't all be thieves. Surely there's one bad apple who turned out to be something worthwhile – like a scientist?'

He grinned. 'Thievery *is* something of a family business. We have a long history of collecting shiny things belonging to other people.'

'And why is that?'

'Because we like shiny things?' His eyes twinkled at me. 'Why did sea dragons attack boats?'

'Because most were too lazy to work, and boats were easy pickings back in those days.' It was a guess on my part, but from the dim memories I had of my uncles, I was betting I was right. None of them seemed to have too much responsibility on their plates. Of course, I was viewing them through the memories of a child, so maybe I was doing them a grave injustice. I added, 'So your skills come courtesy of family training?'

'Nope. Unwanted bastards don't get much of a run in the family business.' Despite the sarcastic edge to his words, I could almost taste the anger in him. I could certainly feel the tension running through his body and arm. 'Hell, draman weren't supposed to get the family skills in *any* way, shape, or form, but something has gone wrong with my generation.'

I slid my arm around his waist, and though I was sure this man wasn't after any kind of support or sympathy, said, 'Or something went right.'

He flicked the end of my nose with his free hand. 'Right for us. Wrong for them.'

'Why? I mean, if your father is going to fling it around with all and sundry, he has to expect that some of his so-called unwanted are going to get the full family genes – and all the skills that might go with them.'

'That's just it. It doesn't happen. It's never happened, not in hundreds of years of history.'

That raised my eyebrows again. 'How would they even know that if they have a history of killing draman at birth?'

'They didn't kill *every* draman. They kept enough alive to work the farm and the fields.'

'So maybe they were killing the ones that showed dragon signs, which is why they've never picked up until now that draman were inheriting dragon skills.'

'Maybe.' He hugged me closer, so that my body was pressed hard against the warmth of his and I could feel the ripple of muscle as he took each step, each breath. Goose bumps ran across my skin, and I wasn't entirely sure whether it was desire or that sliver of fear again. Or perhaps even both.

Because while my mind was urging caution, my body still wanted to fling it to the wind and just give in to the moment and this man and what was growing between us.

And yet if I did, I had a horrible feeling things would go to hell in a handbasket.

I mean, when had anything ever gone right for me in the years since my childhood?

Of course, that was mostly due to the fact I tended to rush headlong into situations I'd been warned against. Like when I'd hit eighteen and become determined to find my mom, despite my dad's warnings. I frowned as memories surged. He'd been so angry with me that day. Truly angry. Yet, reflecting back, I could see that the anger had been based in fear. He hadn't wanted to lose me like he'd lost my mother. And however much he might have wanted to come with me, he couldn't, because by then his arm was gone. He couldn't fly, and while I'm sure he would have taken a plane if it had been practical, he couldn't take the risk of being caught over there without someone close who knew about his condition and how to treat it.

Trae and I made our way through the overgrown gardens, the sweet aroma of the evening primrose that was running rampant through the beds almost overpowering the salty taste of the breeze and the heady scent of man. The house loomed through the darkness, windows like eyes frowning down on us.

For no particular reason, I found myself slowing. And I wasn't the only one. Trae came to a sudden halt, forcing me to do the same.

'What?' I said, voice soft.

'The flashlight battery was starting to die, so I turned on the kitchen light when I left. We should be able to see the glow of it from here.'

I studied the darkened kitchen windows, then said, 'Maybe the bulb just blew.'

'Maybe.'

But he removed his arm from my shoulder, and the night felt suddenly colder. Even though he grasped my fingers, the chill seemed to take hold. Or maybe that was simply the fear that was never very far away from the pit of my stomach.

'We can't stand here all night, you know.' Though part of me wanted to. The night and the cold were better companions than whatever might be inside that house.

His smile flashed, sexy and dangerous. 'I have no intention

of just standing here.' He tugged me forward. 'And if they want us, they're going to have to catch us. Come on.'

He led me forward, quickly and quietly. My bare feet made little noise on the stones, and though he was wearing boots, he was as silent as a ghost. I wondered how he managed it, but didn't dare ask because we were too close to the building. The wind would carry any sound we made directly toward those in the house. If there was anyone in the house.

He moved into the deeper shadows, keeping low as he snuck past windows, forcing me to do the same. No sound rode the night – nothing touched the wind but the soft sound of our breathing. Mine fast, his even.

When we neared the kitchen, he stopped, then pressed me back against the clapboards. 'Wait here.'

'But—'

He touched my lips gently, halting my protest. 'Sneaking is my trade – and it's not me they want. Stay here, and stay safe.'

I nodded. He dropped his hand, then disappeared into the night, becoming one with the shadows within seconds. I hunkered down, using the bushes as cover, straining to hear what was going on.

But the night remained hushed, the wind free of any sounds that didn't belong in the darkness.

After what seemed like ages, awareness tingled across my skin and I looked up to see Trae striding toward me, an almost contrite smile touching his lips.

'What?' I whispered, as I stood up.

'Turns out it *was* a blown bulb.' He shrugged and held out his hand. 'Come on, let's get you inside and warm.'

I placed my hand in his, and let him lead me again. The house was no warmer than outside, but at least it was free of the wind.

He'd left the flashlight on this time, though with the battery on its last legs, the light it gave out wasn't very bright. But he'd also left his laptop on and open, and the screen's brightness washed across the shadows, providing enough light to see where we were going.

'Did you manage to come up with a plan to raid the old lady's house?' I stopped near the bench and studied the floor plans on the screen. 'That place is huge – the damn safe could be anywhere.'

'It'll be in the library or the office, most likely.' He reached across the bench and picked up the plastic bags filled with the clothes he'd bought me. 'You want to go get dressed?'

I looked at the clothes, then at him. 'You sure you want me to do that?'

He gave me a crooked smile that was filled with little boy cheekiness, and yet there was nothing innocent about the desire and need in his eyes. 'To be honest, no. But you lost a lot of blood today and no matter how you feel or how well that wound has healed, you're still looking a little pale. You need to rest, not exert yourself even more.'

I raised an eyebrow, a smile teasing my lips. 'Might be my one and only offer.'

'I doubt it.'

'See, there's that arrogance coming to the fore again.'

'Go get changed, then I'll tell you about our plans for tomorrow.'

I gave a theatrical sigh, and he chuckled lightly and pushed me toward the door. 'Trust me, sweetheart, this restraint is only going to last as long as your recovery. Enjoy it while you can.' He tossed me the T-shirt. 'Use that to dry yourself.'

I went. After stripping off his jacket, I toweled myself dry and dragged on the underclothing, jeans, and sweatshirt he'd bought. The man was a good judge of women's sizes, because they all fit like a glove. I shoved the jacket back on, not only because the night was getting colder, but it smelled so good, and headed back out.

His gaze swept down my length, and an approving sort of smile touched his lips. 'Now, that's what I call a hip-hugging pair of jeans.'

'One has to wonder how many girlfriends you've had over the years to be able to judge a woman's size so well.' I tossed the empty plastic bag and damp T-shirt on the bench, then began to finger-comb my hair.

'Ain't denying there's been a few.' He shrugged. 'I'm a man. That's what men do.'

I raised an eyebrow. 'So you're admitting to being a whore?'

'Nope. Just oversexed.'

'Says the man who recently said no.'

'Hey, that was consideration. A rare event you should appreciate, not sneer at.'

I gave a disdainful sniff. 'I believe you promised to share your plans for tomorrow once I was dressed.'

He caught my arm and tugged me closer. 'The house is up for sale—'

'She's selling? That can't be a good thing.'

'And maybe she simply wants a smaller house,' Trae said, amusement in his eyes. 'Trust me, she's not living in some little beach shack.'

'Maybe.' But I couldn't help feeling that it *did* mean something. Or was that simply my pessimistic half coming to the fore again, and refusing to believe anything could actually go right for a change?

'So her selling the house helps us how?'

'You and I are going to play newlyweds doing a little house hunting.' His lips were so close to mine his breath teased my lips with warmth. 'Think you can manage that?'

I snuggled closer, pressing my hips against his, even as I

pursed my lips. 'I don't know. That could take more acting skills than I'll possess tomorrow.'

'What can I do to convince you it'll be worthwhile?'

He dropped a kiss first on my left cheek, then on my right, and finally on the tip of my nose. Frustration and warmth shivered through me.

'You could stop teasing and just get down to business.'

'That depends on what you mean by business.' His blue eyes were bright with mischief and desire and something else, something that seemed to fire right through my soul, setting it alight.

'Will you just kiss me, idiot?'

He took possession of my lips even before the last word left my mouth, taking them, tasting them. Claiming them in a way that was all male, all possession, all desire. No one had ever kissed me like that. No one. Walking into the sea tonight might have felt like a homecoming, but in very many ways, so did this kiss.

And for all that I kept saying that I couldn't afford to get more involved with this man than I already was, I couldn't force myself to break away, either. I needed this man's kiss, his taste, his closeness, almost as much as I had needed the sea earlier.

A sharp buzzing ripped through the silence, breaking our kiss, making me jump and my heart race. Trae swore and instantly turned off the flashlight, plunging us into darkness.

'What was that?' I said, my voice a strained whisper.

'The early warning system.' He moved quickly but silently across to the window. 'Someone's broken the beam.'

I peered over his shoulder. The night was dark and the only thing that seemed to be moving were the tree branches, tugged about by the sharpening breeze.

And yet . . .

Was that a darker shape near the gate? Was it a car, or just my overwrought imagination?

I squinted, but couldn't make it out clearly enough. It was simply too far away.

'Could a cat or dog have set the alarm off?'

He shook his head. 'I set it higher up the post so that wouldn't happen.' He looked at me. 'Gather all the food. We're getting out of here.'

I spun around and walked back to the bench. After sweeping the food into several plastic bags, I grabbed the laptop and the discarded T-shirt.

'Okay, got everything.'

'I hid the car round the back of the property, near a broken part of the fence—'

'You really *do* believe in always being prepared, don't you?'

'A good thief *always* has his escape routes planned.' He glanced at me, eyes bright and dangerous. 'Take the path along the cliff top and follow it until you reach the fence line. The car is hidden in the trees a hundred or so yards from there.'

'And what will you be doing?'

'Following our trackers and ensuring they can't follow us.'

'Via another accidental fire?'

His sudden grin was a fearsome thing. 'No. I think we might have attracted enough attention with our stunt yesterday. Besides, it's night. Go, Destiny.'

I went, slipping out the back door and into the stillness of the night. Though it wasn't really still, not with the wind tugging at the bushes and whistling through the trees that surrounded the old house.

I kept to the deeper shadows, slipping around the building quickly and quietly. Once beyond the protection of the house, the wind grabbed at me, pushing me forward, seeming to hurry me along even as it slapped and rustled the plastic bags I was carrying.

But held within the fingers of the wind came the purr of an engine. No lights pierced the night, but the crunch of tires against the stone that lined the driveway was unmistakable. And it was getting closer.

Fear gave my feet wings. I practically flew across the open ground, barely watching where I was going, trusting to instinct and the surety of my big feet as my gaze roamed the darkness.

Movement caught my eye. Was that the shadow of a man slipping through the trees to my left?

I didn't stop to look. Didn't dare. It was probably Trae,

anyway – air dragons could move with the speed of the wind when they wanted to.

The sudden sharpness of salt riding the breeze warned of the closeness of the cliff face. I looked forward, saw land give way to the blackness of night and the starry horizon, and swerved left, following what looked like a goat track. I hoped Trae did whatever it was he had to do in a hurry so we could just get out of here. The car at the gate might not be my pursuers – it might just be the cops doing their rounds, or something equally innocent – but instinct suggested that it probably was.

The wind suddenly gusted and in the sharpness of the air came the sudden sound of a footstep.

And it was close. Too close.

I swung around. Saw the looming shadow, the arms outstretched. The pungent smell of chloroform grew suddenly thick in the night, the scent coming from the cloth the man held in one hand. My skin burned at the very thought of letting it get near me.

When used on humans, chloroform slowed down their central nervous system as well as put them out. On us, it burned like acid. But it also happened to be one of the few drugs that could knock us out fully.

I backpedaled fast and swung the plastic bags of food as hard as I could. One bag broke, spewing cans and packaged cakes across the path, but the other took the stranger hard in the gut.

He grunted, but lunged past the bag, his free hand grabbing, searching for purchase of any kind. And the chloroform waited.

I chopped down with my hand, smashing away his fingers, then spun, lashing out with a bare heel. The blow took him in the chin, forcing him back.

But not stopping him.

He regained his balance and shook his head, a wry grin stretching his thin lips. 'Got a bit of fight in you for a change, hey, little fish?'

His accent was American, not Scottish. But then, very few of the scientists had been Scottish.

'I've always had fight in me. Your kind have just never seen it.'

He took a step forward. I took one back, watching his eyes carefully, balancing on my toes as I waited for the leap that would undoubtedly come.

His smile grew. 'The night clouds your judgment and slows your actions. It's the reason we caught your mother. It's the reason we'll recapture you.'

He lunged even before he'd finished speaking. I spun away, out of his reach, then swung the other bag and smashed it against the back of his head. There was a crack, and a spurt of blood, and he staggered forward. The wind chose that moment to gust, pushing him farther, harder, toward the cliff face. There was a moment when he teetered, when his arms flailed and the realization he was about to fall hit him. I could have stepped in then, could have pulled him back and saved him.

I didn't.

He fell into the darkness with a scream, and all I could feel was relief.

Chapter Eight

When the screaming abruptly stopped, I gathered what I could of the fallen groceries, shoving them in the other plastic bags until they, too, were threatening to break, then hurried on.

I couldn't feel guilty over what I'd done. Not when I could remember what they'd done to me, and Egan, and my mom. Not to mention the little ones.

Did that give me the right to idly stand by and watch a man fall from a cliff when I could have easily saved him? Probably not.

But I still couldn't get worked up about it. And if that made me a bad person, then so be it. I could live with that.

One of the plastic bags slapped heavily against my shin, and

I tripped, going down hard, my knees hitting a rock and sending a shock of pain that reverberated right up to my brain. I cursed softly and sat there for a moment, catching my breath and trying to stop the instinctive need to get up and keep running.

I couldn't afford to panic. Besides, what would it gain me other than more damn bruises?

I pushed to my feet and hobbled along the faint path. Eventually, the pain in my knees subsided. I found the fence and followed it to the left, finding the trees and the car. It was locked, so I deposited the bags and the laptop near the trunk, then shook my hands to get the blood circulating through my fingers as my gaze swept the night.

No sign of Trae.

No indication that anything or anyone was moving through the night.

I bit my lip and shifted my weight from one foot to the other, fighting the instinct – no, the need – to go back out there and see if he needed help.

But he was right when he'd said earlier that they weren't looking for him. If I went out there, it would only make things worse.

Although my would-be captor had screamed as he'd fallen. Would the wind have snatched the sound away, or would those who'd come with him have heard it?

I didn't know, and it was as frustrating as ever.

Needing to do something, I walked to the edge of the trees. This area near the cliff was higher than the house, so it provided a good vantage point from which to view the surrounds. There was no one moving down there. No dark shadow of a car. Nothing to indicate there was another soul breathing in the night besides me.

Yet that man hadn't come from thin air. And he surely *wouldn't* be alone. They never were. There was always one who hung back, armed and ready to take action if needed ...

Goose bumps ran across my skin and the hairs along the back of my neck stood on end. I swung around, saw a broad chest covered in a brown sweatshirt, then he was on me, grabbing me, his arm locking around my throat as he tried to raise a stinking white rag to my nose and mouth.

I twisted in his grip and bit his arm as hard as I could. The chloroform-soaked rag hit my neck and shoulder instead of my face, and instantly my skin began to burn. Pain surged, and a scream ripped up my throat. But I used the energy of that pain to bite harder, and my teeth drew blood, even through the material. My attacker hissed, but didn't release me, so I stomped down on his toes.

He cursed and pushed me away. I staggered several steps before I caught my balance, then pivoted on one foot, my heel smashing him in the face as he lunged toward me. He went down hard and didn't move.

I left him lying there and ran across to the trunk of the car, upending the plastic bags until I found the bottles of water. After untwisting the cap, I leaned forward and tipped the contents over my neck and shoulder, trying to stop the burning, trying to wash the foul stuff from my clothes. It took three bottles to ease the burning and a fourth before I felt totally safe.

'Jesus, Destiny, are you all right?'

The voice came out of the night, scaring the shit out of me. I jumped around, fist raised before I fully realized it was Trae, not another attacker.

He stopped abruptly and held up his hands. 'Whoa. It's me. You're safe.'

'Sorry.' I lowered my hand with a grimace. 'But those bastards have a habit of sneaking up on me.'

'Next time I'll whistle "Dixie" before I get within punching distance.' He glanced at the man on the ground, then back at me. 'What happened to your neck?'

'They tried to chloroform me.' I grabbed another bottle but this time drank it. My mouth felt drier than the Sahara, and I very much suspected the cause was fear rather than a result of exertion.

But it wasn't fear for myself. It was fear for my mom, fear for my dad. Fear that I wouldn't be able to fulfill all the promises I'd made.

That in the end, I'd have to sacrifice one promise over another, one parent for the other. I needed to get the codes that would free my mom and the kids, but would the cost be not getting to Maine in time to see my dad and say good-bye? To tell him the love of his life was alive, and that she'd meet him on the forever plains? He had to know that before he died. Had to. Otherwise, when his soul answered the call of dawn's rising, he'd be fated to haunt this reality, forever trying to ease the ache of his heart.

It was the way of his kind.

The way of my mother's kind – even if the ceremonies prayed for the guidance of very different Gods.

I briefly closed my eyes against the sudden prickle of tears. I could do this. I just had to keep trying, keep believing.

'Chloroform?' Trae stepped closer and, with gentle fingers, brushed wet strands of hair away from my neck. 'That looks more like an acid burn.'

'Chloroform does that to sea dragons. We're hypersensitive to it.'

'But why would the scientists even use chloroform? There's a lot of drugs on the market that are safer and work faster.'

'But they won't work on us. Chloroform does. Something to do with our body makeup.' I offered him the water. 'Were there any others?'

He nodded and took the drink. 'Two of them. They split off,

which is why I'm late getting back here. It was easier to take them out one by one but it took longer.'

'And what does "take out" mean, exactly?'

'It means just that. Taking them out of the picture and making sure they can never hurt you – or anyone else – ever again.'

I closed my eyes and took a deep breath. It was bad enough that *I* had blood on my hands, but now *he* did, too.

'But if the bodies are found here—'

'They won't be,' he cut in. 'I flew them out to sea. And I seriously doubt anyone is going to report them missing. Not if what you're saying about Marsten is true. He wouldn't want *any* investigation happening that could shed serious light on what he's doing.'

That was true. I glanced back at the man I'd knocked out. 'And what about him?'

He hesitated. 'What do you want me to do about him?'

'Leave him.'

'That could be a decision that comes back and bites you in the ass. We don't know how many more are out there, remember.'

'I know, but killing in cold blood is different than killing in a fight. I just can't—'

'Then we won't.'

Relief slithered through me. 'What about their car?'

'I drove it off the property and abandoned it several miles up the road. It's wiped clean of prints.'

'Good.' I bent to pick up the scattered groceries. 'At least we should be safe from them for a while.'

'Unless they've got another way of tracking you.'

I glanced at him sharply. 'What do you mean?'

He shrugged. 'You said yourself that you underwent a lot of examinations and operations. It's not beyond the realm of possibility that they've got another way of finding you.' He must have sensed the panic that was surging through me, because he smiled and added, 'It's unlikely, but we've still got to be aware of the possibility. We can't afford to relax just yet, that's all I'm saying.'

I blew out a breath, then nodded. He slammed the trunk back down, then walked around me and opened the passenger door. 'Let's get moving before that man awakens.'

'Good idea, Ninety-nine.'

He snorted. 'Do I have breasts and dark hair?'

'No, but Ninety-nine was the smart one, remember? Although it probably wasn't hard to be smarter than Maxwell Smart, if the show had been anything to go by.'

He laughed, slammed the door shut, then ran around to the driver's side. The sudden brightness of the headlights as the car started up had me blinking.

He drove cautiously through the trees, edged the car through a smashed section of fence, then we bumped our way along a barely-there track, moving through the dunes and grasses for what seemed like ages.

When we finally hit the road, Trae turned right and gunned the engine.

'Feels like we're in the middle of nowhere,' I said.

'Basically, we are.' He didn't offer up other information, though, asking instead, 'How were you planning to get to Maine?'

'I haven't even thought about it yet.'

'You haven't got ID, so we won't be able to take a flight.' He glanced at me. '*I* could fly you there. It would be quicker than driving.'

I shifted in the seat a little, my heart racing at the thought of being carried high and free. 'Can an air dragon carry a full-grown human in flight?'

'Depends on the wingspan of the dragon, and the size of the human.' He glanced at me, devilment in his eyes. 'You're just lucky I happen to be one of the bigger ones.'

'So you keep boasting,' I said dryly. 'But I've seen very little evidence of it so far.'

'Just waiting for the right time, sweetheart.'

I rolled my eyes at the endearment. 'It's a long flight from here to Maine. Even if you *are* one of the larger dragons, can you carry me for that long?'

'I honestly don't know. If your weight does prove to be a problem, we'll fly in short bursts.'

I wrinkled my nose. 'It's probably better if I swim. At least I wouldn't have to worry about being dropped from a great height.'

'It'll take longer to swim.'

I knew that. And a sea dragon going through the Panama Canal – the only shortcut between the Pacific and Atlantic oceans – would be more than a little noticeable, so that was out, too.

'It's still a better option.'

'You really think I'd drop you?' He looked offended that I'd even think that.

I grinned. 'It's more a matter of not wanting to tire you out before that "right moment" gets here.'

'Ah, well, I guess I'll have to accept *that* excuse, won't I?' He glanced at me, and there was concern mixed with the amusement in his bright eyes. 'Why don't you catch some sleep? You've had a rough few days, and it'll be at least an hour before we get to Florence.'

'I doubt that I'll be able to.'

'Try.'

I tried. And surprisingly, I did.

The car door slamming closed woke me some time later. I stretched like a cat, then peered through the windshield. Trae had said he was getting a cheap motel, but the one sitting in front of us, with its white painted walls and slate gray roof, was surprisingly pretty. Especially with all the potted red and yellow flowers near each of the rooms. There weren't many cars around, but given the chill that suggested winter was coming around fast, that wasn't really surprising.

I glanced around as Trae came back, simply enjoying watching him walk. God, the confident – even arrogant – way that man moved was decidedly sexy.

He climbed into the car and tossed me a set of keys. 'Room three,' he said, as he started the car.

'Are we staying here the whole night?'

'We got rid of the bug, so it shouldn't be a problem.'

Unless, as he'd suggested, they had another means of tracking me. But if that were the case, then we wouldn't be safe anywhere.

And I guess the only way we were going to find out one way or the other was to stop, giving them time to regroup and find us again. If they did, then we'd know.

He drove across the courtyard to a parking spot in front of one of the rooms. The headlights illuminated the large golden number sitting in the middle of the white painted door. We were close to the office and the entrance, meaning the headlights of any cars that drove in would shine directly through the window into our room. A good warning system, if we needed one.

He climbed out of the car, then walked around and opened my door. I couldn't help grinning as I climbed out. 'The thief is being a gentleman.'

He slid his hand under my elbow and guided me to the door. 'Don't mock it, or it won't happen again.'

'Oh, I'm not mocking. Just surprised you'd bother.'

'Maybe I'm still worried about you.' He opened the door and ushered me through, then tossed the keys on the flowery spread covering the queen bed. 'You want to make some coffee while I get the gear out of the car?'

I nodded and hunted around until I found the coffeemaker, and then the coffee. As it began to burble and spurt, Trae dumped the last of the bags and his laptop on the chair near the bed, then said, 'I think I'll get rid of this car and get a new one. That scientist you knocked out could remember the plate number. And the original owners would probably have noticed it missing by now.'

'Most people would notice the car is not where they parked it the night before,' I agreed dryly.

'It makes the life of a thief more hazardous, I tell you. And cops tend to get antsy when they discover you're driving a stolen car.'

'Well, maybe that's because it *is* against the law.'

'And yet it's practically a national pastime.'

'Doesn't make it right, my friend.'

'Depends on your definition of right, doesn't it?' Amusement played about his mouth. 'I should be back before dawn. You stay here and get some more rest.'

'You really have a thing about me being rested, don't you?'

His sudden grin made my pulse jump about like a crazy thing. 'Maybe I have an ulterior motive.'

'Oh, of that I have no doubt,' I said dryly. 'The thief always has a plan, doesn't he?'

'You can bet your life on it, sweetheart.' He glanced at his watch, then added, 'Don't unlock the door for anyone.'

'Except you.'

'I'll have the key.'

'Oh. Okay.'

His gaze skimmed my body, then he muttered something and spun on his heel, walking out the door.

Leaving me smiling. The thief *definitely* wanted me as much as I wanted him.

God, was it only yesterday I was telling myself I had to show a little restraint to honor Egan's memory?

It seemed restraint and I weren't exactly on speaking terms right now. I closed my eyes and tried to picture Egan in my mind. But his image was blurred – like a photo in which the subject had moved.

And the image that remained looked an awful lot like Trae.

Egan, I'm sorry I'm not stronger. I'm sorry I can't honor you as much as I had hoped.

He'd understand. I knew that. We were both sensual beings, but our lovemaking had always been a matter of need rather than desire. And at least now I understood *why* he had always seemed distant. His soul mate was dead, killed by his own father, and his heart had been shattered in the process.

Mine, however, had not.

And I wanted what he'd had so very briefly. Wanted what my parents had, even now, after all the years of being apart. And I knew, deep down, that it was here for the taking. If I was brave enough. Or maybe that should be if I was foolish enough. After all, my life right now wasn't exactly sane.

I poured myself a coffee. After taking a sip, I grabbed a microwave meal from the bags, zapped it in the small microwave that was really the only cooking facility provided beyond the coffeemaker and small toaster, then sat down on the bed to watch TV.

An hour later, bored with the TV and growing tired of waiting for Trae, I stripped the covers back and climbed into bed. I was asleep within minutes of my head hitting the pillow.

When I woke, it was to the warmth of the sun streaming across my face and the heat of flesh pressed against my spine. His arm was slung casually over my hip, his fingertips lightly resting on my stomach. He wasn't moving, and his breathing was soft, even. Asleep, even as I was suddenly, gloriously, awake.

I didn't move, and as tempting as it was to press back against him, to stir him to life as I was stirring to life, I didn't. Even a thief needed his sleep, and I had no idea how long he'd been out last night.

So I lay there, wrapped in the spicy, tangy scent of him, listening to him breathe and feeling the warm wash of his breath across one shoulder. My skin tingled, my body ached like crazy, and every little movement he made had shivers of delight flashing across my nerve endings.

Naturally, he slept for what seemed like forever.

In reality, it was probably only another hour or so. Certainly the light streaming into the room hadn't journeyed very far up the wall as the sun began its daily track through the sky.

His waking was done in several brief, delicious moments that were filled with a combination of growing awareness and desire. The twitch of fingertips across my stomach. His growing erection, pressing ever more forcefully against my butt. The quickening of breath across my shoulder. The butterfly kiss of lips on the base of my neck.

'Morning, sweetheart,' he murmured, and hugged me closer, until his erection was snuggled firmly against my butt cheeks. 'What a lovely way to wake up.'

And it'd be even more lovely if he actually got down to business. Good grief, couldn't he sense I was just about bursting with wanting him?

I reached backward, lightly running a hand up and down his hip. 'What time did you get in last night?'

I felt more than saw his shrug. 'Fairly late. It took a while to find a new car. You were asleep when I came in, so I didn't bother waking you.'

'Thanks. I think I needed the sleep.'

'Mmmm.'

His voice was as distracted as any woman could wish, and the thought warmed me almost as much as his touch. His lips found my neck, then my earlobe, kissing them lightly, and the warmth became a shiver of pure delight.

'Anything else you need?' he murmured, his breath washing heat into my ear.

'That depends on what's on offer.' I let my hand dip past his hip, lightly caressing the heated hardness of his erection. A tremor ran through him, and I smiled. There would be no hesitation this morning, no stepping back from the brink.

'What do you want to be on offer?' His hand began to move across my stomach, his touch so light, so tender. Heat pooled under his fingertips, sending little flashes of desire shooting through every nerve ending. Lord, how I wanted this man's touch. No, not *just* his touch, but his scent on my skin, his mouth on mine. His body *in* mine.

His spirit wrapped around mine.

'Everything,' I said, my voice little more than a tremor of air. 'All that you have, and all that you're willing to give.'

He chuckled softly. 'I'll see what I can do.'

'Please.' And before I combusted in sheer frustration.

His touch began to slide slowly upward. When his thumb brushed the underside of a breast, my breath hitched, then became more rapid.

He began to caress, tease, and kiss my upper body and breasts. I closed my eyes, savoring the sensations flooding through every part of me. Loving his firm, hard body pressed against mine, the way he brushed my aching nipples with his thumbs. Enjoying the press of his erection against my hand as I stroked and cupped him. Savoring the rich scent of him, breathing it in deep, until it felt like his essence had flooded through every part of me. Becoming a part of me, in a way that went beyond mere pleasure.

When his caress moved down to that warm, wet part of me that was aching to feel the full length of him, part of me wanted to shout in sheer relief. But I was too busy simply enjoying to waste air like that. He caressed me, toyed with me, until my body was slick with sweat and aching with desire. When he finally slid a finger into me, I could only gasp in pleasure. My inner muscles pulsed around one finger, then two, and the sensation of him delving in and out was incredible. I pushed back against him, riding his hand with increasing urgency, until the low-down trembling bloomed, spreading across my skin like wildfire. But before the orgasm could crest, he pulled away, simply kissing my shoulder, caressing my breasts, until the tremors eased. Then he started again.

This time, when he finally pressed his thumb against my clit, my groan of pleasure could probably be heard in the next room. As he stroked me, caressed me, he let his other fingers slide through my slickness, until he was teasing me inside and out. My whole body shook as pleasure mounted, and my breathing became little more than short, sharp gasps. As the tremors of orgasm began to mount a second time, he finally shifted over me. His flesh was as slick as mine, his body trembling with the effort of control.

But I didn't want control. I wanted him.

I wrapped my legs around his hips, trying to force him closer, desperate to feel him inside. When only the tip of him slid in, I whimpered, wanting – *needing* – so much more.

He chuckled softly, then said in a voice that was all smoky desire, 'Patience, sweetheart.'

'Patience be damned,' I panted, arching up to meet him.

He didn't pull away, and the sensation of him sliding so deep had me groaning.

It was a sound he swallowed in a kiss that was fierce and possessive, and so damn hot it felt like I was going to explode.

Only then did he begin to thrust, his movements deep and

long. I groaned again, a rich sound of gratification he echoed. His movements became harder, faster, until it felt like he was trying to claim my entire body. But this was more than just a physical act – more than just a meeting of bodies. In this one perfect moment of unity, our spirits soared around each other, until it felt like his soul was trying to claim mine as fiercely as his body. I went there willingly, wanting the possession, needing it. Needing *him*. Now. Forever.

The rich ache grew, spreading like wildfire, becoming a kaleidoscope of sensations that washed through every single part of my body, building gloriously until I could barely even breathe. Then the shuddering truly took hold and I gasped, grabbing his shoulders, holding him closer, thrusting him deeper.

As the orgasm raked me, he came, his roar echoing through my ears as I twitched and moaned in sheer pleasure, until even that faded and all that was left was an amazing sense of peace and contentment.

He leaned his sweaty forehead against mine for a moment, blowing out a breath that washed warm air across my face, then slid to one side and gathered me close.

It was a nice sensation, being held so tenderly.

But it was also scary. Not just because I barely even knew this man, but because I now knew, without a doubt, that this was more than mere lust. This was the real deal.

And the timing absolutely sucked.

I closed my eyes against the sudden rush of fear and panic. Damn it, why would fate do this to me? Why throw my future in my face when my present was so full of danger? I might have ditched the tracker, but until I freed my mom and the kids, the scientists would remain a dark specter on my horizon. A specter that had proven more than ready to kill.

And I didn't want to have to pray for Trae's soul in the predawn morning as I had Egan's.

'You okay?' Trae said softly.

I shoved the fears aside and forced a smile. 'Yeah. Just a little mind-blown.'

'That *was* pretty amazing, wasn't it?'

'Totally.'

After a bit more snuggling, he added, 'We really can't stay here like this.'

'I know.' But I didn't move, wanting to delay that moment and enjoy the warmth of his body wrapped around mine just a little bit longer. 'What time are we going to the house?'

He pulled away a little, and air swirled in between us, cooling the sweat still dotting my skin.

'The agent's meeting us at ten. Which gives us about an hour.'

I frowned, and twisted around to look at him. 'Agent? How can we possibly raid the safe if we have a real estate agent dogging our every move?'

'Because she won't be dogging our heels. I'll arrange a little distraction, then you'll keep the old girl occupied while I find and raid the safe.'

'Will that work?'

I couldn't help the doubt in my voice, and he smiled. 'It has in the past.'

'You raid homes in broad daylight?'

'Best time. People are less watchful during the day.'

'And it's more of an adrenaline rush, undoubtedly.'

His smile grew. 'Undoubtedly. You want first shower? I'll make coffee.'

I tossed off the covers and got out of bed. As I walked toward the bathroom, the daylight caressed my skin as warmly as Trae had minutes before. Part of me wanted to go back to his arms, to taste more of what he had to offer.

But time wasn't something I had a lot of, and dallying in bed when I needed to be elsewhere would be nothing short of foolishness.

And I'd been foolish enough recently. But not, I thought, this morning. Whatever else happened, at least I had that moment to take with me.

I took a long, hot shower, and when I finally stepped out, I felt a muted echo of the vitality I felt every time I stepped out of the sea.

Unfortunately, this time there was no yummy man within

eyesight to warm my skin to even greater levels and set my pulse rate soaring. But he was near – and the clink of a spoon against china and the delicious aroma of coffee invading the air suggested he hadn't been idle while I'd drenched myself under the hot water.

I dried off quickly, then wrapped the towel around my body and headed out.

He looked up as I entered the main room, his cool blue gaze sweeping the length of me before coming back to rest on mine. He held out the mug of coffee and said, 'I've made some toast, or there's some cereal if you want it.'

I accepted the coffee and took a sip. Its taste was more bitter than I liked, but compared to the muck the scientists used to give us, anything short of mud would have tasted divine. And as the thought ran through my mind, an image rose. A cherub-cheeked man with a cheerful smile and blue eyes bringing us coffee. The same cherub-cheeked man holding a gun to Egan's forehead. The cold light in his eyes as he threatened to press the trigger unless I dropped the gun I was holding. The splatter of his brains across the wall as I fired the weapon rather than release it.

'Destiny?'

I blinked, but the image of the blood and bone and brain matter seeping down the wall remained frozen in my thoughts, and suddenly I was shaking in cold and horror.

A hand grabbed mine and pried the coffee cup from my fingers. Then his arms engulfed me, pulling me close. And it felt good, safe, and gradually the shaking and the image subsided.

'What just happened?' he said, after a while.

I took a deep, shuddery breath, then said, 'You remember asking me when we first met if I'd killed someone?'

'Yes.'

'Well, I have.'

'We both have, Destiny. But with good reasons, I'm sure.'

'You mean you've killed someone other than those men at the house?' I pulled back, and let my gaze search his. Darkness lay below the brightness. Darkness and old anger. 'I thought you said that you hadn't?'

'I never actually answered the question.' He shrugged. 'I didn't want to scare you off.'

I laughed. 'After almost running me over?'

He raised a hand and placed it over his heart. 'I swear, the only reason *that* almost happened was your beauty. It had me entranced.'

I snorted. 'This from the man who called me less than appealing?'

'Well, that was true at the time, too.'

'You have such a charming way with compliments.' I picked up my coffee and took a sip. My hands were still a little shaky, but nowhere near as bad as they had been. 'Tell me about the other person you killed.'

The amusement died from his eyes. 'Egan and I went after the men my father contracted to kill Sila.'

'So he didn't actually do the deed himself?'

'No. But the intent was there, which was why Egan arranged for the ring to be stolen.'

'And that was the last time you saw him?'

He nodded. 'He knew he had to disappear for a while, because our father would not stop until the ring was found and the thief was caught and killed.'

'So your father didn't know Egan was behind the ring's theft?'

'No. He thought he was pissed off and sulking. He'd been away from the clique for over a week when it was snatched.'

'Who did Egan hire to snatch the ring?'

'A will-o'-the-wisp.'

I blinked. 'He hired a malevolent spirit?'

'They aren't spirits, and they certainly aren't malevolent. More mischievous. They've gotten something of a bad rap over the years.'

'The habit of leading travelers to their doom will do that.'

He laughed. The warm sound sent delicious shivers down my spine. 'Just like air dragons consuming virgins and sea dragons attacking boats have given us a bad name?'

He had a point. 'So how did he go about hiring this will-o'-the-wisp?'

'I've actually known her for a while – we protected each other's backs while learning the trade together, and she owed me a favor.' He shrugged. 'She made sure she was briefly seen, so that no suspicion could fall on Egan or me.'

'Then if no suspicion fell on you or Egan, why is your father basically blackmailing you into finding the ring?'

'Because I need the information he holds, as I said before.' He shrugged. 'Tell about the man you killed. What did he do?'

'He gave us coffee.'

He laughed, but the amusement touching his lips faded as his gaze searched mine. 'Seriously?'

I nodded. 'He was one of the men responsible for bringing us food and coffee. He was on the evening shift.'

'And the coffee was so bad that you had to shoot him?'

His words were light, but his gaze was not. He was studying me, judging me, as so many had judged me over the years. Only Egan had really seen beneath the surface, and yet even Egan had never really known the true me.

Sometimes I wondered if even *I* could make that claim. Because after years of hiding things I could do, pretending to be what I wasn't, the line between who I was and who I wasn't had begun to blur.

'I shot him because he was holding a gun to Egan's head and

threatening to kill him.' I hesitated, and dredged up a smile from somewhere. 'Though, trust me, the coffee there seriously sucked.'

'Where did this happen?'

I rubbed my free hand across my eyes. 'At the loch. Just after we'd started the fire.'

'So you shooting the man was what set off the alarm?'

I shook my head. 'The fire set off the alarm. He was simply in the wrong place at the wrong time. We ran after I shot him, but by then it was almost too late, because the fire had spread faster than we'd expected.'

'Until Egan controlled it enough to get you out.'

Again I nodded. 'I didn't know you dragons could do that when in human form.' Certainly I'd never seen Dad do it, but then, he was always too aware of the need to appear human to everyone who lived around us. Even when we were safe at home, he rarely played with the fires that were his heritage. Yet, at the same time, he'd always made sure that I knew – and could control – every skill that came with me being a sea dragon.

Of course, I was only *half* sea dragon, so it was entirely possible I might have inherited some skills from my father. Certainly I warmed with the sun, whereas most sea dragons remained a little cool. But I'd never been able to raise fire, and had never attained an air dragon's shape.

Not that I'd ever *really* tried, because for as long as I could remember, Dad had discouraged such explorations. Better to be a sea dragon, he'd once said, than to be one of the hunted and the butchered. He'd never really explained that remark, but I'd figured it was connected to the horrible scars on his body. They'd always frightened me enough *not* to explore the other half of my nature.

'Full air dragons can control fire in either form, as long as there's a slither of daylight around.' Trae's smile was thin, filled with an amusement that was cold and hateful. 'It's me that shouldn't be able to do it.'

'If they're so worried about draman inheriting dragon skills, why don't they simply stop mating with humans? I mean, if they want to run under human radar, it's a bit stupid having humans around the cliques anyway, isn't it?'

'Someone has to do the menial work,' he said dryly. 'You don't think the oh-so-superior ones are going to lift a finger to clean something, do you?'

I raised my eyebrows at the sarcasm. 'Egan wasn't like that.'

'Most of the younger generation aren't. It's the older ones.'

'So can all draman change shape and create fire?'

He shook his head. 'No. My sister, for instance, can't shift shape, but she can control fire – and she can control it at night, which is something even full bloods can't do.'

'So her being a draman has its advantages, in some ways.'

'Yeah. Although she was mighty pissed off when she discovered she couldn't shift shape like I could.'

'I can imagine.' I glanced at the time, then said, 'We really need to get moving if we're to make that appointment this morning.'

He glanced at the clock himself, then said, 'You want to pack everything up once you've eaten? I'll go shower.'

I watched him walk into the bathroom, admiring not only the burned gold and silver swirl of his dragon stain, but the strength of his shoulders, the V of his back to his hips, then I sighed and pushed the lusty thoughts away.

Not only did I have a dad to see, but I had kids and a mom depending on me to get them out of hell. Lusty thoughts were not going to achieve either aim.

I packed up most of the breakfast stuff, then munched on some cereal, using the tiny cartons of milk in the room's bar fridge. Outside, the sunshine was giving way to clouds, as the storm I'd sensed coming last night began to roll in.

I was halfway through my breakfast when a car pulled up at reception and a man got out. His clothes had seen better days and his left arm was wrapped in bandages. The driver sported a huge shiner, and even from this distance, looked a little worse for wear. There was a third man in the rear seat, but I couldn't really see him.

I didn't need to.

These weren't strangers.

They were our remaining hunters.

Chapter Nine

I swallowed hastily and the cereal went down the wrong way. Caught between coughing and choking, I shoved the bowl away and ran into the bathroom.

Trae was toweling himself dry, and raised his eyebrow, amusement deep in his eyes. 'Want some water for that cough?'

I shook my head and somehow managed to gasp, 'Hunters.'

His amusement fled and he swore. 'Where?'

'Outside.'

He touched my shoulders, forcing me to one side, and left the bathroom. I followed. He grabbed his clothes off the chair as he passed it, and began dressing as he stopped near the window.

'Red car?'

'Yeah.' I peered past him. 'One of them was the man I knocked out last night, and the other – the one that's inside reception – was wearing bandages.'

'He's probably one of the three that got singed by the car fire.'

'Maybe you should have done more than singed them.'

'I didn't exactly know what we were dealing with then.' His glance was grim. 'If they've found us here, then they definitely have another means of tracking you.'

'Obviously. But where would it be? You searched every inch.'

'Yeah, but nanotechnology is minute. It really could be any-where, even internal rather than just under the skin.'

'How the hell are we supposed to get at something that's not only tiny, but could also be internal?'

'Simple answer is, we don't.'

The reception door opened and the man with bandages came out. He spoke briefly to the guys in the car, then the man in the backseat got out of the car and headed toward the first room.

'Get into the bathroom,' Trae said. 'Don't come out until I tell you to.'

'But won't they recognize you from the car explosion?'

'The man approaching wasn't there, and I have no intentions of being seen by the others. Go, Destiny.'

I spun, grabbed my coffee cup, the bowl, and the extra plate of toast he'd made – all of them giveaways that more than one person shared this room – then ran into the bathroom.

About three seconds later there was a rough knock on the door.

'Sorry to disturb you,' a strange voice said, 'but we've had reports of an escaped felon in the area. You haven't seen anyone resembling this woman, have you?'

'I don't believe I'd *want* to see her. She's a mean-looking one,' Trae said, with just the slightest touch of amusement in his voice. 'What's she done?'

'She's wanted in connection to several burglaries.' The stranger hesitated. 'You alone here, sir?'

'Yes. You a cop?'

'No, sir. I'm a bail bondsman.' He hesitated. 'The couple in room two reported you had company. They said you came in with someone last night. Someone resembling this woman.'

'If you call both of them having black hair similar, then yeah, I guess she was.'

'Is she here now?'

'No. At the rates she charged, I couldn't afford her for anything more than an hour or so.' Trae's voice was dry. 'And if you're not a cop, then I have no reason to answer any more questions. Good day, sir.'

The stranger grunted. It didn't sound like a happy grunt. 'Thank you for your help, sir.'

The door closed. A few seconds later, Trae appeared in the bathroom doorway. 'He didn't believe me.'

'Maybe he didn't believe you're the type to use hookers.' I took a sip of coffee, then raised an eyebrow and asked, 'Are you?'

'On occasion. When the need arises and the help of a good woman isn't near.' He shrugged, his gaze on the small bathroom window at the back of the shower. 'You think you could get through that?'

'I think a better question would be, why would I want to get through that?'

'Because they'll be watching me leave, which means you can't be with me. It's either stay here, or climb out through that window and meet me down the road somewhere.'

I grabbed a bit of toast and munched on it while I contemplated the window. 'It'll be tight, but I can manage.'

'Good.' He stepped up to the window, slid it all the way open, and peered out. 'There's a line of pines just past the back fence. Once there, head to the right. There's a side street just up the road – I'll meet you there.'

'What about the tracker still in me?'

'If those men look to be leaving before me, I'll take them out.'

'Be careful. They know what you're capable of now, and they'll be watchful for an attack.'

'Sweetheart, I'm always careful.'

'And arrogant.'

He merely grinned. I took a swig of my coffee, then said, 'And if those men follow you?'

'I'll drive past the trees and take them on a scenic tour. You grab a cab and head into Florence.'

'Where will I meet you?'

'I'll call you.'

'I don't have a phone.'

'I'll give you mine. Once I'm clear, I'll find somewhere for us to meet.'

'Just don't take any risks. If they have a dragon tracker with them, they can bring you down, just like they brought Egan down.'

He smiled and touched a hand lightly to my cheek. Warmth slithered across my skin and reached deep into my soul.

'This thief knows how to sneak. It's the fish who needs to be careful.'

'They suspect you, Trae. That was evident in his tone. If it goes beyond suspicion, they'll react, and react nastily. You don't know what they're capable—'

'Nor do they know me.' He leaned forward and dropped a quick, warm kiss on my lips. 'You need to get out that window.'

'Now? Why?'

'Because the minute I look ready to leave, you can bet one of those men will be watching for other avenues of escape.'

'Oh.' I put down the toast, then picked up the coffee and gulped it down quickly. 'Let's do it.'

I followed him over. He cupped his hands, then boosted me up. I grabbed the window frame and began to shove myself through the gap feetfirst. I went flat on my back rather than sideways because the window was wider than it was high. It was a tight fit all the same, with my shoulders and breasts scraping. But I got through and dropped to the ground, retaining my balance by grabbing the outside wall.

'You okay?' Trae's face appeared in the window.

'Yep.' I dusted off my hands and gave him a smile. 'Give me the bag of my clothes, and I'll get out of here.'

He passed the bag through the window, then handed me a cell phone. 'If I can't meet you up the road, I'll call as soon as I can.'

I nodded and, as I turned away, I heard the window shut. I climbed through the wire fence, and walked into the shadowed coolness of the thick stand of pine trees. I'd barely taken a dozen steps when the hair along the back of my neck began to stand on end. I stopped behind the gnarled trunk of one of the pines and looked around.

A man stood at the far end of the motel. A dark-skinned man with a large nose and big hands. Not the man I'd attacked last night, but someone else. Someone whose features scratched at my nerves like a bad case of hives.

Because I knew him. He was one of the dragon-born, and a tracker working for the scientists. He was also the man responsible for capturing me in the first place. Cold sweat broke out across my forehead and my hands began to shake. I would have liked to think it was fury, but I knew that was far from the case.

I couldn't be caught by this man a second time.

I *wouldn't*.

I backed away slowly, carefully, until the shadowed greenness of the pines was deep and thick around me. Then I moved forward, taking care with each step, trying to be as silent as possible.

When I looked over my shoulder again, he was following. Not that I could see him. I could *sense* him. Sense the forbidding gloom of his presence. The thick, peppery smell of him.

A shiver ran down my spine, and panic surged. My fingers clenched around the plastic bag containing my clothes, and it was tempting, so tempting, to reach inside and grab the cell phone, to call Trae and tell him to get me the hell out of here. Only he didn't have a phone, so that was a pretty useless urge.

Besides, while I had no doubt he would help me, I wouldn't have called him even if I could have. I'd already killed his brother. I couldn't risk his life as well.

No, this particular battle was mine, and no matter how much it scared me, I was *not* helpless.

I might not have flame in my weaponry, but the sea was

mine to call. And if I was close enough, it was a power I could use.

I just had to get close enough.

I drew in a deep breath, and released it slowly. Then I forced my feet on, walking through the thick shadows, heading for the road Trae mentioned. The trees eventually began to thin out, and bright sunshine started dancing through the pine needles all around me, sprinkling the air with slivers of gold and green. The ground began to slope downward, and a road became visible. I couldn't see Trae's car, which was a blessing. I didn't need to drag him deeper into this.

I stepped onto the pavement and paused briefly, tasting the air, searching for the scent of the sea. Its touch was light on the cooling breeze, hinting at distance.

I crossed the road and turned right, walking up the hill. After a while, my neck tingled, and the tang of pepper scented the breeze. The dark man had come out of the pines.

I clenched my hands and resisted the urge to run. He would follow, biding his time, waiting for the perfect moment. Until we were alone, I was safe.

I swung left, onto another street, following the scent of the sea. Traffic was heavier in this street, and the pavement more crowded. People walked by, some smiling and nodding in greeting, some not. I was one of the latter – fear of the man who followed made me incapable of anything but forward movement.

I crossed another street and walked down another sidewalk, edging closer to the sea and some sense of safety. Occasionally I caught a glimpse of my dark-skinned hunter via the storefront windows as I passed, but mostly it was just a sense, a certainty, that he was near.

The scent of the sea was thicker on the wind now, drawing me on, making it difficult not to run. I kept my pace even, trying to ignore the tingles down my spine, the feeling that at any moment, his fat fingers would be on my neck, squeezing tight.

I shivered and ran across the road. Another turn, and the sea was suddenly visible – a thick blue line that had my soul breathing a sigh of relief.

But I wasn't safe yet. Not by a long shot.

I walked on, hoping I had the time, hoping the man behind me wouldn't risk getting too near until we were all but alone.

But there weren't many people on the beach. Just a handful of joggers and a couple of swimmers brave enough to risk the chill of the water. I stepped onto the sand, the grit of it harsh against my toes. After stripping off my pants and sweatshirt, I strode toward the water. When I was near enough, I dropped the bag and placed my clothes on top. It wouldn't stop a thief, but I could only hope there were few of them around at this hour. Not that I had much to steal – just some cash, a stolen credit card, and a borrowed cell phone. None of which I could actually afford to lose.

Fingers of sea foam reached for my toes as I neared the water, running across my skin, their touch cold and somehow comforting. I strode on, my heart in my mouth, my nose filled with the twin scents of sea and pepper.

He was near. So near.

Despite the iciness of air and water, sweat began dribbling down my spine, soaking through in coin-sized patches on my T-shirt. It was all I could do to hold my pace, to not panic.

The water reached my knees, moved up to my thighs. Safety was close, so close. I let my fingers trail in the water, feeling for the energy running underneath the waves. It danced around my fingertips, little sparks of electricity no one else would ever feel, let alone see. I closed my eyes briefly and called it to me.

And then I heard it. The soft click of a gun's safety being disengaged.

'Stop,' he said. His voice was guttural with an accent I'd never been able to place. 'Don't move any farther into the sea.'

I had no doubt he'd shoot, and that knowledge was powerful enough to not only halt my steps, but to have my heart leaping up into the vicinity of my throat. But I hadn't come all this way to let him catch me so easily. The sea was my home, the one place where I *could* fight him, and I'd be damned if I'd let him take me here. I bit my lip and forced myself to keep moving.

Are you totally insane? part of me screamed. Probably. But in many respects, I'd rather be dead than go back to those cells. And if he *did* kill me, at least the sea would protect my body. She would whisk it away so it could never be used by those men.

But I had no intentions of being killed today. Not by this man. Not if I could help it.

I heard a click – a sound so faint he was obviously using a silencer. Felt the vibration of the shot run across the air, across my skin.

I dove sideways.

I wasn't fast enough to avoid the bullet – not that I really expected to be.

The metal tore through skin and muscle before blasting its way back out of my shoulder – the same damn shoulder as before. The water went red and pain rolled through me, flooding my body, making it difficult to concentrate. But I battled the darkness threatening to swamp my senses. If I gave in to the call of unconsciousness, I would be his.

So I called to the energy of the sea and let it fill me. It raced through my muscles, energizing and renewing. Giving me the strength I needed to fight. I dove deep, keeping low and close to the sandy bottom, swimming out to deeper waters. But not too deep. I needed to draw him out.

Needed him to feel safe while doing so.

And for that, he'd need his feet on the bottom. He knew

how well I could swim, so he'd neither risk going too deep nor bother shifting shape. Air dragons couldn't breathe underwater like we could, and it was harder for them to take off from deeper water – there wasn't enough room for the full sweep of their wings. Besides, while the beach wasn't packed, there were still people about, and if there was one thing the scientists were fanatical about, it was not revealing our presence. Marsten didn't want to share the glory with *anyone*.

It was probably the one thing he and the dragon communities would ever agree on.

When the depth was right, I headed for the light and the air. As I neared the surface, I let myself go and simply floated on the waves, as if unconscious. My arms were outstretched, my fingers in the water.

And still I called to the power of the sea and the waves, gathering it to me, letting it build, until the energy swirled around me, an unseen vortex ready to be unleashed.

For several minutes, there was no reaction from the dark-skinned man. No vibration or movement disturbing the waves rolling toward the beach.

Then I felt it. One step. Then another. Soon he was splashing through the waves, hurrying toward me. I moved my fingers slowly through the water, caressing the power, readying it.

Fingers touched my foot tentatively. Tension ran through the water, thick and heavy, as the man who held my foot braced himself against the slightest hint of movement.

I didn't twitch.

His grip against my foot became firmer. Tentatively, he tugged me backward. The power of the sea surged against my control, as if eager to grab my assailant. I held it back, felt the anger of it roar through my body. Knew I wouldn't be able to control it for very much longer.

His chuckle filled the air. A satisfied sound if ever I'd heard one. So I flicked my fingers wide, unleashing the vortex. It swirled past, sending me spinning, and hit the dark-skinned man hard, sucking him down into the ocean.

I flipped around, taking a breath of air, then ducked under the water. The hunter was spinning under the surface, held there by the vortex. Even if he changed, it wouldn't have helped. The vortex was too strong, too powerful, and would have ripped his wings to pieces. Besides, shifting shape wasn't an instantaneous thing, and he probably would have drowned in the process. The fear etched on his face suggested he knew that.

I spread my hands wide, flicking my fingers toward the surface, raising the vortex and allowing him to grab a breath before yanking him back down again. It was a pattern I kept as I swept him out to sea, until there was no beach, no nothing. Just ocean. Endless blue ocean.

And us.

Even then, I didn't set him entirely free, keeping him locked within the vortex but no longer spinning. Just because I believed that dragons couldn't take off in deep water didn't mean that they couldn't. It was definitely better to be safe than sorry with these bastards.

'Oh God, oh God,' he said, over and over as he fought to get free, movements panicked and almost believable.

Almost. Someone else might have bought it, but I knew what he was, and what he could do. Panic and a killer just didn't go together.

'I know you're a dragon, so quit the histrionics,' I said dryly. 'I also know you'll try and kill—'

I didn't even get the sentence finished before he'd raised his hand. Fire erupted from his fingertips and burned across the waves.

I swore and ducked under the water, watching the thick flames fire past me. When they were gone, I raised a hand and yanked him deep, flinging him about like a useless bit of seaweed before pushing him back to the surface.

He spluttered and coughed, and glared at me with hateful eyes.

'Do that again, and I will kill you,' I said softly.

'How did you do this?' he asked, waving his arm angrily at the swirling water holding him captive. 'They said your power comes at dawn or dusk, not during the day itself.'

I smiled. 'Just goes to prove that the scientists don't know as much about me as they think they do, doesn't it?'

He glared at me, face pinched, eyes narrowed. 'What do you want?'

I stared at him, seeing the fear buried deep behind the anger. 'I want answers.'

'Or what? You'll drown me? Go ahead. It won't stop them coming after you.'

'I don't care if they come after me.' A lie, of course, but he wasn't to know that.

'Then what do you want?'

'I want to free my mother and the kids.'

He snorted. 'That will never happen. The Drumnadrochit facility has been locked up tight, and no one, not even a flame-throwing dragon, will get anywhere near the place.' He paused, and his sudden grin was malicious. 'Oh, I forgot, your pet flamethrower bit the big one, didn't he?'

Anger surged through me. I ducked under the water, grabbed his ankle, and yanked down hard. This time I pulled him deep into the dark coldness of the water, watching his struggle to hold his breath, until his face went dark and the realization he was about to drown hit him.

Only then did I push him upward and let him breathe air rather than water.

He took several long, shuddering gasps, then somehow said, 'Bitch.'

'Totally. And right now, you're relying on this bitch to survive.'

He shuddered and wiped a hand across his red, splotchy features. 'What do you want to know?'

'Tell me about the security at Drumnadrochit.'

'It's been upgraded since your escape. A bird can't fart now without security knowing about it.'

'What about the loch?'

'Sensors along the shoreline.'

'The whole shoreline?'

He hesitated. 'Most of it.'

He was lying. The loch was too big, too wild, for such thoroughness. They'd probably only done the area near my mother's lands. 'Infrared sensors?'

He nodded. 'And movement sensors.'

'What about the security codes – do you know them?'

'It's all handprint-coded now. Everyone working there is registered with the computer. No one else gets in without clearance from the big man himself.'

Which meant we'd been doing nothing but wasting time here in Florence. Even if we'd managed to raid the old lady's

208

house successfully, it wouldn't have mattered a damn. We couldn't slide in a new password because Marsten would have final approval, and we couldn't use someone else's because of the whole handprint deal.

God, we should have figured something like this would happen, but I guess Egan and I had been working blind. We weren't security experts – even if Egan had trained in the family 'business' of stealing. Security equipment had probably zoomed ahead in leaps and bounds in the ten years he'd been locked up.

'So the security net around the research center is tight? There are no gaps anywhere at all in the system?'

'None that I'm aware of.'

Crap. Of course, he could be lying his pants off, but part of me doubted it. Fear lurked in his eyes, and I really didn't think his loyalty to the scientists ran *that* deep. 'Tell me how you've been finding us so successfully.'

'Tracker.'

'Where?'

He hesitated, then said, somewhat reluctantly, 'In your foot.'

'Which we pulled out last night and destroyed. So how did you find us at the hotel?'

'Luck,' he muttered.

But his eyes did a shifty little sideways flicker, telling me he was lying. Or at least, not admitting the entire truth. 'I know there's another tracker, so just tell me where.'

He didn't say anything. I raised my fingers, entangling the full power of the ocean once again, letting it tug lightly at his feet and twist him around. Fear flashed across his sullen features.

'Okay, okay, there *is* another one.'

'Where?'

'In your mouth, in one of the fillings. It's short-range microchip.'

Oh, just great. And here was me with no time and no cash to visit a dentist. Though how on earth would I explain having a tracker in my mouth? 'Which tooth?'

He just smiled. 'Take me back to the shore and I'll tell you.'

'Yeah, right.' If I took him back to shore, he'd either immediately create a fuss that'd attract unwanted attention, or one of the idiots who'd been in the car with him would take a second shot at me. And this time, they might not just get a shoulder.

'You need to get help for that shoulder, you know,' he said. 'Otherwise you'll bleed to death.'

'The sea will heal it.'

He snorted. 'Yeah. The sea is all powerful, all healing. That's why I was able to catch you so easily the first time.'

The sea had nothing to do with that because I was near the loch rather than the ocean. Besides, he'd caught me so easily because I was a fool. I'd naively believed him when he said he could get me inside the research center and help me rescue my mom.

Of course, he'd kept *half* his word. He'd gotten me into the compound all right – and led me straight into the trap the scientists had waiting. I'd called the loch for help, but the loch was freshwater, not sea, and while waters as ancient as the loch *did* contain a powerful energy, it didn't have the same sort of magic as the sea. Not for me as a half breed, anyway. She'd answered, but nowhere near quick enough. The scientists had knocked me out very quickly, and I doubted they would have even noticed a brief rise of water up the shoreline.

'Tell me the range of the microchip.'

He hesitated, then muttered, 'Five hundred feet.'

'That's not very far.'

'The other one was GPS technology. The tooth was just meant as a backup, and designed mainly for around the lab. If you got out of your cell, it was easier for them to use the short-range stuff than haul out the GPS.'

He was beginning to shiver now, his bottom lip quivering and his skin turning a paler shade. He was treading water rather than simply floating, and therefore using more body heat than necessary. He was also an air dragon, and they didn't do well in cold conditions. Not for very long periods, anyway.

Distant vibrations of power began to lap at my skin, and the sea began whispering of an approaching powerboat. I looked over my shoulder, scanning the horizon and seeing a distant dot. Maybe someone had seen this man being dragged out.

Which meant the time for a decision was coming. I spread my fingers in the water, calling to the power, letting it play lazily around me.

'What other safety measures have been employed since we got out?'

'I've been here, chasing after you, so who knows?'

'How many of you are here in America?'

'Six.'

But again his eyes did that shifty little flick. I raised a hand, let the sea swirl around him a little stronger.

'Okay, okay,' he said quickly. 'There's nine.'

One had been killed in the car explosion, and I'd killed one last night. Trae had gotten rid of two others, so that left five. Four if I got rid of this one. Better odds by far, even if the thought of drowning him had a bitter taste rising in my mouth.

'And who is holding the device that tracks the microchip signal?'

'Take me to shore and I might tell you.'

I raised an eyebrow. 'Do you really think I'm stupid enough to believe that?'

'Then what do you intend to do?'

'What do you think I intend to do?'

He flung fire at me. This time, I stopped it with the waves. He didn't say anything, but the fear that had stayed mostly in the background until now was etched all over his face.

The vibrations in the water were becoming stronger. I looked over my shoulder, saw the boat becoming visible on the horizon.

'Hoy!' he shouted, waving his hand wildly. 'Over here!'

'I wouldn't do that,' I said mildly, gathering the lazy net of energy.

'If that boat is ours,' he said, 'you're in deep shit. And I intend to make you pay—'

I didn't wait for the rest of the threat, just flipped underwater and finally unleashed the dragon within.

Energy ran across my limbs – energy that twisted and changed my form, until what floated under the water was long and slender, with scales that ran from the deepest green to the brightest blue. In looks, we were very close to the traditional depictions of Chinese dragons, but there were still some similarities to our winged cousins. The spiked tail and deadly claws, for instance.

With my sea body reclaimed, I unleashed the net of energy I'd been gathering and snagged his legs, dragging him deep down, past the twilight layers and into the dark and gloomy waters that never saw sunshine or surface-dwelling sea life. Down to where the worms, crustaceans, and rattail fish played. Down to where the pressure was beyond even fire dragon endurance and the air in his bloodstream expanded to the point that it blocked the flow of blood to brain and limbs. Death after that was almost instantaneous. If I had to kill, then I would kill quickly. Not that this type of death was in any way easy.

I released the energy of the sea and let his body float away on the current. The rattails would have a good feed for the next few weeks.

I flicked my tail and rose slowly toward the surface. The feel of the cold seawater slithering over my scales was sensual, making me want to wriggle in sheer pleasure. I loved my sea form, and part of me wanted to remain like this for a while. But if that boat *did* belong to the scientists, they might very well have the short-range receiver with them. Which meant I had two choices – destroy the boat and kill those on board, or escape.

I flipped over onto my back and swam slowly toward the vibrations of the boat. Even if they did have the tracker, I was deep enough that they wouldn't see me. But I would see them.

The hull of the boat came into sight. I swam underneath it, then angled away until I could see who was on board. The boat was a luxurious one, so didn't belong to Marsten's men. Unless they'd commandeered it. Inside it were two men. One of the men held what looked to be a cell phone, but when he swung around in my direction, I realized it had to be the receiver.

I spun around and headed under the boat again. The man with the receiver was shouting for the driver to turn, which meant I was left with little option. I couldn't let them follow me again.

I snapped my tail and dove deep, gathering speed. When the ocean was little more than a dark blur roaring past, I flipped around and headed back up, swimming straight at the underbelly of the boat. At the last possible moment, I twisted, hitting the hull with my back, sending it flipping up and over. As those aboard fell into the sea, I located the man with the tracker and swam toward him. He spun and saw me, and frantically began to swim away. As if he could ever beat me in the water. I caught him in an instant, and snapped with my teeth, grabbing the receiver out of his hand and tasting blood in the process. Nausea rose, but I ignored it, crunching down on the device before spitting out the remains.

Then I turned and swam away. I couldn't kill them. I might regret it later, but right now, I had enough blood on my hands. Besides, Marsten's men weren't the real problem – they were just paid employees, doing what they were told. Even the dragons in his employ wouldn't present such a problem once Marsten and the scientists at Drumnadrochit were taken care of.

That had to be my first priority. Leaving a trail of bodies behind me held no appeal, especially when Marsten and his investors had more than enough funds to easily replace those bodies.

I headed for the shore. The sea bottom eventually began to rise and sunlight played through the water, filling my world with pretty shades of blue and green.

As I rose back through the twilight layers and reached the surface levels, I shifted shape once again. In human form, I swam the last few hundred yards, then strode out of the water.

It was just beginning to rain, and there was hardly anyone on the beach. Certainly no one seemed to have noticed that a shot had been fired or a man had gone missing. My plastic bag and clothes were still sitting where I'd left them and, from this distance, didn't appear to have been disturbed. Of course, that didn't mean nothing had been taken. I stripped off my T-shirt and slung it over my shoulder to hide the bullet wound the sea had only half healed, then in my panties and bra, walked up the beach toward my clothes.

Once I'd grabbed my bag, I did a quick check for the phone, credit card, and cash. They were all still there, and relief slithered through me. Some days, luck was just on your side.

I quickly dressed, using a dry shirt as a towel, then finger-combed my hair and headed off the beach. I dug the phone out of the bag, checked that Trae hadn't called, then shoved it in my pocket. The cash and credit card quickly followed.

So what did I do next?

Go find a restaurant and wait for Trae's call?

Fact was, I no longer needed to break into the old lady's house, and I no longer needed the security codes.

I could go find my dad, and give him the message from my mom. Give him the hope that she would find him, and that there was no need to haunt the twilight zone between this world and the next.

I bit my lip, letting my gaze roam across the street and the cars parked nearby, searching for a familiar car. But neither the scientists' red car nor Trae's gray one was anywhere nearby.

Part of me wanted to see Trae's car. Wanted to see Trae. Not just because I missed him already, but because being alone brought back all the old doubts. Doubts about my strength. Doubts about my ability to do the task I'd set myself.

Truth was, the only time I'd ever really been alone was those first few weeks before my capture. After that, there'd always been scientists, and later other dragons, about. Still, it wasn't until Egan joined me that I'd ceased to feel so alone. It was stupid, I know, but Egan's presence had always given me some hope that I could beat them. That together we could do this and win. I'd spent most of my adult life being poked and prodded, having my blood and flesh extracted and examined, and it was only with Egan that I'd found the strength to fight. It was a strength that had eventually freed us.

I didn't know if I could do this alone.

Didn't know if I *wanted* to do it alone.

But even as that thought crossed my mind, a vision rose. Egan running. Stumbling. The blood, splattered across the crystal walls of his home. Its warm stickiness as it slid down my skin. Him dropping to the ground as his life flooded across the gray stones of the home he'd thought so safe.

And then Egan's face became Trae's, Egan's blood Trae's . . .

A sob caught in my throat and suddenly tears were filling my eyes, blurring my vision. I stumbled, and flung out a hand, using the wall of a nearby shop to steady myself.

No, I thought. *No.*

Egan's death was enough. I couldn't handle Trae dying as well. Which meant I had to let him go – at least until being around me no longer spelled death.

And while I very much suspected it wasn't going to be easy to lose my thief, I had to at least try.

Because I had a bad feeling that if Trae got hurt or killed, it would hurt *me* in ways I couldn't even begin to understand.

Chapter Ten

I'd barely made my decision to leave when the cell phone rang. My heart leapt somewhere to the vicinity of my throat, and for several seconds I thought about ignoring it. It was stupid to answer it, stupid to give him advance warning of my intentions. I knew all that.

And yet part of me ached to hear his voice. To hear the timbre of it resonate through my body one more time, warming me as much as his clever hands.

I blew out a breath, then dragged the phone out of my pocket.

'Hello?'

'Destiny? Where are you?'

My gaze went to the sea. I could hear it calling me, telling me not to be long. I closed my eyes, and lied. 'I don't exactly know.'

He paused. Somewhere close behind him, a woman ordered a coffee. Cups clinked. Voices murmured, a general hum that spoke of a smallish crowd. He had to be in a café somewhere. 'What the hell is that supposed to mean?'

'It means I don't need to visit that house anymore.'

'Why not?' His voice was sharp, filled with the threat of anger.

'I had a nice chat with one of the men in the red car. Apparently, they no longer use key codes, but rather handprint scans.'

'He could have been lying—'

'He wasn't.'

Again he paused. 'And the man?'

'Still swimming deep, as far as I know.'

'Destiny—'

'No,' I cut in, ignoring the deepening anger in his voice. Ignoring the shiver that was part fear, part desire. 'Sorry, Trae, but I'm not willing to let you pay the price that Egan did. They still have the means to find me, and enough is enough.'

'I won't let—'

'I'm going to get my mother,' I cut in again. 'I'm sorry, Trae. Sorry I can't help you.'

'Damn it, Destiny, we had a deal—'

I hit the end button, cutting him off mid-sentence. For several seconds, I just stared at the phone, waiting for it to ring, for him to call back. When he didn't, an odd mix of relief and disappointment ran through me.

Not wanting to examine *that* particular mix of emotions any more than necessary, I shoved the phone into the bag, then tied it up tight. Of course, the plastic wasn't watertight, and the phone would more than likely be destroyed by the deeper ocean waters, but I'd rather that than leaving it here for him to find. I didn't want to give him an easy reference point for my leaving.

It was time to go see my dad.

Before it really *was* too late.

I tied the plastic bag to my wrist and strode back into the sea. And tried not to think about how angry my dad was going to be when he saw me again. He might be crippled, and he might be dying, but I had no doubt his fury would be *fearsome*. I'd gone against his orders to go after my mom, and had disappeared for years. And yet I knew a lot of the anger would be aimed at himself as much as me. Aimed at the disease that was slowly killing him, and his inability to do anything to help either me or my mother.

Sadness rose like a tide, and suddenly I was blinking back tears. 'What goes around comes around' had been a favorite saying of his when I was younger. Well, where the hell was the payback for the scientists who were destroying my family? When was fate going to step in and say enough is enough?

Or was that now my lot? To mete out the justice they had coming?

I bit my bottom lip and dove under the waves. The problem was, I didn't actually *want* justice. I just wanted my mother free. Just wanted us to live as a family again.

Of course, the scientists knew we were out here in the oceans now, just like they knew the air dragons were here. No matter what I did, that knowledge would remain. Surely it would only be a matter of time before the news spread through the scientific ranks and the hunt for us all became even more intense.

But there wasn't a lot I could do about that, and gnawing over it like a dog with a bone would get me nowhere fast.

One step at a time, I thought.

I shifted shape when I was deep enough, and began the long trek down the North American coast, heading for the tip of South America.

It was a tedious trip. I kept myself amused by skimming the waves and chasing the sea life that darted like quicksilver flashes in front of me, but the day rolled into the night and back into the day until the hours just seemed to blur together.

For the first time in my life, I wished I'd taken after Dad more than Mom. Right now, wings would have been bonus. At least I could have flown directly across the continent rather than having to swim around South America before heading back home. It was time wasted – time that could be better spent with my dad.

But the only way I could have flown was to ask Trae. And not only would that have selfishly put him into danger yet again, there was also the worry as to whether he could actually do it.

Air dragons *could* carry people. There were enough myths and tales about fiery beasts dragging off human sacrifices to have at least some basis in fact – but could they manage it for long periods? Somehow, I doubted it. Even birds of prey didn't carry their kills for great distances.

I wondered what it would be like to soar through the clouds. How different would flying be to cutting through the cold, wild seas? Would there be more of a sense of freedom? I'd always imagined that cutting through sunshine and wind would be far more pleasant than skimming through the ever-cold waters of the deeper oceans, but Egan would never really talk about it much.

I closed my eyes and imagined him soaring through the blue skies, his scales gleaming with fire, gossamer wings outstretched as he soared high and long. He'd been beautiful, truly beautiful, in his dragon form.

Just like Trae.

And it hurt to think I might never see him or his dragon

form again. Because even if he did come after me, he might not want anything more to do with me after the way I'd broken our deal.

The seas got a lot rougher as I rounded the tip of South America and began the long trek up toward the North Atlantic. It was still boring, though, and while I tried desperately not to think about Trae any more than I already had, my thoughts inevitably drifted back to him.

And part of me began to worry. Trae wasn't the type to give up easily, and he wanted the ring as fiercely as I wanted to see my dad and free my mom. Just because I'd left him behind didn't mean he'd actually stay there. And certainly the sheer length of this swim would give him more than enough time to catch up – even if he didn't use his dragon form to fly from Oregon to Maine.

The one good thing was the fact that he didn't know where I was going. I might have told him Maine, but Maine was a big place, and our home wasn't near any major cities anyway. And Trae wouldn't find us in the phone book – our number was unlisted.

Not that *that* would stop a determined man.

Of course, the main problem for me was the fact I had to come in at night – it was difficult enough to swim through the bays without being spotted, let alone get under the bridge at Lubec. *That* would take timing, and high tide. But night also gave Trae an advantage – he could fly high and keep watch. Air dragon sight was sharp – he'd see my shadow, even at night and under the water.

Still, there was little I could do about it, and no point in working myself up any more than I already was.

When I finally rounded the national park and swam into Johnson Bay, excitement began to pulse through my bloodstream. I was home – or close to it. Maybe it wasn't the home where I was supposed to be raised, but it was the home of my heart regardless, and suddenly I was eager to see the old log house my dad had built on the South Bay shore in the years before the disease had really begun to take hold.

The tidal currents were moving fast, and I rode them past the bridge, thankful I'd come in close to high tide. The sea in this section could get low enough to walk through – although the mud could make *that* difficult.

I swam into the deeper waters of the bay, my excitement growing as I made my way through Cobscook Bay and into the waters that had been my home for many years.

It was then a large dark shadow swooped low over the water. Claws bigger than the length of my hands briefly skimmed the tops of the waves, the deadly tips gleaming inches from my nose before the shadow lifted and moved on.

I swore softly and rose to the surface, allowing my snout and eyes to break the water but leaving the rest of my body hidden.

Not that any watchers were likely to notice me when there was a goddamn winged dragon skimming the waves.

And oh, he was *so* beautiful.

His sleek, powerful body looked silvery in the moonlight, but each movement had a ripple of deep gold shimmering across his scales. His wings were gossamer, glittering with every powerful stroke, reminding me of the gleaming beauty of a spider's web after a sun shower.

One wing dipped, the fragile-looking tip momentarily digging into the sea and sending up a huge spray of water as he lazily turned around. His gaze met mine, the blue depths full of fury and warning. Then he was turning back around and heading for the shore.

I followed him. I had little other choice – that brief look had said that well enough.

He didn't change until he had landed on the rocky shoreline. Luckily, it was hours after midnight, and the few houses that were within spotting distance were dark and silent. It was doubtful anyone had seen the dragon take on human shape.

I shifted the shape once the sea bottom began to rise, and strode somewhat reluctantly toward the beach. *This* was not going to be pleasant.

I stopped with my feet still in the sea. There were still several yards between us, but I could see him and hear him, and that was close enough. Not that I thought he'd hurt me, even if his anger was hot enough to burn.

His face might as well have been a brick, for all the emotion he was showing. But I could see the flick of it in his bright eyes. Feel the thunder of it rolling through the air.

'How did you find me?'

'I've been patrolling all night.' His rich voice was as clipped as mine. 'Air dragons may be creatures of air and sun, but we have damn good night vision. A sea dragon is hard to miss, even at night and under the water.'

'Bit risky flying around like that, wasn't it?'

He gave me a cold sort of smile. 'If I fly high up, people just think I'm a large bird.'

Extremely large, I would think. And if those people happened to be near a pair of binoculars, well, there went any resemblance to a large bird. Still, an air dragon flew extremely fast. It was doubtful that even those who had a camera at hand would catch anything more than air swirls.

'What about the laptop and the equipment you had in the car?'

He gave me a dark sort of look. 'I went back to my house and stored them there.'

'Look, Trae—'

'Not here,' he snapped, closing the distance between us, wrapping me in heat and anger. 'The night is freezing, and you're shivering. My car is just up on the road. Let's get somewhere warm before we do this.'

He gripped my arm and propelled me forward several steps. Caught by surprise, I almost fell, and it was only his grip that kept me upright. Once I'd managed to catch my balance, I ripped my elbow out of his grasp and stopped.

'The last thing I need' – I stabbed him in the chest with a finger and tried to ignore the warmth that flared up toward my arm with each tiny touch – 'is some fool acting like a damned he-man. You can't just haul me around as you please. Be civil, or that ring is going to remain sea-bound for eternity.'

He crossed his arms, his eyes flat and dangerous. 'That's not a threat you should be making, sweetheart. Trust me on that.'

I growled low down in my throat and pushed past him. 'Why couldn't you have just accepted the situation and left me alone?'

He followed, a presence I could feel through every pore, in every fiber. In some ways, he felt like sunshine through rain – an inner warmth surrounded by threatening darkness.

'Because we had a deal.' His voice was even, not hinting at the fury vibrating the air. 'And you're *going* to live up to your side of it.'

I swung around and faced him. 'All you need the ring for is to get some information out of your bastard of a father. *I'm* trying to get to mine before he dies. What makes you think I really give a damn about any stupid deal you might have made right now?'

'What makes *you* think that the information I need is any less urgent than you getting to your dad?'

'Because if it *was*, you would have told me.'

'Not when the fucking ring was already out of my reach and couldn't be immediately retrieved.' He eyed me for a minute, the heat of his fury washing over me again despite the tight control he obviously had over his emotions. 'Agreeing to the deal gave me the ring in a couple of days. And that was okay, because it helped me, and it helped you, as Egan had wished.'

I studied him for a moment, then said, 'So what sort of information does your father hold that is so important?'

He sighed, and thrust a hand through his hair. 'My sister has gone missing, and my mom feels sure that she's in some sort of trouble.'

'Is this a kin intuition thing?'

'She's human, remember, so the kin intuition doesn't apply. She just occasionally gets these feelings about things, and they mostly come true.'

'Then why the *hell* didn't you tell me all this in the first place?' My voice was sharper than I'd intended, but damn it, he deserved it. If his sister was in trouble, he *should* have told me. 'Why do such a botched job of stealing it?'

'Because we're conditioned not talk about the clique or

clique business. Besides, I had no idea what had happened to my brother, who you were, and whether I could trust you. Running with the ring just seemed easier at the time.'

'You could have just explained the situation, Trae.'

His gaze searched mine. 'Would you have believed me? Especially considering you had no idea until our meeting that Egan even had siblings?'

'Honestly? I don't know,' I said. 'Maybe not when we'd first met, because I didn't know you any better than you knew me. But later, yeah, I would have. Either way, stealing it wasn't the answer.'

'So I discovered.'

This, I thought sourly, was a complete and utter shambles. And why? Because neither of us had trusted the other enough to just come out and explain things. But at least this was one mess that was easily fixed.

I swung around on my heel and marched back to the sea. I couldn't change the delay I'd caused – a delay that might very well endanger his sister – but I could do this. I could summon the ring from the sea and give it back to him.

'Destiny, the car is—'

'I don't care about the car. I'm getting the ring.'

'It's nearly dawn—' he said.

'Which is the best time for this sort of magic.' I swung around and faced him. 'I have enough blood on my hands already, Trae. I don't want your sister's on them as well. When I get the ring, I want you to go. Get the information you need, and go find your sister.'

'But—'

'Promise me,' I cut in sharply, 'that you'll take the ring and go.'

He hesitated, then said, 'Okay. I promise.'

'Good. You might want to get some blankets from the car, though. This could be a bit of a wait.'

I turned back around and walked to the water. The waves hissed over my feet, welcoming me back, wanting me to go deeper, wanting me to play. I ignored them, wading out until the water was thigh deep. Once there, I stopped and waited for the dawn.

It stirred gradually through the darkness. Slivers of pink and gold began to breach the night, dousing the stars and lending a glory to the predawn darkness. The energy in the air gradually increased, becoming more and more frantic, reaching toward its crescendo as the slivers became a river that flooded the sky. As the beat of energy came to a peak, and the air came alive with the hum and power of a new day, I raised my left hand and held it palm up to the skies.

'To the Gods of the sea, I call on thee.'

The ritual words rode across the silence, holding the energy, shaping it, becoming a thing of beauty and command. The waters around me began to stir and swirl, and the rush of waves were momentarily lost against that gathering whirl. Droplets of water shot into the sky, sparkling like diamonds in the gathering brightness.

'To my brothers of deep, dark waters, and my sisters of the quick shallows, I call on thee.'

More energy touched the air, a deep, bass thrum that spoke of vast, cold places. It flooded through me, filling me, completing me, in a way no human touch ever would.

The droplets came together, becoming a water spout that glittered and spun and danced upon the rich, dark waters.

'Return the ring you've kept safe and unfound. Return it to me now from the dark and secret places.'

Thunder rumbled in the distance, and the energy stirred, then leapt away. The turbulence stilled and the waves returned. I turned around and waded back up to the shoreline.

Trae was waiting, and there were blankets at his feet. 'Now what?' he said, his fingers briefly touching my cheek, washing warmth across my skin.

'Now we wait.' I grabbed a blanket and wrapped it around me cocoon-like, then sat down. 'What did you mean before, when you said you were conditioned not to talk about the clique?'

'Just that.' He picked up a blanket and wrapped it loosely around his shoulders, then sat down beside me. Even though we weren't touching, his warmth flowed around me, heating the chill from my skin far swifter than the rising brightness of the day. 'We are conditioned from the cradle not to talk about the clique. Every single day of our childhood we were told that those who talk about family business to outsiders will die. You hear it so often it becomes a part of your very nature.'

Disbelief surged, and I looked at him. 'Surely they wouldn't actually—'

'Not they. *Him.* The bastard we call king. And I've seen it done, many times. Our clique is a law unto itself in this matter – and no one, absolutely no one, dares to defy that law.' He looked at me, eyes glimmering in the growing light. 'I have told you more about the clique than I have ever told anyone. But the training is still there, and it is very hard to break. Especially when it involves those that I love.'

'So you think your sister is in danger rather than just trouble?'

'I don't know. But would you take the risk?'

'No.' I leaned a little closer to him, so that our shoulders touched. 'Was she living at home with your mom before she disappeared?'

He snorted softly. 'Most of us half breeds get out as quick as we can. We're protected from the worst excesses of the clique until we reach sixteen, but after that it's open season.'

I frowned. 'What do you mean by that?'

'Let's just say that young male air dragons tend to like testing their strength and their sexual prowess, and a lot of them aren't particular about gender.'

I raised my eyebrows. 'Air dragons are bisexual?'

'Mostly, no, but in our clique there aren't a lot of breeding females. Hence the abundance of draman like myself. Those who can't find human release often turn to each other.'

'But if there's twelve other cliques, why don't they just go elsewhere? Surely the female shortage doesn't run through all the cliques?'

'I suspect it doesn't, but air dragons are notoriously protective over what they class as "their own." It's that whole not-sharing-the-loot mentality that was apparently prevalent in the early days.'

'So did any of these young dragons ever try their wily ways on you?'

Amusement glimmered briefly in his eyes. 'Only one. I handed him back his balls on a platter and was never bothered after that.'

'Not surprising.'

'No. Mercy was pretty self-sufficient, as well, but she was attacked several times. Most of the time, I was there to stop it before it went too far, but once I was forced out—' He hesitated and shrugged. 'She pretty much left when she hit sixteen.

She came to San Francisco and lived with me while she finished school and studied journalism, then got an apartment with several friends.'

'If your mom's so worried about her, why wouldn't she go talk to the police?'

'Because talking to the police would be involving outsiders. And that would jeopardize my mother.'

'But she's human, not dragon.'

'Yes, but she's been employed by the clique since she was eighteen, and considers them her family. If she calls the cops, she'd lose that family – either by losing her life, or being thrown out of the clique.'

'Just how big is your clique?'

He hesitated. 'There would be over a hundred and fifty, if you just counted dragons.'

'*That* many dragons cannot go unnoticed forever. Not in this day and age.'

'Ah, but they rarely take dragon form these days. Even the young are taught to fly in the early hours of dawn, when few humans are about.' He shrugged. 'The cliques have thousands of years of practice melding into civilization while remaining apart. They might capture the odd individual, but they will never find more than that.'

I wasn't so sure. Especially given the scientists now had dragons working for them.

'Your sister didn't leave a contact number or a message with any of her friends?'

'She did leave a message with a friend saying she had a tip about a story, and was going to investigate it. That was weeks ago.'

'Why can't *you* report her disappearance? I mean, you don't give a damn about clique politics, and you have no position within the clique to lose.'

'But again, my mom has, and if I did report it, she would be punished for it.' He shrugged, seemingly accepting of the situation despite the surge of anger I could feel in him. 'Besides, we don't know where she actually went. Hard to track someone – or prove they're missing – if they've already told you they'll be out of contact for a while.'

'So how does your dad know her whereabouts?'

'Apparently the Arizona clique sent word about her.'

'Meaning she's probably in Arizona. Have you searched the area?'

He glanced at me. 'Of course. But Arizona isn't exactly a small state.'

'And the Arizona clique won't help?'

He snorted. 'Help the unwanted bastard son of a California clique? Not likely.'

I raised an eyebrow. 'So despite the fact the cliques work together for self-protection from humans, they don't exactly get along?'

'You could say that.' Amusement ran through his voice, and a tremor that was all desire tripped across my skin.

'Meaning your father might not actually know anything. He could be lying in an effort to get the ring back.'

'He could, and I certainly don't trust him one iota, but I do believe he knows *something*.' His sudden smile was cold. Hard. 'His strength is waning rapidly and he's desperate for the ring. I think, in this case, he'll tell me what he knows.'

I studied him for a moment, then asked, 'So why did the conditioning break now? Why not before?'

He smiled and reached under the blanket to gently clasp my hand. His skin was slightly rough against mine, but so warm. I opened my hand, letting his fingers slide between mine, feeling an odd rightness in the gesture.

'Because the conditioning only works with strangers. You have become far more than that to me now.'

'And you to me.' It sounded so lame, and there was so much more I wished I could say, but suddenly my stupid tongue was all tied in knots and the words I really wanted to say got stuck in my throat.

But maybe that was for the best. With everything I still had to do, what was the point of pouring my heart out?

I watched the sea for a while, looking for any sign that the magic was returning, then said, 'What if she's met a nice man and is having the time of her life?'

His sudden grin had a wry twist to it. 'Are there any nice men still out here in the world?'

'I don't know. I haven't met any lately.'

He glanced at me, eyebrows raised and a devilish twinkle in his eyes. 'I could play nice, if you want.'

'I know the sort of nice you're talking about,' I replied dryly. 'But if you want that ring, we'd better behave. The sea doesn't like to be kept waiting.'

'Later, then.'

'Much later.' When this was all over, and everyone was safe.

Silence fell again, and day grew around us, bringing houses and the bay to life. I dragged my knees close to my chest, watching the water, watching the dance of sunlight across the waves. Feeling the growing sense of power rumbling underneath them.

Eventually I tossed off the blanket and walked back into the water. The sense of power grew stronger, swirling around my legs. Farther out in the bay, a long plume of water became visible, its silver droplets twinkling and gleaming like rainbows as something rushed toward me.

I held out my hand, palm up, as the plume of water drew ever closer. Then there was a flash of silver, the warm kiss of water across my palm, and the ring was returned.

'Thank you.'

The quick dance of sparkling droplets said the words had

been accepted and acknowledged by the deeper energy of the sea, then they, too, were gone.

I glanced at the ring sitting in the middle of my palm. The dragon's jeweled eyes still gleamed like blood dripping from a wound, and the ring itself remained heavy and cold against my skin. Reluctantly, I closed my fingers around it, then turned and headed back to the beach.

'Here,' I said, holding out my hand. 'I hope it helps you find your sister.'

He opened his palm and I dropped the thing into it. The red eyes seemed to gleam ominously before he closed his fingers around it and shoved it in his pocket. As if he, too, felt the coldness in the thing.

His gaze met mine, the rich depths gleaming brightly in the sunlight, as if lit from behind. 'Thanks.'

I shrugged, trying for casual, knowing there was no other choice. 'If you're no longer going to use the car, can I take it? I can't swim in the bay at this hour in either form – there are too many boats and people about.'

He took the keys from his other pocket and dropped them into my hand. 'It's the red Ford with the white top. You can't miss it.'

I clenched my fingers around the keys, pressing them into my palm, using the pain of it to help stop the tears that were threatening to spill.

'This is not the end for us, Destiny,' he said softly.

My gaze rose to his, and something in my soul sighed at the determination I saw in those bright depths. 'Good, because I don't *want* this to be an end for us. But I also don't want to be responsible for your death. Egan was enough. Go find your sister, do what you have to do, and maybe we can meet up at your big old house a month or so down the track.'

'Egan made his choices, Destiny. You're not responsible for what happened because of them.'

'Egan died because he chose to escape with me, and no amount of prettying it will change that fact.' I half turned away, then added, 'Good-bye, Trae. Good luck with your sister.'

'Damn it,' he said, then stepped forward, grabbing my arm and pulling me backward, into his arms. His mouth claimed mine, and it was all heat and intensity and raw emotion. It was a kiss that said everything that remained unsaid between us, a kiss that held so many promises that my heart ached and my stomach churned.

Because I couldn't afford to hang on to those promises, I really couldn't. There was just too much uncertainty in my present.

He broke the kiss as suddenly as he started it. He stared at me for several seconds, his breathing harsh and blue eyes stormy, then simply said, 'A month, then. Make sure you're there.'

'I will be.' I turned and walked away. But as I began to climb the steps to the parking lot, I looked back. I thought I saw a muscle tick along his jawline. Thought I saw his fingers twitch, and then clench. But he didn't say anything, didn't move, and I didn't stop.

When I finally reached the parking lot, I gave in to the urge to look around again.

Trae was gone.

Chapter Eleven

It was a lonely drive to my dad's. But as the miles slipped by and I got closer to home, tension began to crawl through my body. Tension that was an odd mix of excitement and anxiety. I hadn't seen my dad in nearly eleven years, and I had no idea how badly he'd been ravaged by the diabetes.

Part of me didn't actually *want* to see what the disease had done to him. I wanted to remember him as he was back then, not as he was now. Which was selfish of me, I guess.

I swung the car into our street and slowed as I neared the beautiful old maple tree that marked the road that led down to our house. But something caught my eye – the brief glint of sunlight off glass deep in the trees. It took me a moment to realize what it was.

The windshield of another car.

A chill ran down my spine. They were waiting for me. So much for them not knowing where my dad lived.

I pressed the accelerator and zoomed past. No car came out of the trees to follow.

God, all these years of thinking he was safe, of thinking that the scientists didn't know about him and couldn't bother him – and yet at any moment they could have so easily swept him into their vicious little net.

So why hadn't they?

Marsten wasn't one to hold back from acquiring more test subjects, so maybe they simply didn't realize Dad was dragon. Maybe they'd been watching him for a while, but had never seen him change, never seen him play with fire, and just presumed he was human.

But how would they have known where he lived in the first place? It wasn't something Mom could have told them, because she didn't know. They'd snatched her before we'd moved to America.

And all I'd taken over to Scotland with me was some cash and a couple of credit cards. I'd had no intentions of being there long, and had figured I'd have no reason not to be there illegally. God, I'd been so arrogantly confident – and a stupidly easy target.

Could I have told them?

As I'd told Trae, I'd been knocked out many a time over the years. Maybe they'd found some sort of truth drug that worked with our body chemistry. Maybe I'd babbled my heart out, and just hadn't known about it.

And if that were the case, it was just as well I didn't know all that much about my relatives. At least I wouldn't have been able to betray them as well.

So what did I do now?

With a short-range tracker embedded in one of my teeth, I couldn't go too near those men. It'd be my luck that they'd have a receiver.

But I still had to get to the house. Still had to see how my dad was. And that left me only the option of going through the trees and walking along the shore. That should put enough distance between the tracker in my tooth and any receiver the men might have.

I drove off the highway and followed what looked to be little more than a deer track deep into the trees, until there was nothing more to see than shadows and tree trunks. After switching off the engine, I opened the door and got out. The scent of balsam and rotting leaf matter filled the air, but I could feel the closeness of the bay. The energy of it seemed to caress my skin, making it tingle.

Home, I thought, and felt a smile touch my lips.

I shoved the car keys into my pocket and walked through the

tree trunks, following the faint whiff of water down to the bay's boulder-strewn shoreline.

I had no real memories of Loch Ness. I might have been born in its dark, murky waters, but Dad and I had moved here when I was barely six years old. This was the home of my heart. It was here I'd been raised, here I'd learned how to swim and dive, to hunt and fish, and to be all that a sea dragon could be. All under my dad's watchful gaze and tutelage.

The image of him sitting on a chair, casually drinking a beer as the moonlight played through his blond hair, had tears stinging my eyes. Damn it, I *missed* him. Missed him so much my heart seemed to ache under the weight of it.

And suddenly I was running up the beach. Waves lapped at my toes, tingling touches of power that seemed filled with welcoming. But I no time to stop and play, because time was running out for my dad.

Our old log home, with its sharply angled green-iron roof and vast array of windows, came into view. Despite the urgency hammering at my soul, I slowed. There was no sign of movement near the house, and no sound to be heard other than the whisper of water across stone and sand. There was no sign that anyone had been near the place for months, but that didn't mean there wasn't.

I jogged into the shadows offered by the pines, spruces, and cedars that formed a U-shaped windbreak around our house, and slowed as I neared one of the side windows. With every sense alert to catch any sound or movement, I crept forward and peered past the sill. The living room was filled with sunshine, and dust lay thick on the coffee table and along the top of the old leather sofas. Dad had never been the world's best housekeeper, but even he wouldn't let the dust get this thick.

Frowning, trying to ignore the fear beginning to clog my throat, I ducked past the window and moved to the back door. Again, no one appeared to be near. After another quick look around, I slipped my hand past the potted remains of a sorry-looking raspberry bush and lightly dug at the soil. My fingers touched metal and relief slithered through me. At least some things hadn't changed.

I pulled out the key, wiped off the dirt, then slipped along the porch to the door. The key slid in after a bit of jiggling, and the door opened.

The ticking of the grandfather clock sitting in the dining room filled the silence, and the air was thick with age and dust. I walked through the mudroom and laundry room into the kitchen. The dishes that lay in the sink were coated with sludge so thick it had to have been brewing for weeks, at least.

Dad wasn't here. And he hadn't been here for some time, if those dishes were anything to go by.

Again fear ran through me, thicker than before. I took several deep breaths to calm myself, and tried to remember who he might have turned to if things had taken a turn for the worse. Really, there would only be one person. Our family had never been big on making friends, and we'd pretty much kept to ourselves over our years here. I had friends at school, of course, but none of them ever knew what I was. Or what Dad was. *That* was a secret I had never been tempted to reveal – not after my mother's kidnapping and our subsequent flight.

I couldn't remember Dad with friends. It was always just him and me, and I think he preferred it that way. Which meant he could only have turned to old Doc Macy for help.

One of the boards on the back porch creaked. My heart just about jumped out of my chest and my mouth went dry. I flattened back against the refrigerator and reached for the cooking pot that was always sitting on the stove top. I wrapped my fingers around the wooden handle, my knuckles just about white as I listened to the whisper-soft footsteps moving toward the door.

'Destiny?' Trae said softly.

I blew out a breath, twin surges of relief and anger flying through me. Anger won. 'What the hell are you doing here? You promised to leave.'

He stepped into the room somewhat cautiously. He glanced at the pot still clenched in my hand, and amusement briefly touched his lips. 'I did leave.'

'But you weren't *supposed* to come back. You were supposed

to be returning the ring to your father so you could find your sister.' I slammed the pot back on the stove. 'You know, the one that's in trouble? Remember?'

Annoyance flared in his eyes. 'Of course I remember.'

'So why are you standing here instead?'

'Damn it, how can I leave when Egan is dead, and *you* came so close to death?' His voice rose slightly, anger, frustration, and worry all evident in the rich depths. 'Those bastards are still out there, and they still have a means of tracking you. I couldn't live with myself if something happened to you. I couldn't live without you.'

Warmth flared through my heart, through my soul, and my feet wanted to do a happy little dance, even though I knew that *this* was wrong, that he should be more worried about his sister than me. *She* was family. I wasn't. Not yet.

'But what if something happens to your sister when you're here helping me? Could you live with that?'

'No.' He thrust a hand through his hair, and blew out a breath. 'I rang my mother and asked her what she was feeling about Mercy. She still feels she's in trouble, but it's not life or death type trouble. I'm trusting her instinct. It's all I can do.'

'But—'

'No,' he said forcefully. 'This is my decision, my right, my choice. If something does happen, I'll deal with it. But I can't leave you to handle this situation alone. I won't.'

248

I studied him for a moment, then stepped forward and wrapped my arms around his neck, hugging him close. Listening to his breathing, feeling the rapid beating of his heart.

He sighed and wrapped his arms around my waist, pulling me closer still as his lips brushed the top of my head.

'If something happens to her, then I'm going to have to live with it, too,' I said softly, my words getting lost against the wool of his sweater.

'If something *does* happen, it will not be your fault, just as Egan's death was not your fault. You cannot take the blame for other people's decisions, Des. That's not fair to *them*.'

I didn't say anything. I didn't agree, and no amount of words would ever take away the guilt that lingered deep inside, but there was no point in going on about it. It was just something we were never going to agree on.

And I just hoped that his sister's trouble wasn't anything too big or life-threatening.

'Where's your dad?' he said, after a while.

I pulled away from the warmth of his arms. 'Not here. He hasn't been here for a few weeks, by the look of it.'

I walked past him into the dust-covered living room and then up the stairs that led to the bedrooms. Dad's was the closest to the landing, mine up at the far end. A bathroom and a study separated the two rooms, and a quick glance inside the study revealed the usual array of books and papers surrounding

Dad's computer. He might have lost one of his arms, but he'd never lost his love for reading and writing. As I looked at all the piles of paper scattered about, I wondered if he'd achieved his dream of being published in the eleven years I'd been gone. I hoped so. It just wouldn't be fair to have *all* his dreams amount to nothing.

Tears stung my eyes again, but I blinked them back. Find him first, I thought. Cry later. Trae briefly touched my shoulder, but it was a touch so light it would have been easy to believe I was imagining it. Except for the fact that warmth spread like wildfire through my body, filling me with strength and momentarily washing away the sadness.

'We'll find him,' he said softly.

'I know.' I pushed Dad's bedroom door open. The bed was unmade, the patchwork comforter I'd made for his eightieth birthday trailing on the floor. A dragon's life span was usually at least double that of a human, but we'd both known the diabetes would snatch him from this world well before he ever reached those sort of illustrious years. But I'd always expected him to at least hit a hundred and ten.

My eyes went to the bedside table. The phone was on the hook, but the address book was open. I walked across. Doc Macy's number stood out starkly on the page. I picked up the phone and dialed.

'Lubec Medical Center. How may I help you?'

My mouth suddenly felt dry again, and I had to swallow before I could speak. 'I'd like to speak to Doc Macy, please.'

'One moment, please.'

And then I was on hold, listening to what sounded like elevator music for a good five minutes. Trae moved up behind me, not actually touching, but close enough that the heat of him pressed into my spine. It felt safer – which I guess was odd considering the man himself was as far from safe as I could ever get.

'Doc Macy here,' a deep voice suddenly said into the receiver, making me jump a little. 'How can I help you?'

'Doc, it's Destiny here. Rian McCree's daughter.'

'Jesus, girl, where have you been for these last eleven years? Your dad worried himself sick.'

'It's a long story, Doc, and not one I can explain over the phone. Where's my dad?'

'He's in Lubec. We had to move him into a nursing home.'

I rubbed a hand across my eyes, fighting the sting. Fighting the fear. 'How bad is he?'

'Pretty bad. The disease has taken his feet, and most of his internals are on their last legs. I don't actually know how he's holding on.'

He's waiting for me, I thought. He knows I'm coming. 'Where is he?'

'Twin Pines Nursing Home. It's run by a friend of mine – one who understands your dad's needs.'

Understood what he was, in other words. At least we didn't have to worry about medical staff uncovering odd genetic differences and reporting them. 'Then you'll know he won't want to die in that place.'

'No.' Doc Macy paused. 'I'd advise heading straight there, Destiny. He hasn't got long.'

I closed my eyes, but really, he wasn't telling me anything I didn't already know. 'Can you arrange his release, then?'

'I'll call as soon as we finish up here.'

'Thanks for looking after him, Doc.'

'There's few enough of us left in this world, my girl. We have no choice but to look after each other.' He paused, and I heard papers shuffling. 'I'll get Mike to look after all the official stuff.'

'Thanks.'

I hung up the phone and turned around. Trae's arms went around me, and for a moment I allowed myself to melt into his embrace, to sink deep in the sense of strength and resolve that was so much a part of this man's makeup.

'He's in a nursing home in Lubec,' I said softly. My face was pressed against his chest, and the beat of his heart was a rhythm that seemed to flow from his skin to mine, making it seem in that brief moment we weren't two but one.

His lips brushed the top of my head, a feather-light kiss that sent heat shivering through every nerve ending, making me tingle.

'You want to leave right away?'

'I have to,' I said, and pulled away from his arms. The day felt suddenly colder. 'But there's a car in the trees at the driveway entrance, and I think they're Marsten's men. We need to deal with them on the off chance they pick up the tracker signal as we pass.'

'They're not a problem at the moment. I knocked them out and tied them up when I first got here. The car is pretty unnoticeable, so we should have some leeway before anyone realizes they're missing.'

'Good. We'll need it.'

He raised a hand and gently brushed the hair from my cheek. 'Why is time so important?'

'Because as I said, Dad is dying, and he wants to do it here, not in some nursing home.'

Understanding dawned in his eyes. 'A sunrise cremation?'

I nodded even as tears filled my eyes again. I ducked my gaze away from his, and reached down to grab the comforter. 'We'll need this to wrap him in. He'd like that.'

Trae raised an eyebrow but didn't question me. I dug the keys out of my pocket and handed them to him. 'You drive, I'll direct.'

We left the house and made our way back to the car. It didn't take us that long to drive to Lubec, but I had to stop and ask for directions to Twin Pines, because I had no idea where it was. The town had grown since I'd last seen it.

Two massive red pines marked the entrance to the nursing home. We drove in through the wrought-iron gates and followed the curved driveway through the mix of pines and elms until the main buildings came into view. They were an L-shaped and double-story brick affair, surround by lush gardens and yet more elms. Very pretty. Trae stopped the car in the parking area to the left of the building, and I climbed out.

My gaze went automatically to the windows, and I wondered which room was Dad's.

'Ready?' Trae said.

My gaze jumped to his. 'Part of me is afraid.'

'That's only natural.' He held out his hand. I grabbed the comforter from the car, then walked around and twined my fingers through his. 'Come on, let's go.'

He gave my fingers a slight squeeze, and suddenly I was glad that he was here with me. His presence gave me strength and helped bolster my courage to face what this disease had done to my dad.

We followed the concrete path up to the main reception area. Trae opened the door and ushered me through. A pretty blonde at the reception desk looked up and smiled as we entered.

'Welcome to Twin Pines,' she said cheerfully. 'How may we help you?'

'I'm here to see Rian McCree.' I stopped near the desk and

shoved my hands in my pockets so that nobody could see just how badly they were shaking.

'You'd be Destiny, then? Doctor Jones has been expecting you. He said to go straight up, and he'll join you as soon as he finishes his rounds.'

'Thanks. What room is Dad in?'

'He's in the left wing, subacute care. Just take the elevator to the next floor, then follow the left corridor along to room two twenty-five.'

'Thanks,' I repeated.

Trae cupped my elbow, gently guiding me across to the elevators. He pressed the up button, then reached down and twined his fingers back through mine. 'You okay?'

I nodded. I couldn't speak. My throat was too dry.

The elevator doors dinged open. I pressed the button for the next floor and the doors slid shut. The elevator rose smoothly. I guess it would have to in a nursing home.

We got out on the second floor and followed the long left corridor through a double set of swing doors and into an area that was obviously subacute care. The rooms were more sterile than homey, and the sharp smell of antiseptic stung the air.

My stomach was churning so hard as we neared the room I thought I was going to be physically sick. Trae squeezed my hand, and it was his presence more than my own courage that got me through the door.

The frail man on the hospital bed was not the man I remembered. His good arm, visible outside the sheet, was pale and emaciated, and the body under the sheet looked much the same. He had no feet, just heavily wrapped stumps that the sheet only half covered. And the smell ... Even under the harshness of the antiseptic, I could smell the rot. They hadn't stopped the gangrene, despite taking his feet.

I stopped, but he must have heard me, because he opened his eyes and looked at me. His face was pale, gaunt, filled with lines that started from his eyes and ran down his cheeks to his chin, until it seemed his skin was little more than a network of deeply drawn trenches. His once-golden hair was white and scraggly, curling around his ears and straggling across his bony forehead.

But his sudden smile was the smile I remembered, filled with warmth and caring and love, even if the body behind it was puckered and sunken.

'Desi,' he whispered, his blue eyes bright with relief and love. 'I knew you'd come.'

I bit back a sob and half ran across the room, taking his hand in mine and holding it up to my cheek. 'I'm sorry, Dad. Sorry that I ran off, sorry that I wasn't here when you needed—'

'Hush,' he interrupted. 'None of that's important now.'

But it *was* important. Important because while I didn't regret the reason I left him, the fact was I hadn't achieved most of the things that I'd set out to do and, as a result, wasn't here when he needed me.

I kissed his fingers, then said, 'I found her, Dad. She's alive, and she sends her love.'

He closed his eyes. 'I knew. I always knew.'

'I couldn't free her. But she wanted me to come here, wanted me to tell you—' I hesitated, took a deep, quivering breath. 'That she will meet you on the forever plains very, very soon.'

He smiled, and it was a good smile, a happy smile. A smile that said he could finally die a contented man. 'It'll be wonderful to see her, after all these years apart.'

'She'll be there, Dad. It won't be long now.' I hesitated, and looked around at Trae. 'Dad, I'd like you to meet a friend of mine. Trae Wilson. He and his brother helped me get here.'

'Then I owe you a debt, young man.'

'There's no need to feel indebted.' The graveness in Trae's voice was at odds with the sudden mischievousness in his blue eyes as he looked at me and added, 'It was my pleasure. Honestly.'

And mine, I thought with a wry smile. Even if he was sometimes one of the most infuriating men I'd ever met.

I squeezed my dad's hand, and looked around as a man walked into the room. He was tall, slender, and had a wildness about his eyes that wasn't quite human. 'Doctor Jones?'

He nodded and walked over to the bed, his white coat flapping back and almost looking like wings. He picked up the clipboard at the end of the bed, and scrawled something onto it.

'It's all been arranged,' he said. 'Your dad has been released into your care for the night. I'll come out after my shift is over and check on him. If death doesn't come tonight, we'll extend the home care until it does.'

My vision blurred with tears again. I blinked and looked back at my dad. He was still smiling.

'I've called some nurses in, and we'll get him into a wheel-chair for you.' The doctor glanced at Trae. 'If you'd like, you can bring the car around to the main doors.'

Trae nodded, touched my back lightly, then left.

'Will anyone question events?'

'There is a private cemetery and crematorium on the grounds, and it is not unusual for the families of residents to make use of the facilities, even if the death occurs during leave. We'll have a small memorial service. There will be no questions about his death, trust me.'

I did trust him. Like Doc Macy, this man exuded a confidence and a warmth that made it almost impossible to do otherwise.

The nurses came in, and Dad was bundled into a wheelchair. He made no sound, but the pain of his injuries filled the air nevertheless. I had to bite my lip against the urge to tell them to stop, that they were hurting him.

Because *everything* was hurting him. Even the mere act of breathing.

Once he was settled in the chair and all his tubes and bags were sorted, I stepped forward and wrapped the comforter around his legs. He touched it lightly and his face lit up. 'Ah, I remember when you made me this. Took you weeks.'

'Months,' I corrected. 'You thought I was doing homework, but I was stitching this.'

He chuckled. 'I remember being afraid to wash it.'

'My stitching isn't *that* bad.'

'It is, my girl, it is.'

I grinned and bent down, dropping a kiss on his cheek. 'I missed you.'

He touched my cheek lightly. 'And I you. We are not designed to be solitary creatures, unfortunately.'

'No,' I agreed, and wondered how he'd found the strength to cope all these years. At least I'd had company, and a reason to keep on fighting. My dad only ever had a stubborn belief that we *would* return.

One of the nurses stepped behind the wheelchair and began rolling my dad toward the door. I walked beside him, my fingers lightly twined in his. As we rolled into the elevator, the trembling in his fingers grew. I knew it was excitement. The knowledge that he would soon be home and free to die as he'd wished. In the open, under the stars, so that the power of dawn would caress his body and guide him on to the after-world.

And though the thought had tears flooding my eyes again, I could wish for nothing else. It was what he wanted, what he'd been holding on for. After all my years away from him, I could do nothing less than give him his last wishes in his final moments on this earth.

Doctor Jones held open the front door and the nurse wheeled him into the outside air. Dad raised his face to the sky then breathed deep. His pale skin seemed to flood with color and he sighed. It had to be hard for a man of sunshine and heat to be cooped up inside endlessly, unable to even raise a finger-tip to the caress of day. It might not be as deadly as being restrained from water and wave was for me, but it couldn't have been pleasant. And it was something he shouldn't have had to face.

I bit my lip, and wished I could bite down the guilt as easily.

Trae climbed out of the car and opened the rear door. The doctor and two nurses struggled to get Dad into the car and comfortable. He didn't complain. Just smiled his happy-to-be-free smile.

Once he was in and buckled up, Doc Jones came over and gave me his best 'doctor' smile. 'He should be comfortable for the next twelve hours.'

'We both know he won't last twelve hours.'

'I didn't think he'd last as long as he has. Your father is a man of amazing strength.'

'Yeah, he is.'

I shook the doctor's hand, then climbed into the backseat beside my dad. I took his hand in mine, not saying anything – not needing to say anything. Touch was enough for now.

Trae drove us back to our house, but again parked in the trees – though closer to the house than before.

'What's going on?' Dad said. 'This isn't our place.'

'One of the trees came down over the driveway,' I said. 'We have to walk a bit.'

'Then take me straight to the beach, not the house. I want to feel the sun for a while. Let it heat my bones.'

I nodded and scrambled out of the car before he could hear the sob that careened up my throat. Trae caught my hand before I could move around the back of the car, and pulled me toward him. 'You're amazing,' he said softly, and dropped a sweet kiss on my lips.

I resisted the desire to melt into his arms and allow the warmth of him to chase away the ache in my heart. Dad had waited long enough for this, and even the few minutes a brief hug would have taken from him just wasn't fair.

'I'll get him out and carry him,' Trae said. 'It'll be easier. Can you carry the chair?'

He reached back into the car and popped the trunk, then moved around to Dad. I dragged the wheelchair out, hooking the awkward thing with my arms and carrying it in front of me.

I led the way through the trees, holding back branches and crushing aside bushes that got in the way. The wind had picked up, sighing through the pines and rustling the dying leaves of the various aspen. The chill of night was already in the air, but it didn't seem to matter to Dad. His smile grew the nearer we got to the water and the sunshine. When we finally broke free of the trees, he laughed. It was such a carefree, joyous sound, it brought a smile to my lips.

We walked along the sand until we neared the house, then I set up the chair. Trae placed Dad in it carefully, then attached the bags to their spots on either side of the arms.

'I'll go check out that tree problem,' Trae said, as he stood. 'You want me to collect anything to eat on the way back?'

'I'm not sure what's in the house, but yeah, if you can find something.'

He kissed me again, soft and lingering, then left. I watched him walk up the beach and disappear into the trees, then returned my attention to my dad.

'You like that one, don't you?' he said.

I smiled. '*That* one is a whole lot of trouble.'

'The good ones always are.' He closed his eyes and leaned

his head back, once again allowing the sunlight to caress his skin. 'Tell me about your mom, Desi. Tell me what happened.'

So I did. Everything I could remember, as well as some stuff that was more guesswork than fact. Trae came back about halfway through, handing me a cup of coffee and several crackers.

As the day ran into night, conversation faded. We sat in companionable silence and watched the stars grow bright in the sky. When the moon began its track across the night, Trae rose and retrieved a couple of blankets, wrapping one around my shoulders and the other around Dad's. I flipped one end of the blanket open and he sat beside me, his presence keeping me warmer than any blanket ever could.

Doc Jones joined us sometime after midnight. He sat back in the trees, a witness to events but not a part of them.

Dad was still smiling when he passed away in the early hours of the morning. I continued to hold his hand, feeling the warmth of his skin gradually leaving his body. But the deeper burning – the fires of the dragon waiting for the dawn and the final journey – were still present.

The air began to hum with power long before the first vestiges of dawn began to crack the night. Energy flitted across my skin, little sparks of power that were very visible in the blackness that surrounded us. But the crazy tingling did little to ease the ache in my soul. I doubted anything could right now.

I studied the horizon, waiting, as the hum of power grew and intensified, and slivers of red and gold broke across the sky – bright flags of color that heralded the coming of day and the beginning of my dad's last journey.

Even as the warmth of the coming day flooded through my body, breaking the chill of night, it caressed my dad's body and stirred the waiting dragon to life. His skin grew warmer to the touch, beginning to glow with that inner heat. It forced me to release his hand, even though I didn't want to.

The day grew brighter, my dad's skin warmer, until it seemed the sun itself burned under his flesh. Finally, the fires of the dragon broke free – gloriously, finally free – and reached skyward with exuberant fingers.

'May the Gods of sun and sky and air guide you on your journey, Dad,' I whispered, my eyes on the flaming brightness and my throat so constricted with tears I could barely speak the ritual words. 'May you find the peace and happiness in the forever lands that you could not find in this.'

The streaming fingers of sunlight seemed to twirl and dance, as if in answer, and then they were gone, lost to the brightness of the coming day.

The radiance caressing my skin died, taking with it the underlying hum of energy. All that remained of my dad were a few ashes and the remaining scraps of a comforter that the wind snatched up and scattered.

He was gone. Forever.

I closed my eyes and let the grief flow free.

Chapter Twelve

I don't know how long I cried. I just couldn't seem to get my act together, and much of that was guilt. It was ridiculous to feel that way, I knew, because the past couldn't be changed no matter how much I might wish otherwise. I'd done what I'd done. I'd left knowing Dad was ill, that the diabetes was getting worse. But in the foolishness of youth, I hadn't figured it would be so hard to free my mom. Hadn't counted on getting caught myself. I'd been too confident in what I was and what I could do to worry about such things as capture by the very people who held my mother.

Through all the tears, Trae was there. Holding me when I needed to be held, making love to me when I needed the intimacy, leaving me alone when I wanted to be alone. He fed me and looked after me, and was patient with me when my grief ran into the need to rant and rage.

But I couldn't stay in that pit of despair and guilt forever, especially not when I still had promises that needed to be kept. Besides, the more I delayed, the longer Trae was away from his sister.

It was well after midnight several days after the memorial service at the hospital when I turned in the warm circle of Trae's arms and said, 'We should leave here tomorrow.'

He touched my cheek, running his finger down the length of it until he reached my lips, then lightly began to trace them with a fingertip. 'Are you sure you're up to it?'

I nodded and stretched out languorously, so that my body was pressed more fully against his. 'It's probably best to swim to Scotland. Or fly, in your case. I wouldn't put it past them to have someone watching the airports.' Or be paying one of the customs officers to keep an eye out for them.

'I *could* acquire you a new passport, if that's your worry.'

His touch moved down my neck and across my right shoulder. Desire trembled through me, but I held still. That feather-light caress felt too good to move on to more intimate pursuits just yet.

'In this day and age, with all the massive security checks they have at airports, faking it is not worth it.'

'Faking it never is in the long run.' Amusement played

around his lush mouth as his fingers drifted toward my breasts.

I arched my back a little and pressed into his hand. 'And do you often fake it?'

He cupped one breast and flicked his thumb over the erect nipple, sending little arrows of pleasure shooting across the rest of me. His blue eyes twinkled mischievously in the night. 'Never when it's important.'

'And this *is* important?' I said softly. Emphatically.

'The most important thing in my life,' he said. 'And not only for this moment.'

Then he kissed me.

It was a kiss that was deep and long, a kiss that explored and aroused. A kiss that spoke of emotions that had been hinted at, and talked around, but never actually said. They were there nevertheless, thick and real.

'The trouble with a moment,' I said when I could, my voice more than a little breathless, 'is that it *does* only last a moment.'

'I think I should be offended by that comment.' His voice was dry. 'I'll have you know, my stamina is legendary. I've been known to last for hours.'

'Then prove it.'

He chuckled softly. 'A challenge you may yet regret, my girl.'

'Not when you're still talking rather than doing.'

He grinned and sat up on the bed, shaking free of the sheets and blankets. Then he picked up my right foot and began massaging my toes with warm fingers.

Frustrated amusement rolled through me. 'This isn't exactly what I had in mind.'

'Hush, and let the master work.'

I snorted. 'You're not my master.'

'Ah, but that's where you're wrong. I'm the master of your seduction, and you will be putty in my hand by the time I'm finished. Now shut up and enjoy.'

I shut up as ordered and closed my eyes, enjoying the press of his fingers against my foot. Enjoying the warmth that flooded up my leg and across my torso. Enjoying the tingle of expectation as the minutes ticked by, and the desire – need – for him to move on grew.

Eventually, he did, paying similar attention to my calves, and then my thighs. I made a small sound of disappointment when he skipped the hot spot at the junction of my legs and moved up to my belly. He chuckled softly, but that disappointed sound moved into a sigh of contentment when he began to caress my breasts. But he moved on all too quickly, working his way up to my shoulders and down each arm, before finally – thankfully – he began his teasing, erotic journey back down my body to the one point he'd missed. Even before his fingers slid over my clit, I was shuddering with pleasure, but that softest of touches had me moaning. God, if he didn't get on with it soon, I'd surely burst.

He kept up that teasing caress until I was squirming and pressing myself harder against his hand, wanting – needing – the orgasm that loomed so close. When he finally slipped two fingers inside me, I gasped and came undone, shuddering and groaning and thrusting into his touch.

When the shudders began to ease, he started again, this time with his tongue, savoring every glorious inch of me, until sweat sheened my body and every fiber vibrated with the need for release.

When his tongue slipped over my clitoris, I made a sound that was little more than a gargled half scream, and thrust up against him, so that his face was buried in the warm heat of me. And he licked and sucked and delved his tongue deep inside of me, until my body was afire and I was begging him to take me fully.

He finally relented and slid up my body, capturing my lips as he slid slowly, deeply inside. As my flesh enveloped him, a low groan of pleasure vibrated against the back of my throat. God, was there a greater sensation on this earth than the completeness of this one moment?

I began to move against him, but he held me still and continued to kiss me. Not urgently, not desperately, but slowly, passionately, like he had all the time in the world. I answered in kind, even though my body was trembling with the need for completion. I slid my hands up his back and around his neck.

And I knew, in that moment, that we were one. Not just physically but spiritually, our souls entwined and eternally linked.

'Look at me,' he ordered softly.

I opened my eyes and gazed into his, and felt like I was falling into a bright ocean. Caught, once and for all – and forever.

He began to move then, slowly at first but gradually gaining in intensity, until he was thrusting deep and strong. And suddenly the control and the calm were gone, and our lovemaking became all passion and heat and intensity. All I could think about, all I *wanted* to think about, was this man and this moment. Pleasure spiraled so quickly my body was shaking with the force of it, and when my climax finally – gloriously – hit, the convulsions stole what little breath I had left and tore a strangled sound from my throat. He came a heartbeat later, his body slamming into mine, the force of it echoing through my being.

When I remembered how to breathe again, I took his face between my palms and kissed him long and slow. 'That was amazing.'

He rolled to one side and gathered me in his arms. 'I told you I was a master of the art.'

I snuggled closer to his warm, sweaty body and breathed a sigh of contentment. 'Would that be the art of bullshit you're talking about?'

He chuckled softly and gently tucked a sweaty strand of hair behind my ear. 'That would be my other specialty.'

'No doubt about that,' I murmured, and drifted off to sleep.

When I woke the following morning, I was alone in the bed, but the smell of cinnamon toast and coffee filled the air, making my stomach rumble.

I shoved the blankets aside and got out of bed. The day beyond the windows was bright, filled with blue sky and few clouds. But the way the spruces swayed suggested the wind was pretty fierce. And if it was coming straight off the sea, I had no doubt it would also be icy.

I grabbed my old terry bathrobe from a wardrobe still filled with all my clothes and pulled it on, doing up the sash as I clattered barefoot down the stairs.

'That smells good,' I said, as I entered the kitchen.

He looked over his shoulder and gave me a warm smile. 'I should hope so. I've been slaving away in the kitchen for hours.' I raised an eyebrow, and his smile became a grin. 'Well, a good ten minutes, at least.'

I stood on tiptoes and gave him a quick kiss. 'Mmmm, you taste better than the food smells.'

'As much as it pains me to admit it, you need food more than you need more of me at the moment. Here.'

I grabbed the plate and began to munch. It was as delicious as it smelled.

'I exchanged some cash after I rang my mom,' he said, dropping some dishes in the sink and washing them. A house-trained man who also could cook – you had to love that, I thought with an inner grin. 'So we'll have some usable money when we get over there.'

'Unfortunately, I lost my credit cards when the scientists snatched me in Scotland,' I said, around a mouthful of toast. 'But I found a new ATM card when I was going through some of the mail.'

Which the Doc had given me after the small memorial service, along with a small bag of Dad's possessions. Tears touched my eyes again, and I blinked them away. He was gone, but at least he'd gone the way he'd wanted to go. I'd given him that, if nothing else.

'I think we need to hit them fast,' Trae said, 'before they've got time to realize we're even there.'

'I agree, but we can't be too fast. That's what got me caught the last time.' I finished the last of the toast, then gulped down the hot coffee. 'I'll go upstairs and have a shower.'

He nodded. 'I checked the tides. We need to leave within the hour if you're going to make it under the Lubec bridge in time.'

'I'll be ready in ten minutes.'

'Does a woman ever really mean that when she says it?' he asked, voice dry but a twinkle in his eyes as his gaze met mine.

'Time me,' I said, and raced up the stairs.

273

After the quickest shower in recorded history – for me, at least – I dried myself, then padded naked into my bedroom to raid my wardrobe, picking out a pair of jeans, an old Nirvana T-shirt, and a woolen sweater that would keep me warm even when it was wet. I dug an old pair of Nikes from the thick dust under my bed, then grabbed the waterproof food carryall my dad had made when I was a teenager who constantly needed to be fed and yet who was prone to wandering unheeding of time under the sea, and filled it with extra clothes and a coat. At least I'd have something dry to change into once I was in Scotland.

That done, I picked it up and clattered back down the stairs.

He glanced at his watch. 'Ten minutes and forty-five seconds. You're late.'

'So I'll make it up to you later. There is, however, hot water left, so maybe you should be thanking me.'

'Maybe I should.' He put his coffee cup down on the bench, then walked across to give me a quick kiss. 'Hmmm. Nice.'

'Shower,' I said, smiling as I stepped away from him. 'Otherwise we're never going to get out of here.'

'A bossy woman,' he muttered, the twinkle in his eyes belying the edge in his voice. 'Just my luck.'

'Get,' I said, imperiously pointing toward the stairs.

He got. I poured myself a coffee, then turned off the machine and leaned back on the bench, sipping the hot, sweet liquid and listening to the shower, imagining all that water running over lean, hard, golden flesh.

He rattled down the stairs ten minutes later, as sexy as all get-out in jeans and one of my dad's old black sweaters. My body began to ache at the mere sight of him, but now was not the time. We had people to rescue, and they'd all spent too much time locked in hell already.

'Got everything you need?' he asked, switching the kitchen light off then grabbing the car keys from the counter.

I nodded and rinsed out the rest of the coffee under the tap, then followed him out the back door. The wind whipped around me as I stepped onto the porch, flinging my still-damp hair in every direction. I shivered and locked the door, then shoved the key in my pocket. No need to put it in the plant anymore. There was no one else left who needed it – not unless I rescued my mother.

'What happened to those men who were waiting for us?' I asked, a slight catch in my voice that could have been caused by either fear of what I still had to do or the cold itself. Maybe even a bit of both.

He strode ahead of me, already in the trees, and for a moment, I didn't think he'd heard me. Then he flung over his shoulder, 'I flew them off the property. Dumped them and a few supplies in some secluded forest in Canada and took their cell phones. It'll take them days to get anywhere without phones.'

And by the time they did get somewhere, we'd be long gone.

I followed Trae through the trees and down to the beach. The wind in the open was even colder, filled with the scent of the sea, a scent that called me on.

I gripped my bag tightly, and stopped beside Trae. 'Talk to you in Scotland,' he said, and dropped a kiss on my cheek.

'You'd better have a coffee ready,' I said, 'because I'm going to be fucking freezing by the time I get to those shores.'

He laughed, and flung an arm around my shoulders, hugging me briefly but fiercely. 'There's better ways than coffee to warm you up,' he said, giving me another swift kiss, then letting me go.

I walked down to the water. The sea greeted me with its usual enthusiasm, and a smile touched my lips. I dove into the water and kept under the waves, swimming far out. When I finally surfaced, Trae had already gone.

The journey to Scotland was a long and, in many ways, a lonely one. Trae occasionally swooped above me, his gold and silver form bright against the blue of the skies, but mostly I was alone, deep under the water, with only the occasional pod of dolphins to keep me company.

I didn't stop, though tiredness was a weight that made my body ache. Stopping gave me time to think about Mom and the kids and what they might have gone through while I was

276

away, and those were thoughts I just couldn't handle right now.

I made my way around the Hebrides and Orkney Islands and finally swam down through the North Sea to the Moray Firth near Inverness. Night had leeched the warmth from the sky by the time I got near the River Ness, and the lights of the city washed brightness across the river. I swam upstream for as long as I could, then, when the water would no longer cover or hide my dragon form, shifted shape and swam toward the shore.

To say I was dripping wet and freezing cold by the time I climbed up the grassy bank would have been the understatement of the year. I splashed out of the water and looked around, wondering where the hell Trae was. I hadn't seen him for at least six hours, and given how densely packed with humanity this area was, he wouldn't have been able to land anywhere near.

I just about had a heart attack when a voice behind me said, in a thick Scottish brogue, 'Jesus, girl, are you all right?'

Totally glad I'd decided to keep my clothes on rather than swim naked, I turned around and gave the stout, gray-haired man standing in front of me a wan smile. 'Yeah. I fell into the water while trying to retrieve my cell phone.'

'That's a dangerous thing to be doing at this hour of the evening.'

I crossed my arms and shivered. 'Stupid, more likely.'

'Aye. Are you staying nearby, lass? Can I drive you anywhere?'

'I'm not staying far away, and I'll be fine walking. But thanks for the offer.'

He nodded, then shoved his hands deep into the pockets of his big old coat and continued on his way. I thought about pulling out my own coat, but given my sodden state, that would be pointless. It'd be wet in no time and I'd end up just as cold. I resolutely turned and splashed my way up the pavement, following the river and that tiny spark inside that said the home of my ancestors was close. A spark that drew me on, even though exhaustion and cold were trembling through my limbs.

About five minutes later a car rolled to a stop beside me and the passenger window slid down. 'Need a lift, gorgeous?'

'Only if you have coffee.'

'I can do better than that,' he said, eyes gleaming with amusement. 'I can take you where it's warm and feed you.'

'I'm yours,' I said, and jumped into the back of the car.

Trae laughed. 'Too right, woman.'

I leaned over the seat and gave him a warm, lingering kiss that did a whole lot to chase the chill from my body.

'Nice to see you again,' I murmured, when I could.

'She says through chattering teeth. Even your damned lips are freezing cold. I think you'd better get changed. Blue doesn't suit your human form.'

I laughed and dropped back onto the seat. I undid the carryall and dragged out some dry clothes, then somewhat awkwardly stripped off the sodden stuff and wriggled into the dry stuff, all the while aware of Trae's heated gaze watching me, and feeling warmer because of it. I wrung out my hair as much as I could, finger-combed it into some semblance of order, then clambered into the front of the car.

'I believe you promised food.'

'I believe I did.' He started the car, turned the heater to full blast, then drove on.

It was late evening, so the streets weren't packed with people, but they were around. Their laughter and music rode the air. He eventually pulled into a parking space outside an old, weatherworn inn. Despite its rundown appearance, inside it looked warm and it was packed with people – more locals than tourists, if the thick brogue filling the air was anything to go by.

We got out and went inside, Trae guiding me with one hand at my back. We found a table near the huge old fireplace, and for several minutes I did nothing more than stand in front of it and melt the ice from my bones.

A few hours, a few ales, and a good meal later, I was feeling decidedly better and sat back with a sigh.

'Feel human again?' Trae asked, a smile teasing his lips.

'As human as I could ever feel.' I drained the last of the ale from my glass, then said, 'I guess we'd better move. We need to find somewhere to stay up near the loch, and it's getting rather late.'

'I've already booked us a cabin near Strone Point, which didn't look that far down from Drumnadrochit's main center. The owners advertised the cottage as overlooking Urquhart Bay and the loch, so I thought that would be handy.'

'It will be.' Because it would also overlook the sharp hills of my mom's lands, and the house the scientists were using as their base. I needed to watch that house for a while. Needed to get a feel for their rhythms and movements. I had no idea how we were going to get in, let alone rescue my mother and the kids, but one thing was certain. It could not be rushed.

Still, Mom would feel me near. Would know I'd come back to rescue her, as I'd promised.

'I told the proprietor we'd be arriving a little late.' He glanced at his watch. 'She's going to meet us there with the keys in about half an hour.'

'Should be plenty of time.' I somewhat reluctantly pushed to my feet. Trae held out his hand, and I wrapped my fingers through his, letting him lead me through the crowd.

Once back in the car, I stared out the side window, watching the bright lights of Inverness fade into hills and darkness. Trae turned on the radio, and the gentle melodies that filled the car were restful rather than intrusive. After days of swimming, it was tempting to let my eyes close and drift off to sleep, but that was pretty pointless given that Strone was only fifteen miles away.

Twenty minutes later, the headlights were sweeping across a little white cottage, highlighting the stonework and the pretty little window boxes. Its curtains were drawn and there were no lights on inside.

'She's obviously not here yet,' Trae said, stopping the car and turning off the lights.

'No,' I agreed, and climbed out of the car. The wind stirred around me, tugging at my hair and chilling my face. I breathed deep, letting its crispness fill my lungs.

This might not be the place of my heart, but it *was* the land of my ancestors. Standing here in the night and the cold, feeling the grass and the soil under the worn heels of my Nikes, hearing the lap of wind-stirred water against unseen shores, sent a huge wave of rightness and belonging through me.

I might not have been raised here, but sea dragons had used this area as a refuge long before humans had come to claim the lands for their own. We were a part of the very foundation of this place, and it a part of us. And no matter how much I loved my home in West Lubec, there was no escaping the power of this place.

No escaping the simple joy of merely standing here.

Lights swept across the night, twin points of brightness that pinned me where I stood. Trae climbed out of the car and walked around to stand beside me, wrapping one arm across my shoulders and pulling me close to him. The warmth of his body battered away the chill of the night.

I raised a hand to protect my eyes from the lights, and watched the car approach. It pulled to a halt a few yards from where I stood, and an older-looking lady climbed out.

'Oh dear, you'd be Trae and Des Jones, then?' she said, looking us up and down. 'I wasn't expecting a couple.'

Trae had obviously given her a false surname, meaning he was a whole lot smarter than I'd been when I'd first come here. 'Is that a problem, Mrs Molloy?'

'Oh, no. It's just that I've given you the bigger cottage, the one with several bedrooms. It's a bit more expensive, though.'

Trae gave her a smile that brought heat to her cheeks, and said, 'That'll actually work out well, because we've some friends who were thinking of coming over from England to join us.'

'Ah, good then. And it's nice and quiet out in these parts. Except when the trucks go past on the A82.' She fetched a silver key from her pocket and bustled toward the door. 'You two here for a bit of monster-spotting, then?'

'Not really,' Trae answered, his glance at me full of amusement. 'But we're told we can't tour Scotland without at least having a look at Nessie's loch.'

'Well, there haven't been many sightings of her since those

damn scientists moved in up there.' She waved a straightened finger toward the hills of my mother's lands.

I raised an eyebrow, feigning surprise. 'Scientists?'

'They've been here for years. Don't know why – they debunk the monster myth every chance they get.' She sniffed and pushed open the door. 'Hasn't harmed tourism, but I'll be glad when they leave, all the same.'

My heart just about stopped. 'They're leaving?'

'That's the talk. Certainly they've been a bit more frantic in their activity of late.'

'But why would they be leaving?'

'Maybe they're finally believing their own words.' She swept on the lights and shrugged. 'Most researchers give up after a while. The loch holds her secrets well, and even the most well-financed venture must run out of cash.'

I hesitated, then asked, 'So they've had no sight of the monster?'

She looked at me. 'Oh, that's one for conjecture.'

'So despite what they're saying, you think they have?'

'I think they've found something, lass. Whether it's the monster or not is anyone's guess.'

I smiled. 'You don't believe in her?'

'Oh, I do. But I believe she's far too clever to be caught by the likes of them. After all, she's lived in these parts for centuries. She'd have to be a canny one.'

Canny didn't take into account modern equipment or hunting methods. And it certainly didn't take into account being betrayed by some greedier members of the dragon community.

Even so, perhaps my mother, like the locals, *had* been too complacent, too confident the loch would hold her secrets against all comers.

But then, that affliction had also been my downfall. I'd been so damn confident in my skills that I'd waltzed straight into their trap. Well, not again. Not without some planning beforehand, anyway.

But the five-hundred-foot range of the tracker in my tooth would make planning my assault a whole lot tougher. The minute I entered that place, they could find me. If they suspected I was there, that was.

The question, of course, was whether they actually had the receivers here, or whether they were all in America with those who were still trying to capture me. I had to hope they were, but I couldn't actually bank on it. They knew I wanted my mother out of there, after all.

I ducked in front of Trae and stepped into the cottage. The front room was small, but homely, and filled with flowers whose sweet scent warmed the slightly stale air.

'Haven't had time to give it a good airing, but open a window or two, and it should be right.' She walked across the room. 'There's three bedrooms along the hall through here, the bathroom to my right, and there's a small kitchen diner to your left.'

'It's lovely,' I said.

She beamed. 'Will you be needing breakfast?'

I hesitated, and glanced at Trae. 'Would you prefer breakfast early or late?'

I put a slight emphasis on 'late,' and he raised his eyebrows, amusement bright in his eyes. 'Late would be better. I'd prefer to sleep in after the flight over we had.'

'Late, then. About ninish?'

She nodded, and Trae gave her the cash for the cottage. She bustled back out the door, a woman who was all energy and good cheer.

'Now what?' he said, once she'd left.

'Now I need to go talk to the loch.'

'Just let me bring in the bags.'

While he did so, I opened a few windows, allowing the cold night breeze to meander in and freshen up the place, and lit the fire with the kindling and logs provided. Then I kicked off my shoes, picked up the keys, and chucked them toward Trae as he came out of the bedroom.

'Barefoot?' he said, as he caught sight of my feet. 'I hope that's not a requirement around these parts, because I'm just not built for it.'

I grinned and tucked my arm under his. 'Don't worry, I'll keep you warm.'

He snorted softly. 'You can hardly keep yourself warm at night. I mean, look at your toes. They're blue.'

'But it's a very fetching shade of blue.'

He laughed and dropped a quick kiss on my lips. 'Come on, let's get down to the water so we can get back up here to the warmth.'

We headed out, picking our way across the grass and then highway, before walking down the slope to the dark shores of the loch. To our right, the stony remains of Urquhart Castle were silhouetted against the moon-washed water and the hills beyond, and only the occasional twinkle of a house light, or the bright beam of headlights sweeping past on the A82, shattered the illusion of being alone in the wilderness.

I stopped when the water began to lap at my toes and his boots, but the touch of it filled me with a delicious sense of power and welcome. It was almost as if the loch had long mourned the loss of her dragons. Part of me ached to dive in, to swim deep and enjoy the murky depths, surrounding myself in the sense of strength, power, and history that the loch represented to my family. But given that the scientists might have sensors located along the loch, if not in it, that just wasn't wise. I'd have to wait a while yet before I could enjoy such freedom.

'That's my mom's land over there,' I said, pointing left,

across the bay to the sharp, tree-covered hill that had been the ancestral lands of my family right down through the generations. Few lights shone through the thickness of the trees, certainly none coming from the old, stony building that was neither house nor castle, but somewhere in between. But even a heavily fortified building that had withstood time and weather hadn't been able to withstand the invasion by the scientists.

He frowned. 'There's not much evidence to be seen that there's a whole underground scientific study going on over there.'

'That's why he's been able to get away with it for so many years.'

He scanned the tree line for a moment, then said, 'So there really is another castle over there?'

'Well, it's not what you'd call a traditional castle – there's no massive towers and stuff.' Although it *did* have turrets. 'It's more like a great big fortified house. Dad used to draw me pictures of it.'

I couldn't actually remember a whole lot about the place. What I knew about the history behind it was thanks to the pictures and the stories he'd told me. He'd loved the old house, and had for years studied the ancient texts that were hopefully still locked securely within the secret vaults. He probably knew more about all the different generations of sea dragons who had lived and died within its walls than my mother did. Thanks to him, I knew my past, even if I had no real acquaintance with this land.

'Meaning it's a protected building?'

'Yeah.'

'Then the scientists shouldn't have been able to do much alteration without someone knowing about it.'

'I'm guessing they didn't bother to apply for permits.' There'd been basements there already, of course, but they'd added to them. Added the pools and the cells that had become our home within home for far too long.

My gaze ran across the hill again. 'It *is* odd that we can't see any lights. The last time I was here, the outside walls were lit all night.'

Hell, they turned off the lights in our cells for a bare six hours, and only then because they'd finally realized Egan wouldn't come near me unless it was dark.

'Does the no-lights factor mean they have already left?'

'God, I hope not.' But my heart began to race at the thought. It would have been ironic indeed to have come all this way for naught. Ironic, cruel, and yet somewhat fitting, given the way my life had been turning out of late.

I took a deep breath, trying to calm the sick fear that was churning my stomach and not entirely succeeding.

'I could do a flyover and check,' Trae suggested.

I was shaking my head before he'd finished. 'Too risky. Besides, there's a better way.'

I let go of his arm and stepped a little deeper into the water. The waves tugged against my legs, as if urging me to go deeper still. I smiled and squatted, slipping one hand into the water and caressing it with my fingers.

Ripples of power ran away from my touch, a steady vibration of energy only one other would notice or feel.

If she was close to a source of loch water, that was, and wasn't out of her mind with the drugs.

And she should be near water. The scientists had learned very early the importance of water to us sea dragons. While they'd originally used tap water in our ponds, they'd quickly discovered that if they wanted *happy* sea dragons, then they'd at least better use the loch water.

I continued caressing the water, and the power grew, until the night seemed filled with a sense of raw expectancy.

And then something stirred across the far side of the loch. An energy that was almost lethargic, and yet whose very presence made the dark water shiver in anticipation.

Mom, responding to my call.

What, she said, her mind speech slurred, but nevertheless strong and filled with so much anger, *the fuck are you doing here?*

Chapter Thirteen

I blinked. To say I was surprised by her response would be something of an understatement. I'd spent so many years trying to contact her and not being able to, that to do it so easily now was shocking. Almost as shocking as her words, in fact.

It could only mean that she was no longer being drugged. But why would they do that, when they knew how dangerous she could be?

And if she wasn't drugged, why had she not called the loch and escaped? Or did she, like me, fear that the little ones might not survive the experience?

I told you I'd come back.

And I told you to go to your father.

I did. He – I hesitated, gulping down pain. *He awaits you on the forever plains.*

She was silent for a long moment, then said, *So you reached him before he died?*

Yes.

Thank the Gods of sea and loch.

The relief, the loneliness, and the sheer and utter tiredness behind that statement had my eyes stinging. She'd been locked away from everything and everyone she'd loved for well over twenty years, and yet somehow, she'd clung to life. That must have taken more strength than I could ever imagine owning.

I'm here to get you and the kids out, Mom. Just like I promised.

Don't. You'll be caught again. She hesitated again, and the thick sense of energy that was her presence seemed to fade from the water. *It's too late for me anyway.*

The words were soft, filled with a weariness that spoke of an acceptance of fate. Fear rushed through me and, for a second, I couldn't even breathe. Because something was wrong. Something was *horribly* wrong.

Damn it, what had they done to her now?

I couldn't lose her now. I *wouldn't* lose her now. Not so soon after losing my dad.

You may not care about living or dying in that place, but the kids don't deserve it. There was more anger in my voice than I realized, and I could feel her shock ripple down the psychic lines.

No, you're right. They need to get out, before it's too late for them, too.

Fear slivered through me. *What do you mean?*

She didn't answer, and the power of her presence faded. I hit the water with my free hand in frustration, sending up a huge splash. Damn it, what the hell was going on over there? I continued to caress the water as my gaze ran across the dark hills, but there was absolutely nothing to see and no further response from my mother.

'No luck?' Trae said softly.

'Yes and no.' I rose and stepped out of the water, much to the disappointment of the waves. 'I managed to contact her, but she keeps saying I can't help her.'

He wrapped his arms around me and held me close. The beat of his heart was strong and sure against my chest, his arms filled with a strength I knew I could depend on no matter what.

'What now?' he murmured, his breath gently stirring the hairs on the top of my head.

'Now, we go to bed. I'll summon the dawn magic to do a more thorough investigation, and we can decide how to proceed from there.'

'That,' he said with a smile in his voice, 'is the best suggestion I've heard yet.'

We made our way back to the cottage and then to bed, but sleep didn't figure a whole lot into the equation. The night was a long one, filled with passion and tenderness, richened by the emotion that lay in every caress, every kiss, every sigh. We never said the words, but we didn't need to. Not yet.

We finally fell asleep entwined in each other's arms, sated and exhausted. If I dreamed, I didn't remember it.

It was still dark when we woke the following morning. After showering and getting dressed, we headed out into the predawn darkness. Slithers of pink had barely begun to caress the sky with their warmth, and the air tingled with the power yet to come. It played across my skin, an energy that seemed more dangerous, and a lot wilder, than the energy that came from most lakes.

We crossed the A82 and walked down to the rocky shoreline, following it around the bay. As the streaks of pink intensified and changed, becoming bands of red and yellow that tainted the dark skies, the morning mist folded down across the hills, hanging so low it danced in wispy streams across the water, making loch and the surrounding land look somewhat dark and mysterious.

Once again, part of me longed to dive into those waters, to cavort and play and simply enjoy, as my ancestors had done for centuries. But I couldn't – not until the scientists were gone and it was once again safe for my kind.

But there were things I *could* do – powers I could still call on – that might help my quest to free my mother. And the scientists, for all their equipment and sensors, wouldn't have a clue as to what I was doing.

'Is it true they have a fiberglass statue of the monster over there?' Trae asked, his soft tones riding the stillness without jarring against it. 'One that the kids climb all over?'

I pulled my gaze away from the loch and looked toward Drumnadrochit, a smile touching my lips. 'I think so. Dad used to tell me stories about it when I was a kid, and about how he and Mom used to go get photographed beside it on special occasions, just for the fun of it.'

'How right did they get the shape?'

I smiled. 'From what Dad said, she looks more like a castoff from the dinosaur period. Even pregnant sea dragons don't look *that* bad.'

He grinned. 'So I gather the color is wrong, too?'

'Yeah. They seem to think gray is a good color for sea dragons, but I think that's the only color we *don't* have.'

'Maybe they're just too used to dolphins and whales, and think loch monsters would fancy the same shades.'

'Or it's just a lack of imagination on the artists' part. I mean, all they have to do is look at the other sea life. It's not all gray. Far from it.'

Dawn's energy began to beat through the air, flaying my skin with its raw power. I breathed it deep, feeling it fill me, warm me. Welcome me.

'It's time,' I said softly to Trae, and untwined my fingers from his. 'Wait here.'

I stepped into the water, letting the dark energy of the loch lap around my ankles and mingle with the force of the rising day.

On the horizon, the slivers of red and gold became a flood, streaking across the sky and obliterating the night. The energy in the air grew frantic, crawling across my skin like fireflies and making my hair stand on end.

There was *so* much raw, untamed power in this place. It filled me, enriched me, made me believe I could do almost anything.

But that had been my downfall last time, and I would not make that mistake again. This time, we'd *take* time. And I would ask for the help of the power that beat all around me.

As the throb of energy reached a peak, and the air came alive with the hum and power of a new day, I raised my arms, holding my palms skyward, letting the raw energy and the trailing mist caress my fingers.

'My brothers of the deep, dark water, and sisters of mist and sky, I beseech thy help.'

In the distance thunder rumbled, a deep earthy sound that made the dark waters tremble. Waves splashed up my legs, soaking past my thighs. The energy in the air seemed to concentrate on my hands, until they glowed with the same red and gold that brightened the skies.

'Show me what happens on our ancient lands,' I continued, my voice soft and yet somehow vibrating across the silence. 'Show me the secret ways so that I may stop those who have invaded the serenity of this place and chased away the dragons.'

Again the thunder rumbled, stronger, deeper than before, and for a moment it seemed that the very land under my feet trembled. The mist stirred, and so did the loch, her waters shifting, moving, as if several fingers of current had suddenly formed. The energy encasing my hands leapt away with them, one following the lead of the water, the other following the streams of mist.

I closed my eyes and waited. Even through my closed lids, I could feel the day brightening. Her fingers of light were spreading ever farther, sucking away at the energy of the dawn.

Then the sky rumbled, long and slow, and again the loch stirred. Water hit my legs, swirling upward, soaking my thighs and my stomach, even as it whispered of old ways and secret passages. Then the mist returned, and with it the bright remainders of dawn's power, regaining its perch on my hands before crawling up my arms and spinning around my hair. Images filled me. Buildings, stairs, and secret ways, along with people, trucks, and boxes.

The scientists were indeed getting ready to move.

'Thank you, brothers of the darkness, and sisters of mist and skies.'

Water slapped at my legs, then leapt away. The energy in the air went with it, leaving me feeling suddenly cold, and more weary than I'd thought possible.

I turned around and walked back into Trae's arms. 'How did it go?' he asked softly.

'I found a way in.' But it wasn't one he could use, and he wasn't going to be happy about it. I hesitated, then added, 'There's an ancient passage that runs from the bottom of the loch up to the original basements of our house. The passages that run beyond it lead to the cells where the kids and my mom are being held.'

He released me and stepped back a little. Gold glinted in his still damp hair, warmed by the growing light of day. 'If that's the case, the scientists would be aware of it. It'll be alarmed.'

'The passage is disguised as a well and is covered for safety. It appears locked from above, but can easily be opened from the inside. It was apparently designed that way.'

Of course, it *was* highly possible that the passages outside the well room were monitored – in which case, how far I got would depend greatly on how close the scientists were to leaving, and how closely they were watching the security monitors.

He raised an eyebrow. 'So it was an escape route for your ancestors?'

I shrugged. 'More a refuge from those who would hunt the so-called Loch Ness Monster.'

'I thought it was scientifically impossible for caves and tunnels to form in the rock around the loch. Isn't it the wrong sort of stone or something?'

'That I can't say, not being up on all the geology of the area, but this passage wasn't made by nature. It was made by my ancestors.'

'Ah.' He studied me for a moment, then asked, 'How far down is this passage? And how long is the tunnel?'

'There's no way you can use the tunnel, Trae. You can't hold your breath long enough to get anywhere near the passage, let alone through it.'

He looked at me, then, and the bright blue of his eyes had given way to the steel of determination. 'You are not going in there alone.'

'We have no choice in this. The passage was designed for sea dragons in *human* form.'

'Destiny—'

'No,' I said, so forcefully he raised his eyebrows. 'I won't let you risk it, Trae. It's not worth your life.'

He didn't say anything for a moment, just bent to pick up a stone and throw it in the loch. It landed in the water hard, throwing up a huge splash. The droplets seemed to hang in the air for a moment, glittering and sparkling in the growing brightness of the day.

'I cannot simply sit here and let you walk into a dangerous situation,' he said, his voice edged with an anger I could feel as much as I could see. 'I promised to protect and help you, and I fully intend to keep that promise.'

'But not at the cost of your own life.'

'Nor yours.' He glared at me, determination fierce in his eyes. 'There's no way that, with all the security that's going to be in and around that place, you're going to get in and out unseen. No way.'

'If I *can* get in unseen, then I can get out the same way. We have no other choice.'

'There's always more than one choice. Besides, I'm a very good thief, and I know more than a little about getting through high security.'

I hugged my arms around my chest. 'Trae—'

'No. Either I help you, or I'll stop you.' There was a finality in his voice that brooked no argument. 'Besides, there's one thing you seem to have forgotten.'

I frowned. 'What?'

'The kids. If I can't swim in or out that tunnel, then they're sure as hell not going to be able to.'

God, he was right. I was an idiot. I sat down on a nearby

rock and rested my head in my hands. 'Then how are we going to get them out?'

'Easy. I create a diversion while you go in and free the kids and your mom.'

'That still leaves the problem of getting them out of the compound.'

His gaze ran across the water and studied the trees on the opposite shore. 'How old are the kids again?'

'The oldest is fifteen, the youngest is seven.'

'So most of them should be able to shift shape and fly?'

I nodded. 'All the boys can. Carli can shift, but she can't hold shape very long. They took her too young and she just hasn't had the practice.'

'But the others should at least be able to fly across the lake?'

I nodded, and studied him for a moment, watching the glint of sunshine run through the stubble lining his cheeks. Watching his blue eyes glitter and burn. 'You have an idea?'

He nodded. 'The best way to ensure they don't notice you sneaking in is to give them something else to worry about.'

'But that could be dangerous. They know how to capture dragons, remember.'

'Not this dragon. Besides, I thrive on danger.' His words were gently mocking, but there was nothing mocking about the caring or determination in his eyes.

'But your skills are sunshine-linked. Our best chance of getting the kids and Mom out unseen is at night.'

'I agree, and yes, my flames *are* sunshine-linked. But there are other ways to light fires. Hell, matches have been around for ages.'

Matches meant getting a whole lot closer, though, and that was dangerous. But the resolve so evident in his eyes said there was no swaying him. 'What about the kids, then?'

'Is there a way up onto the roof?'

I nodded. 'There's an old set of stairs near the cells, actually. I think the scientists have them locked off, but we could break the locks easily enough.'

'Good. Get the kids out first, and send them up the stairs. Twenty minutes after I start the diversion, I'll make my way up there. I can carry little Carli, and the boys can fly after me.'

'Where to, though? It won't be safe to bring them back here – they know the little ones can't fly far, and will search through the closer villages.'

'The scientists are going to be too busy saving their asses and their work to immediately worry about finding the kids *or* you.'

I gave him a twisted smile. 'The scientists never do what you expect them to – and they have a habit of anticipating my moves.'

'Then we book a cottage across the other side of the loch,

somewhere that won't strain the capabilities of young dragons who haven't flown much.'

'That'll work.' I studied him for a moment, then added, 'Once the kids are safe, I can get Mom out through the well.'

He nodded. 'It's a good plan. Trust me.'

'I *do* trust you. I just don't trust the scientists.'

He squatted down beside me, and touched a hand to my cheek. His soft caress sent a shiver of delight through every part of me. 'Don't forget that, no matter what, you can protect yourself. The loch is nearby – use the power of it if you need to.'

'I will.' But if one of the scientists had a gun, then the loch wouldn't be of much use. I sighed and pushed the thought away. What was the point of dwelling on such things? There was enough fear churning my stomach already. 'We should go back and eat breakfast.'

'The second best suggestion I've heard for while,' he said with a smile. He rose to his feet and offered me a hand up.

I let him tug me to my feet, then, hand in hand, we left the shoreline and walked up the hill, waiting until several trucks rolled past before crossing the road and making our way back to the pretty little cottage.

Breakfast was waiting in a hamper near the door. Trae scooped it up, then lifted the tea towel covering the top and sniffed deep. 'Ah, lovely.' He tugged the towel completely off.

302

'There's fresh breads, homemade jams, and something that looks suspiciously like lumpy paste, but it's hot.'

I laughed as I opened the door. 'That's probably going to be porridge. A favorite around these parts, according to my dad, who hated the stuff.'

'It's not something my clique ever thought about eating, I can tell you.'

'It's apparently good for keeping the belly warm.' I opened the door and ushered him inside. 'You want a coffee?'

'Yep. It may be the only thing that washes down the paste.'

'You eat it with milk and sugar, dope.'

I made the coffee, then brought the two mugs over to the small table. We ate breakfast in comfortable silence, the scent of the breads and jams mingling with the warm spiciness of man, filling my lungs and stirring hunger – for the food, and for him.

But as much as I wanted to give in to the need to caress him, to let my fingers reacquaint themselves with all that tanned muscle, now was not the time.

We couldn't afford to relax now, no matter how good or how pleasurable it would be. The men he'd flown off to the wilds of Canada might very well have gotten to a phone by now, in which case Marsten and his men would know I'd either be here or be on my way here. Maybe that was even why they were packing up. Either way, we had to keep alert. Last night had been a gift – but we dare not steal time like that again.

I sighed softly then rose to grab another cup of coffee. 'So what do we do to fill in the day?' I said, walking across to the nearest window and looking out. A green car was slowly making its way toward our cabin. I wondered if it was Mrs Molloy, back to collect her basket. 'And don't suggest a horizontal tango. We haven't the time.'

'We have all day,' he said dryly.

I gave him a grin. 'Yeah, but there's only one head alert when we're in bed, and it isn't the one with the brain aboard.'

He laughed, a warm rich sound that had my toes curling. 'You could be right there.'

Outside, the green car had slowed even further, allowing me time to study the driver. It was a male, not a female – not Mrs Molloy, as I'd originally thought. He was big, his shadowy features rough-looking.

The sight of him had trepidation racing across my skin. I might not have seen this particular man before, but I knew what he was all the same. *A scientist.*

I stepped to one side of the window, hiding behind the blue and white checked curtains.

'What's wrong?' Trae said quickly.

I held up a hand to silence him, and listened to the sound of the approaching car. It cruised past slowly, not stopping, but remaining at a speed that allowed the driver time to look and study.

They suspected.

But how? Why? I wasn't within tracking distance, and I hadn't done anything to attract attention, hadn't gone anywhere to be noticed. And yet that man was looking at this cottage, not at any of the other houses or cottages nearby. Just this one, and this one alone.

Could Mrs Molloy have told them that two Americans were staying here? She might claim to hate the scientists, but the almighty dollar was a great incentive to overlooking such feelings. I wouldn't put it past the scientists to be paying the nosier folks in the village to keep an eye out for strangers with an American accent. Which I wouldn't have thought would be exactly scarce in a town that thrived on tourism.

The car finally moved on. I peeked out the window, watching until it had disappeared over the hill, then spun around.

'We need to get out of here.' My gaze met the blue of his. 'That was a scientist cruising past.'

'Damn.' He gulped down the rest of his coffee, then rose. 'Was he pointing anything our way?'

'No.' Which didn't mean the receiver couldn't be on the seat next to him. 'But why would they even suspect I'm here? The tracker only has a range of five hundred feet, so they can't have caught the signal from the research center. Besides, if they *had*, why would they merely be doing a drive-by?'

'Maybe the signal was weak or intermittent. Maybe they

want to be sure before they cause a fuss.' He shrugged. 'Either way, it looks like we'll need to go do a bit of sightseeing.'

I blinked. Why did this man always do that to me? 'What?'

'Hiding in the open is always a good policy. People just don't expect it. So, we'll wander up to Urquhart Castle and spend the day there mingling with the tourists and remaining well out of any tracker range.'

'Then let's get out of here.'

I walked into the bedroom and grabbed our bags. Mine mightn't hold much more than clothes, but I wasn't about to leave anything behind that they could examine. It might only confirm any suspicions they had that I *was* here.

Because if they *were* anything more than just suspicious, they'd surely be doing a whole lot more than cruising past.

He took the bags from me and slung them over his own shoulder.

'The cottage hasn't got a back door,' I said, 'so we'll have to use one of the rear windows.'

Amusement played around his mouth. 'Considering the size of my ... ego, do you think I'll get through them easily enough?'

'Just,' I said dryly. I walked back into the kitchen and pushed up the window. 'How about this time you go first?'

'You just want equal ass-viewing time.'

'And is there anything wrong with that?'

'Hell, no.' His words were solemn, but the twinkle in his eyes was very evident. 'I am a very sexy guy with a very sexy ass, after all.'

'And I think Carly Simon sang a song about a man just like you.'

He grinned. 'Impossible. I am unique.'

I was tempted to say 'Thank god,' but given his mood, he'd probably take it as a compliment.

He tossed the bags through the window, then climbed out. After a quick look around, he turned and offered me his hand. I hesitated, then placed my fingers in his. The warmth of his flesh encased mine and sent a crazy tingle rushing across my skin.

My feet had barely hit the ground before he was drawing me toward him for a quick, tantalizing kiss.

'You keep doing that and we're going to get ourselves into trouble,' I muttered, trying to ignore the excited pounding of my pulse and the aching need to melt back into his arms and just keep on kissing him.

'But it's a good kind of trouble,' he said with a grin.

I whacked him lightly. 'Behave. This is serious business.'

'So is the two of us.' His grin faded a little as he picked up the bags and slung them over his shoulder. 'You ready?'

I nodded. 'Are you sure this is going to be safe?'

'I doubt they'll expect us to be playing tourist up at the ruins, and if even the tracker has a range double what you were told, we should be well enough away from them.'

'I hope you're right.'

Because a crowded tourist spot didn't exactly provide a whole lot of places where we could run and hide.

As it turned out, I was worrying over nothing. The sun tracked its way across the sky and we made like regular tourists, examining the ruins and having lunch and afternoon tea in the new visitors' center.

It turned out to be a good day – a slice of everyday normality in a life that had been far from normal. At least for the last eleven years. Egan and I had been lovers, but it had been out of necessity and the need for companionship more than anything else. We'd never had the chance to do any of those things lovers normally do. Not even share after-sex small talk, because Egan had always been too aware of the scientists and their insidious monitors.

But today, with Trae, I got a taste of that – a taste of what it would be like to be his lover, his friend, the person he cared most about – and I had to say, it was nice. More than nice, really, because it was a glimpse of the future that might be mine if I survived the present.

The castle closed at five. We trailed out with everyone else, then made our way down to the shore of the loch, keeping in the shadows of the hill and the castle so that we were less likely to be noticed.

As we neared the shore, I picked up a pebble and tossed it high. It hit the water with a splash, sending glittering droplets spraying into the darkening skies. Ripples ran away from the spot where the stone sank, the circles growing ever stronger rather than weaker.

The loch knew I was near. She was waiting for me.

An odd tremor of excitement ran through me. I needed to get in there. Needed to reclaim that part of my heritage so long denied.

'It's time to go.'

I placed my fingers in his, felt the quiver start deep inside. A quiver that was all desire, all want, all need.

He pulled me close, his body pressed so hard against my own that I could feel the beat of his heart. It was as rapid as mine.

'Promise me one thing,' he said, his words so close they whispered heat across my lips.

'What?' It was softly said, more a sigh than any definite word, but he seemed to understand all the same.

'You'll call if you get into trouble. Scream, rant, rave, do whatever it takes. I'll hear you, and I'll come running.'

'If you promise to be careful. To not get caught.'

'I won't get caught,' he said. 'I'll give you twenty minutes to get into the place, then I'll start the diversion.'

I nodded. There was little else I could do. He smiled, and touched my chin lightly. 'Don't look so fiercely concerned. Trust me, I know what I'm doing. It's why Egan asked me to join you, remember?'

'No, I don't, because I couldn't hear your conversation. And you don't know what they are capable of.'

'It can't be anything worse than what my father is capable of,' he said softly, then kissed me.

It was a good kiss, a kiss that was all heat and desire. A kiss that made promises I knew would never be fulfilled unless we survived the next few hours.

But we *had* to survive, because so many lives – young and old – depended on it.

When the kiss finally ended, I was breathless, aching, and wanting him more than I'd ever wanted anyone in my life. And I knew it was a want I just couldn't act on.

'I have to go,' I said, and pulled away.

'Just promise me you'll be careful.'

'I promise.'

Without looking at him any further, I stripped off my clothes. Once naked, I walked toward the icy waters. He didn't say anything and neither did I.

It was only when the dark, murky waters closed over my head, and that strange sensation ran across my eyes, that I looked back at him. Even through the muck and the peat particles that ran through the water, I could see him quite clearly. The pile of my clothes was pooled around his feet and my bag was still clenched in his right hand.

He looked worried.

Really worried.

I turned around and dove deeper. The passage that had been carved through the rock so long ago lay at the very bottom of the loch, close to where the steep sides joined the flatter bottom. Despite the advances in technology, science had not yet found a way for sonar to cover the whole loch, and few bothered even trying to map the sides. Though given the rumors of tunnels and caves within the loch – rumors that had become almost as legendary as the monsters themselves – many had certainly tried. And with varying degrees of success, from what I'd been able to learn through my research as a teenager.

The passage became visible, even though it was little more than a deeper patch of blackness in the thick darkness that was the water. I slowed, edging into the rough-hewn mouth of the tunnel and wondering how long it had actually taken my ancestors to carve out. Wondering if they'd had help and how they'd protected those helpers once they'd finally broken through the last of the rock and the black water had rushed in.

Though I guess one way to protect a secret is to let none survive who know it – a motto I would yet have to consider if my mother and I were to have any hope of being left alone.

I shivered. I'd killed in the past to protect myself and those I cared about, and I'd undoubtedly kill again if it meant protecting my mother and the kids. But could I kill in cold blood? Was I physically capable of hunting down and killing all those who now knew of our existence?

I really wasn't sure. And that was scary.

I swam on. The passage wasn't arrow straight, as I presumed, but full of twists and turns, snaking through the hard rock. In several places there were rock falls – no doubt caused by some sort of seismic activity, because the rock just looked too heavy and solid for it to be any sort of wear – and the sharp edges scratched my belly as I squeezed past. Trae would have struggled, even if he had been able to hold his breath long enough.

Finally, the water pressure began to ease. Though the water felt no warmer and the visibility was no clearer, I knew I was nearing the top.

My head broke through the water, and I blinked. Once the protective film retreated across my eyes, I looked around.

Though it was pitch black, I could see well enough. I guess that was one of the benefits of being a sea dragon. We had to see in the darkest of waters, as well as through the murk of the loch's deep waters. This well held little in the way of problems.

The walls here were as rough-hewn as the walls of the tunnel, the marks of the picks that had hacked through the rock still very evident even after all this time. Sludge and God knows what else slicked the walls, some of it hanging in thick green tendrils. No light twinkled from high above. Indeed, there was nothing to indicate this well had an exit point at all. The only indication I had that there *was* an escape was the faint stir of fresher air through the dank atmosphere of the well.

I reached for the handholds carved deep into the rock and began to climb.

Chapter Fourteen

The air was cold against my skin, seemingly colder perhaps than the water. It crept across my body, stealing the warmth from my skin, settling into my bones.

I reached the top of the well and pressed a hand against the thick metal cover. It was heavy, thick with rust that flaked away as my fingertips pressed against it, but nevertheless it was basically solid to the touch. I took a deep breath, then pushed with all my might.

The cover slid up and back, and clanged to the ground with an almost bell-like sound. It seemed to reverberate across the silence, a sharp call to arms to anyone who was listening.

I scrambled over the lip of the well and dropped to the cold stone of the ground as the last of the bell-like reverberations faded away and silence returned. I remained there, my muscles taut and limbs trembling – whether with fear or the readiness to run, I couldn't honestly say – listening for anything that might indicate someone had heard the crash of the cover and was coming to investigate.

Nothing. No footsteps, no alarm.

I rose and squeezed my hair to help dry it, then found the stairs and padded upward. My feet slapped lightly against the stones, making little noise.

The door at the top of the stairs was heavy, made of metal like the well cover but nowhere near as rusted. I gripped the knob and turned it carefully. The door creaked open, revealing a long corridor lit by a solitary bulb about halfway down.

These were the corridors I'd briefly glimpsed in the mist this morning, and they were a part of the old sections of the house. The newer additions to the basement – the cells – were ahead and to the left. If I went right, I'd reach the old stone staircase that wound up through the largest of the turrets to the roof. If the morning mist was right, the exits on the other floors were still well hidden. If I could get the kids to the stairs, they'd have a clear run to freedom.

But that was a whole lot of ifs.

I slipped through the doorway and headed down the corridor, keeping to the shadows and hoping they hadn't installed motion detectors in the time I'd been away. I ran through the patch of yellowed brightness, then walked on, passing several semi-open doors. The rooms beyond were silent and dark, and I felt no immediate inclination to investigate. Not until I knew what lay ahead, anyway.

I padded on, my bare feet making little noise on the stone. Each breath sent little puffs of white drifting into the darkness, but I couldn't actually feel the cold. The night and my own nature had seen to that.

I reached the tunnel junction and stopped. In the distance to the left there were voices and music, and it took me a couple of seconds to realize it was a TV, not the guards, I was hearing.

I risked a quick peek around. The guard station had been installed at the junction between these old corridors and the newer ones that led down to the cells. The guard sat in the middle of the room, his feet propped up on the desk and munching on a sandwich as he watched the TV.

To get to my mother and the kids, I'd need to get past that man.

How long had it been since I'd left Trae standing by the loch's edge? Surely it had taken me at least twenty minutes to traverse the twists and turns of the passage? And yet there was no sound, no alarm. Nothing to indicate he'd begun his diversion.

But even if there were only a few minutes left of his twenty-minute limit, I couldn't risk waiting. The longer I stood here, doing nothing, the more chance there was of getting caught. The guards didn't just sit in the box watching TV; they patrolled regularly.

I worried at my lip for several seconds, trying to think of the best way to distract that guard without getting myself caught, then turned around and walked back to the first of the storerooms. Inside were lots of boxes and equipment, but on the shelf lining the back wall, I found a box of tools. I grabbed a heavy wrench and several small screwdrivers, then left.

A quick peek around the corner told me the man hadn't moved. I took a deep, calming breath, then tossed one of the screwdrivers toward the guard's box as hard as I could.

It hit the wall several yards shy of the box, and fell to the ground with a clatter. The guard didn't turn around, didn't move.

I cursed silently and tried again. This time the screwdriver clattered to the ground much closer, and the guard jerked around. I ducked back behind the wall, my breath caught in my throat as I listened for his reaction.

For several seconds there was no sound other than the TV, then the chair creaked and footsteps echoed on the stone. There was a pause, and while I imagined the guard bent over to inspect the screwdrivers, I didn't dare look.

The footsteps started again, coming toward me. I gripped the wrench harder, my knuckles practically glowing as I waited.

Light flashed across the wall opposite as the footsteps got closer, and closer. Despite the chilly air, sweat trickled down my spine. I waited, my fingers aching with the force of my grip on the wrench, as the smell of pine and man began to sting the air. Then the light sharpened abruptly and the guard appeared.

I swung the wrench, smashing it across his face. Blood spurted, spraying across my cheeks and the wall behind me. He barely made a sound, crumpling to the ground almost instantly. The flashlight rolled from his fingers, sending crazy patterns of light across the walls until it came to a halt. I stood over him, sucking in air, the wrench raised and ready in case he moved. He didn't.

I blew out a relieved breath, then scrubbed an arm across my face and stepped past him, turning off the flashlight before heading back to the storage rooms. A search through several more boxes uncovered what I needed – rope.

With the guard on his side so that he didn't drown in his own blood, I tied his feet and hands – ensuring his palms were facing outward rather than inward, so I could place them on the scanners – then patted him down. The keys were in his trouser pocket.

I stepped over him again and moved on into the other passage. The TV still blared in the guard box, and several banks of monitors sat in front of the guard's chair, showing various shots of corridors and cells.

Jace, Tate, and Cooper were all sitting in front of laptops, playing shoot-'em-ups. Carli was sitting cross-legged in front of the TV, watching *The Simpsons* and giggling softly. I couldn't see Sanat or Marco, but the bathroom door was closed in both their cells, so maybe they were in there. I couldn't see my mom, either, but there were only a couple of cells with water in them down this end of the house, so she had to be in one of those. I doubted they'd move her to the end Egan and I had escaped from – the fire had damaged a fair section of that area and it was no longer secure.

I took note of all the cell numbers then glanced at the time. As much as I wanted to flick off all the monitors and race down to free everyone, I couldn't. Not until Trae's distraction started. They might not miss one guard, but someone was sure to notice a whole heap of blank screens.

So I waited, tapping my fingers on the desk, watching the clock and the slow progress of the minute hand. Tension tightened my muscles and sawed at my nerves, and sweat formed at the base of my neck before trickling down my spine. Each minute that passed was another minute wasted.

Finally, all hell broke loose.

An explosion shuddered through the night, followed closely by a shrill alarm, the noise so strident, so loud, it would surely wake the dead. Not that there were any of *those* around here. Or so I hoped, anyway.

My heart began beating like a jackhammer, feeling like it was going to pound right out of my chest. I flexed my fingers, trying to relax, listening to the noises underneath the racket of the alarm.

I looked up at the screens again. Jace and Cooper had abandoned their games and were on their feet, looking toward the ceiling. Jace had a smile on his face.

He knew we'd come for him.

The younger kids hadn't really moved, though Marco had come out of the bathroom and was now standing in the middle of the room, as if wondering what to do next.

From above came the sound of running feet, shouts, then several more explosions ran across the night – a mass of noise that blew away any remaining sense of peacefulness. Tension tightened my muscles, and it was all I could do not to run down the corridor to the cells and free everyone. But to give in to that sort of need would be stupid. *Any* sort of speed or careless movement would be stupid. Trae might have given me his diversion, but these were trained guards we were talking about. It was highly unlikely they'd all leave their posts to go investigate whatever havoc Trae was causing. There'd be guards still around somewhere, and even the slightest hint of something out of place might bring them running.

I'd learned that the hard way.

So I waited until another massive explosion made the old

building shudder, then flipped all the monitor switches. The screens went black – hopefully, the guards above would think the explosions had taken them out.

Hopefully they wouldn't come down to investigate.

I propped open the metal door leading out to the main corridors, then retraced my steps back to the guard. He was still out, and though blood pooled thickly around his head, the bleeding had actually stopped. And he was still breathing, albeit a little shallowly, so I hadn't actually killed him, which was good. I had no idea if a hand scanner needed the prints of a living, breathing person to work.

I blew out a breath, then grabbed him and hauled him up and over my shoulder, letting him flop down my back like a sack of grain. He wasn't a big man, but he was damn heavy, and my back muscles protested. But I ignored them and staggered back to the guard box, then went through the metal door and walked down the brightly lit corridor, hoping I wasn't leaving a blood trail. Hoping no one chose that moment to come around the corner. If they did, I was a goner.

I passed Tate's and Marco's cells, and went straight for Jace. I'd need his calm head and watchful eyes to help me with the little ones. When I reached the metal doorway, I grabbed the guard's limp hand and flattened it against the scanner. A blue light swept across his fingers, then the light above the door flicked from red to green. I shoved the key into the lock and opened the door.

Jace was there, waiting for me, his smile as wide as the Pacific. 'I knew you'd come. I told the others that, every single day.'

I gave him a hug with my free arm. 'I'm just sorry it took so long.'

He shrugged. 'It doesn't matter now, does it?'

I smiled. 'No, it doesn't.'

I shut the door once he was out and relocked it. We moved on and collected the rest of the boys. I then sent Jace and Cooper down the far end to watch for any roaming guards, and walked around the corner to collect Carli.

There was no one in the halls, but smoke poured down the stairs at the far end. Whatever Trae was doing, he was doing it well.

After using the guard's handprint to unlock the door, Marco and Tate propped him against the wall for me, holding him tight so he didn't slide down to the floor. I wiped the sweat from my forehead with a trembling hand, then unlocked Carli's door and pushed it open. Before I could blink, she was flying at me, her little arms wrapping around my neck and holding on tight.

'You came!' she all but shouted. 'Jace said you would.'

'Shhhh, Carli,' I said, wincing a little as her high-pitched squeal reverberated through my eardrums and along the silent halls. 'We have to be quiet until we can get out of here.'

Her eyes went wide, and she whispered, 'Sorry.'

'It's okay.' I gave her a hug, then knelt. 'Hold Sanat's hand and let him look after you while I take care of the guard.'

She nodded, and offered her hand to Sanat. He wrapped his fingers around hers, looking pleased to have some responsibility.

I locked the door, then grabbed the guard again and staggered down to one of the empty cells. I dumped the guard on the far side of the bed, where hopefully he wouldn't be seen. And just in case he woke, I tore some strips off the sheets and gagged him.

Then I closed the cell. I still needed him to get my mom out, but my first priority had to be the kids. If worse came to worst, Mom and I could call the loch and escape with the water. The kids didn't have that choice.

I scooped up Carli, then we ran back down the hall to where Jace and Cooper were watching.

'Nothing,' Jace said, green eyes solemn as he looked at me. 'And the noise has stopped upstairs.'

I nodded, and hoped like hell the silence didn't mean something bad had happened to Trae. 'This way. Quickly.'

I led them back through the guard's box and down the old corridor. At the junction, I stopped long enough to pick up the heavy wrench, then we continued on.

The tunnel seemed to be climbing, and the air was less

fresh – more full of mold and age. The younger boys huddled a little closer to me, but weren't quite touching. Trying to be brave.

A gated doorway appeared. There was a padlock on the door, but it didn't look new. More like one the scientists might have found.

I stopped and handed Carli to Sanat. 'Jace and Cooper, keep your ears open. Tell me if you hear anything that sounds like they might be looking for us.'

They nodded. I raised the wrench and smashed it against the padlock. Sparks flew and sound rang through the darkness. The lock dented, but didn't break. I tried it again. This time, splits appeared in the metal. The third time, it smashed open.

I blew out a relieved breath and opened the gate. Stairs ran upward, highlighted by moonlight that washed in at regular intervals from the arrow slits.

I looked back at the kids. 'Okay, we're going up a secret stairway to the roof. Although the scientists don't know about the other gates, we still need to be as quiet as possible.' I looked at them all. 'Okay?'

They nodded. Marco asked, eyes widening as he studied the darkness of the stairwell, 'Why are we going to the roof?'

'We're going to meet a friend there. He's going to lead you to a safe place.' I stood back and waved them all through. Jace went through first, and the others were so used to following his lead that they didn't even hesitate.

'Egan's not here?' Cooper asked.

I hesitated. 'No, Egan ... couldn't make it. But he sent his brother Trae. That's him upstairs, making all the noise.'

With the kids all through, I closed the gate and put the lock back, so that at least it would appear locked from a distance. I picked up Carli and we began to climb. Up and up, through the dust and the cobwebs, our footsteps echoing quietly across the moonlit shadows and our breathing a rasping accompaniment.

Another explosion ripped through the night, and relief slithered through me. At least Trae wasn't caught yet. We walked on, our pace slowed by the younger boys. None of the kids would have gotten much exercise in their cells, and their unfit state was telling on these stairs. I hoped to God they'd have the energy to fly once we got to the roof.

We passed the first floor, moved up to the second. The dust in the air was lessened here, the cobwebs not so thick, but the scent of smoke and oil and burning rubber was intense. We passed a wall that was fiercely hot, and as I ushered the kids to the other side, I wondered just how close the fire really was.

My legs were beginning to shake by the time we reached the door at the top. I put Carli down, making her hold Jace's hand, then hefted the wrench and brought it down on the old lock.

It shattered straightaway. I gripped the door handle and swung the door open.

The night was ablaze. Flames shot skyward, burning across the darkness and blotting out the stars. In the distance, the flashing lights of emergency vehicles could be seen, but they didn't seem to be moving. Maybe they were having trouble getting through the gates. I wouldn't have put it past the scientists to have kept them locked.

Screams and smoke filled the air, and the smell of burning rubber was more pungent out here. Flames licked one side of the building, washing brightness across the roofline. We'd have to keep low, otherwise we might be spotted. Surely twenty minutes had passed since he'd started the explosions, which meant he should be here soon.

'Okay,' I said, turning around to face the kids. 'We've got to go out onto the roof to wait for Trae. There's some flames on one side, and a bit of smoke, but nothing too dangerous. Everyone keep low, so they won't spot us down below.'

They all nodded. I took Carli's hand, and led the way out, keeping low as we moved to the center of the roof. Two seconds later, there was a scuffing sound from the left, a grunt of air, and Trae appeared, falling more than sliding over the roof battlements.

'That's the good thing about old stone buildings,' he said, his grin all cheek as he rose and dusted off his hands. 'Plenty of handgrips.'

'So glad you're enjoying yourself,' I said dryly. 'But we're a little pressed for time, so if you wouldn't mind hurrying?'

'Did she always nag like this in the cells?' he asked, his gaze sweeping over the kids before coming to rest on Jace. He offered the kid his hand. 'You'd be Jace, then?'

Jace nodded, his face solemn. 'You're Egan's brother?'

'I am. And he had a lot of good things to say about you boys.' He looked at Carli, and knelt down. 'And you're even prettier than he said.'

Carli giggled and pressed lightly against my leg. I smiled, and knelt down beside her. 'Trae's going to make you a seat in his claws, and fly you across the lake. You think you can handle that?'

She looked at Trae, then Jace and the boys, and doubt crossed her features. 'You'll be safe,' Trae said, 'and Jace and the boys will be right there with us.'

'We will, Carli,' they piped up in unison, before Jace added, 'I promise I won't let anything happen to you.'

She studied him for a moment, expression solemn, then nodded. 'Okay,' she said softly.

'Okay.' Trae rose and glanced at me. 'They're going to spot me the minute I change, so perhaps the boys better shift shape first.'

I looked at them. 'You ready?'

They nodded. Sanat and Tate closed their eyes, their

expressions ones of fierce concentration, while Jace, Marco, and Cooper simply reached for the magic in their souls. The haze of changing swept over their bodies, shifting, remolding, and lengthening their forms, until what stood on the roof was a hue of dragons as colorful as the rainbow. Silver, brown, green, blue, and red. They spread their wings, fanning lightly.

'Good lads,' Trae said, then glanced at me. 'You be careful going back in for your mom.'

'I'll be fine.'

'You'd better be.' He took several steps back, and the haze swept across his body, until he was no longer a man, but rather a glorious gold and silver dragon, his scales gleaming like polished copper in the sharp firelight.

'Wow,' Carli said, echoing what I was thinking. I doubted I'd *ever* get tired of seeing his dragon form.

Trae lowered himself down and cupped his front claws so that they formed a chair-like structure. 'Ready?' I said to the little girl.

She looked up at Trae, then nodded solemnly. I led her forward, and helped her get seated. Trae gently closed his claws around her, so that she was locked in tight.

I kissed her cheek, then said, 'You okay?'

Again she nodded. There was fear in her brown eyes, and perhaps the glitter of tears, but she gave me a tremulous smile nevertheless.

'I'll see you soon, okay? Enjoy the ride, Carli. It's lovely, flying right up there with the stars.'

She looked up at that, and her smile blossomed. I touched a hand to Trae's chest, and he looked down at me and winked. I stepped back, well out of the way.

'Get going, everyone.'

Wings swept into action, pumping hard. The boys lifted off somewhat shakily, but soon they were soaring high. Trae glanced at me, blue eyes bright in the darkness, then sprung skyward after them.

Carli's delighted laughter seemed to linger in the air long after they'd disappeared.

There were shouts from below, indicating they'd been spotted. I waited for several precious seconds, scanning the sky and hoping there were no hunters about to spring into the air and give chase. No one did, and relief slithered through me. But it was short-lived. I needed to go rescue my mother, before the scientists got the fires under control and I got trapped.

I turned and ran for the stairs.

The journey downward took a quarter of the time, though I was sweating and breathing heavily by the time I took off the old lock and swung the gate open. The corridors were shadowed and silent, and I prayed to the Gods of sea and lake that they kept that way. I ran down the hallway, my feet slapping against the cold stone, the sound echoing lightly across the silence.

I grabbed the still unconscious guard from the cell, and once again carried him down to the next lot of cells, the muscles in my back and legs on fire. In the second cell along, I sensed my mother.

I flopped the guard against the wall near the scanner, holding him upright with one hand as I wiped the sweat from my eyes and sucked in great gulps of air. I was shaking so hard anyone would think I'd run a marathon – and I suppose in many ways I had. A marathon of fear. Fear for Trae, fear for the kids, fear that I'd be back too late to free my mom.

After several more deep breaths, I grabbed the guard's hand and flattened it against the scanner. Again the scanner read his prints, and the light above the door changed color.

I dragged the guard inside the cell, then turned and looked around. The large room was shadowed and quiet. Water trickled softly to my right, the smell of it warm and familiar. Loch water.

So why hadn't my mother called the loch? She could have, given time and patience.

To the immediate right lay a basic bed. A bedside lamp pooled yellow light across a sparse rug, and highlighted the dust on the cold stone floors. Beyond the bed lay the open bathroom facilities. My mother was in neither the bed nor the bathroom, but she was here somewhere.

'Mom?' I said softly. 'It's me.'

'No.' There was a long pause, as if she were searching for the right thing to say, then, 'I told you not to.'

Her words were slurred, her voice filled with a deep sense of weariness and hopelessness. And pain, great, great pain.

It hurt to think that she'd come to such a point where nothing seemed worth fighting for. But it also hurt that she would think I could simply walk away, leaving her here for these monsters to continually prod, and poke, and sample.

I studied the shadows, trying to pin down her location. 'I won't let you die here, Mom. Come on, I've found a way out for us.'

'There is no point. My time is too near.'

Fear clutched at my heart. She *had* given up on her life. Well and truly given up.

No, part of me wanted to shout. *This isn't like you. We need to fight them. We can't let them win.* Damn it, she'd *always* been a fighter. Even Dad had acknowledged that. I guess that was part of the reason I'd gone to find her when I was old enough. She hadn't come, as Dad had promised she one day would, so I'd gone to find and free her. And in the foolishness of youth, had presumed I'd succeed where she had long failed.

What had the scientists done to her that it had come to this?

I finally spotted her silhouette. She was standing near the air-conditioning vent, not facing it but rather with her back to it, so that the slight breeze stirred her hair and flung the dark strands across her face.

For some reason, fear stirred all the more strongly.

'Mom, I won't leave unless you do.'

'Destiny—'

'No,' I said, more violently than I intended. 'There's no debating this. You're leaving this goddamn place. They've taken you from our lives, taken *your* life. I won't let them take you in death as well.'

She was silent for a moment, then sighed. 'If you wish.'

'I damn well *do* wish.'

She hesitated, then stepped forward, and the lampshade's pale light washed across her face. Or what remained of her face.

My mother had been blinded.

And not just blinded, but disfigured. It almost looked like acid had been splashed across part of her face and her eyes. The left side of her face had an almost melted look, reminding me of the way plastic held too close to a fire softened, then ran. And her eyes – oh God.

I gulped back bile and resisted the urge to look away. One socket had no eye at all. It was just a space filled with scarred and ravaged skin. The other, barely visible under her drooping eyelid, was white. Pure white.

'Not a pretty sight, is it?' she said softly.

There was no bitterness in her voice, no anger, and I think

that was even more shocking than what had been done to her.

'Why?' It was all I could say, all I could think to say.

She smiled, though only half her mouth lifted. 'They got sick of me trying to escape, so they decided to do something about it. I've had a long time to get used to the feel of it, Destiny.'

It certainly explained why they'd never let me see her. I was fiercely glad they hadn't decided to blind *me*, as well, and suddenly wondered if Egan had been my savior in more ways than one. After all, I'd done more than my fair share of attempting to escape in the early years of my capture, and blinding me most certainly would have stopped that.

But maybe they figured that having a mutilated female wouldn't have done their aim to have a breeding pair too much good.

'That's just—' Words fled. Somehow, monstrous and evil just didn't seem to cover what they'd done adequately enough. I took a deep breath in an effort to cut the sick churning in my stomach, then said, 'Was it deliberate?'

'They intended to take my sight, so yes, but my strength took them by surprise and it went slightly wrong.' Bitterness crept into her voice. 'Even after all this time, they are still surprised by the things we do. Despite all their technology, they have not learned that much about us. It is, perhaps, the only blessing in this whole mess.'

Anger swirled through me. 'Damn it, Mom, why didn't you call the loch? Why didn't you punish the bastards for doing this?'

'Because I can't.'

I blinked. 'What?'

'I can't call the loch. At first I think it was drugs, but the longer it went on, the more the restriction became a part of my very nature. I can't control water anymore, Des. It's been too long, and that part of my soul has shriveled up and died.'

Fear slithered through me. 'But controlling water is as much a part of you as flying and fire are to an air dragon. How can your own nature restrict something like that?'

'Because there is a limit to how long a sea dragon can be away from the sea, Destiny. Loch and lake may sustain us for years, but we need to be in the sea if we are to retain the sea in our souls.'

I closed my eyes and took a deep, shuddery breath. I'd speculated that this might be the case, but I'd certainly been hoping that it wasn't true. 'Why didn't you tell me?'

'Because you're a half blood. Because no one – not even me – really knows how the rules apply to a sea dragon who has the fire of the day running through their blood.' She hesitated. 'What was the point in warning you, when the rules might not apply to you? Only . . . it seemed they did.'

A chill ran through me at her words. 'How close had I come to losing my powers?'

'Very.' She rubbed her arms lightly, as if similarly chilled. 'It took five years for my control to fade, Des, and that was longer than I'd thought possible. I could feel the slip of power in you after eleven years. You were walking the edge of losing your soul when you broke out of here.'

And still she hadn't warned me. Maybe she simply didn't want to worry me any further. 'So it wasn't just for Dad's sake that you wanted me out?'

She smiled gently. 'It was for both of you. I didn't want either of you to suffer.'

'And you think Dad or I don't want the same for you? Do you think we don't care whether you die here or die free?'

'Des, the love of my life is dead, and my soul is shattered. The place of my death no longer matters, only death itself.'

The place *did* matter, because without the dawn ceremony, her soul would be as lost as my dad's would have been. It was just more evidence to the fact that she wasn't thinking entirely straight – and whether it was drugs, or losing the sea, or something else entirely didn't matter. She might *sound* reasonable, but she wasn't.

'And,' she continued softly, 'I have no choice in the death matter anyway. The drug they used to keep me calm over the years has done far more than just dampen the abilities I no longer have. Too much has built up in my system and it has poisoned me. It eats away at my insides, and there is no stopping it now. My time is close, Destiny.'

Her words made my heart ache – not just for her pain, but because I was losing her just when I'd finally found her. The family I'd hoped to regain once she was free was nothing more than ashes blowing on the wind. Just like my dad.

I blinked back tears and swept my gaze down the length of her, for the first time noticing how thin she was. Her hands were little more than skin stretched over bones, her ribs and hips protruding. Even if she could have escaped, it was doubtful she'd survive the cold, dark waters of the loch in that condition. There was no padding, no insulation against the cold. And while a dragon's skin might be designed to protect us against the icy depths, tough hide alone was not enough.

'There may be no stopping it, but that doesn't mean you have to die here.' I walked over to her and wrapped my arms around her. I might have been hugging a skeleton, but it felt so good to hold her after all these years of not even being allowed to see her. And to have her taken away so soon after finding her … Tears stung my eyes again but I blinked them back again. Now was not the time for grief. That could come later, when it was all over.

'It's so good to see you,' I whispered, when I could.

She hugged me back, her frail arms displaying a surprising

amount of strength. 'And it's good to finally be able to hold you, my stubborn, beautiful child.'

I squeezed my eyes shut against the run of more tears, and kissed her ruined cheek. I so wanted to do more, to hug her and kiss her and tell her how much I missed her, how much I loved her, but we just didn't have the time. Besides, she knew. It was in her touch. In her gentle, mutilated smile.

I pulled away, and tucked my arm in hers. Her skin was like paper. Brittle, icy paper. And not all of the cold in her skin was the night and the nature of a sea dragon. Some of it was the ice of death. I bit back the rise of bile and anger, and forced a calmness in my voice as I said, 'Let's get out of here. Dad awaits, and you know how impatient he can be.'

She laughed softly. 'Yes. And I'm afraid it's a trait our daughter shares.'

'That, unfortunately, is true.'

I guided her past the pool, around the still unconscious guard and through the door, which I closed behind us. The green light I could do nothing about, not without grabbing the guard and using his fingerprints again – and that was time I didn't want to waste. I had a feeling we didn't have a whole lot of it left anyway.

Another explosion ripped through the air as we began to walk, and the very walls around us seemed to shake. Dust puffed down from the ceiling. Trae had obviously set timers on some of his explosions. I wondered how he'd managed it. And whether we'd actually have an ancestral home to worry about by the time all his diversions had finally gone off.

'What's that?' Mom whispered.

'A little something to sidetrack the scientists.' I tightened my grip on her and tried to hurry her steps a little. Though the hallway itself was quiet, my skin itched with the need to be gone, to get out of this place. My luck might have held so far, but my luck had never been *that* good for long.

A point proven when the sound of rapidly approaching steps whispered across the air.

'Oh, no,' my mother said, her voice cracked and unsteady. 'Not now. We can't be caught now.'

'We won't.'

The footsteps were coming from the corridor in front of the guard's box – the one that ran at an angle to this one – and were still some distance away. I stopped, hoping they'd take another corridor, hoping they'd go into one of the other rooms.

They didn't.

I cursed softly, then guided my mother into the nearest open cell – one that was bigger than some of the others I'd seen. The wide pool was deep, and the dark water smelled fresher than the water in my mother's cell. The ceiling soared above us, the rafters dark with age and decorated with dust and webs. We might be in the basement, but this room rose the full height of the house. Those were roof rafters above us, not the supports of the next floor.

'I know this room,' my mother said, her nose in the air and nostrils flaring. 'They do tests here. Air tests. Underwater tests.'

I didn't need to ask what those tests were, because I'd been put through a few of them in my time in this place. But never here.

I guided her over to the water's edge, then gently pressed her down. 'Hide in the water. If they come in here and discover us, duck under. You may not be able to use the water's power anymore, but you're still a dragon.'

'But you can't—'

'Mom, just trust me.'

'I do trust you. I just don't want these monsters catching you again.'

I smiled. 'I thought we were the only monsters in this world.'

'Monsters come in all shapes and sizes,' she said grimly. 'And many of them are human-born.'

Wasn't that the truth. 'Please, Mom, get into the water. I'll hide over near the door. With any sort of luck, they won't even come this way.' Even as I said the words, I didn't believe them. But as long as *she* did, nothing else mattered.

She hesitated, then slipped into the cold, dark water. As her sigh of pleasure ran across the silence, I walked behind the door. The footsteps drew closer, not stopping at the guard's box but moving on quickly. I flexed my fingers, trying to ease the tension creeping through my muscles and wishing I still had the wrench. But I'd put it down when I'd dragged the guard inside Mom's cell, and I hadn't thought to bring it with me.

The footsteps came closer, then stopped just outside the door. My breath caught somewhere in my throat and refused to budge, and my pulse seemed to beat in my ears, so loud I swear that person outside the door would surely have to hear it.

For several seconds, the stranger didn't move. He just stood there, breathing steadily. I couldn't see him through the crack between the door and the jamb, and he didn't seem to have any particular scent.

Sweat trickled down my spine. I licked my lips, praying he'd move on. But he didn't, and it was pretty easy to guess why.

He knew we were in here. Knew because he held one of the receivers. It didn't matter whether it was my signal or Mom's, because in the end, we were both here and both caught.

'I know you're in the water, Aila. Come out where I can see you.'

My breath caught at the sound of his voice, and my stomach began twisting itself into knots.

Because it wasn't just a guard who stood outside our door. It was the man in charge himself.

Marsten.

The one man I'd been hoping to avoid.

The one man I would probably have to kill if I was ever to have any hope of living a peaceful life.

I flexed my fingers, and forced myself to remain still. He obviously wasn't standing close to the door, otherwise I'd see him. And until he *was* close enough for me to see and assess whether he was armed, I had to remain where I was.

'Aila, we know it's your daughter and her latest flame out there causing problems. If we catch her, we'll kill her. Unless you come out. Unless you stop her.'

I glanced at the dark pool, saw no ripple in the water, nothing to indicate my mother was there or listening. But his words made me frown. Was Marsten picking up my signal, Mom's, or both?

And if it were both, why would he say it was me out there causing problems?

Was he trying to bluff us? Or biding his time and waiting for reinforcements? After all, how much more could there be out there for Trae's little diversions to blow up?

Urgency pulsed and suddenly my feet were itching with the need to move, to get out of here, while we still had the chance. But until Marsten moved, until I knew whether he was armed or not, that really wasn't an option.

Neither was standing here waiting.

I looked around the room. There were various cases around walls, but even if they held something that could be used as a weapon, they were all locked, and therefore useless to me. And the scientists still weren't foolish enough to leave anything that might provide weaponry laying about.

'Aila, you have to the count of three, then I'll start firing. And who knows just what – or who – I'll hit?'

My heart jumped into my throat and seemed to lodge there. *Yup. He knew Mom wasn't in here alone.*

'One.'

There was no movement from the water. I stepped back. I wasn't sure where I was going or what I intended to do. I just knew I didn't want to be near that door when Marsten started firing.

'Two.'

The whisper of a safety being clicked off ran across the silence. Sweat trickled down my spine, and I retreated another step.

'Three.'

Water stirred. Soft ripples of movement ran from the far end of the pool, growing ever stronger as they raced toward us, reaching the end and splashing upward.

'If you want me, Marsten, come and get me. I'm through dancing to your particular tune.'

Though her words were defiant, I could hear the weariness in her voice. The pain. She was closer to joining Dad in the forever lands than I'd imagined.

I blinked back tears, and waited for Marsten's response. It wasn't long in coming. Lights flooded the room, their brightness making me blink.

'Come out of the water, Aila.'

'You come into the room, and maybe I'll consider it.' The words rumbled out of the water, causing little ripples to scurry across its surface.

There was one footstep, then another, and the scent of smoke and sweaty male began to sting the air. Obviously, Marsten had been outside when Trae had begun his diversion.

More steps, then suddenly Marsten was in the room, his silver hair glistening in the brightness as he edged sideways, the weapon clenched in his hands and pointed directly at the water.

More ripples ran across the pool, then suddenly my mother appeared, her head breaking the water just enough to let her ruined eye and nose emerge.

Though I wasn't near the pool, I began to move my fingers, caressing the energy building in the air, calling to the dark water and feeling the eagerness of it slide across my skin – a kiss filled with such fury that the hairs along my arms stood on end.

'Your time here with us has ended, Marsten. Give it up, and walk away, while you still can.'

Amusement flitted briefly across his craggy features. 'Aila, we've seen the worst you can do, and it doesn't scare us. Get out of the water, or I will shoot. Remember, you're just as useful to me dead as alive, so don't for a moment think that I won't.'

I didn't. And I knew my mother wouldn't have cared either way. But I would not let her die in this place – not through a bullet, and not through her own will.

I stepped forward, into his sight.

The gun in Marsten's hand didn't waver. 'I was wondering when you'd move, Destiny.'

I continued to move my fingers as I edged forward, trying to get closer to the water. Trying to raise a barrier between my mother and that gun.

'You gain nothing by shooting either of us, Marsten,' I said, as the energy I was collecting began to pull at my hair and my hands, and tiny sparks seemed to dance across the dark, rippling waters. 'You have no real idea about what my mother and I can do. And you won't ever know just what we're capable of if we're dead.'

'What I know,' he said, 'is that you've killed a number of good scientists, and have proved difficult animals to keep.'

'We're not animals,' I said, glad my voice showed none of the rage and fear that was boiling through me. 'We're still more valuable alive than dead.'

'Actually, you've proved the exact opposite time and time again. And you've destroyed the viability of this facility.'

'And just how have we managed that?' I continued to move

forward, creeping toward the pool's edge inch by tortuous inch, all the while wishing I could simply run to my mom. Yet that was a chance I couldn't take. Any sudden movement might cause him to fire that gun. 'We may have blown up a lab and burned out a bit of equipment here and there, but that's about all we've managed to do.'

'What you've managed to do is destroy the secrecy of this operation. Half of Drumnadrochit probably saw air dragons flying over Loch Ness, and the scientific world will guess we have discovered something and want a piece of it. We needed more time to uncover the secrets hidden in your genes, and that is what you have robbed us of.'

And you've robbed us of life, of humanity, and each other, I wanted to snap back, but what was the point? We might hold human shape, but Marsten was never going to see anything more than an interesting puzzle to unravel.

'You haven't even begun to touch on our secrets, Marsten, and trust me, you need us alive to even begin to understand us.'

'I think I'm the only one who's qualified to be the judge of that,' he said, and pulled the trigger.

'No!' I screamed, and unleashed the waiting energy. The dark water flew up, swirling around my mother, swiftly becoming a thick whirlpool through which nothing would get through. Not even a bullet.

The bullet hit the wall of water and ricocheted away. Marsten swore, then swung the gun and pulled the trigger again. This time straight at me.

I had no time to call the water and protect myself. The most I could do was throw myself sideways. But I wasn't superman. I wasn't even an air dragon. I didn't have wings and certainly couldn't fly. I wouldn't beat that bullet, and I knew that, but that didn't stop me from trying.

The air seemed to scream. Or maybe it was me screaming. I don't know. The safety of the dark water was close, so close, but the bullet was faster than my fall. Metal tore through my thigh, blood, skin, and muscle flying into the air as the bullet punched its way through my leg. I hit the water and went tumbling, crashing into the far edge of the pool, landing half in, and half out of the water.

The air whooshed from my lungs and all I could feel was pain – thick, gut-churning pain – and all I wanted to do was slide into the beckoning darkness of unconsciousness. But it wasn't over yet, not by a long shot, and I fought to remain awake and aware as a slick red puddle began to form around my leg and drip slowly into the pool.

Water splashed, and then my mother was beside me. 'Oh God, oh God,' she said, her frail hands on my face, my neck. Feeling for the wound she could smell but not see.

Behind us both, footsteps approached. My heart accelerated,

pumping fear through every inch of me. Pumping my life out onto the cold concrete.

But with the footsteps came another sound. The air was screaming again. But not from a bullet. Not this time.

Trae was coming.

Relief flooded through me. I didn't care how he knew I needed help. All that mattered was that he was coming, that he was near. All I had to do was keep us both alive until then.

'Mom, get back into the protection of the whirlpool,' I whispered urgently.

'What? Don't be—'

'Mom, shut up and just get into the damn water.'

My voice was little more than a hiss of air. I touched her face lightly, trying to convince her of my urgency, but my gaze went past her and focused again on Marsten. There was no compassion in his dark eyes, no doubt. We were nothing more than a couple of test subjects he had no intention of losing. A shiver went through me. There was no talking sense to someone like that. No way to make him see us as anything more than monsters who had no rights, no voice in this human-filled world.

'Mom,' I added, 'trust me, please. I didn't come all this way to get us both killed.'

She sobbed, but spun and dove into the water. I played my fingers through the water, calling to the energy of the loch, calling to the deep, dark waters that waited beyond this small pool.

'Well, well, well,' Marsten said, as he stopped at my feet. 'That water spout of yours was a very neat trick. It would appear that the littlest sea dragon has been holding out on us.'

'I told you we were more useful alive than dead.' My gaze went past Marsten to the roof high above. *Hurry. Please hurry,* I thought, even though I had no idea whether he could actually hear me.

'If you were less troublesome, I'd probably agree with you. But with all the samples we've collected over the years, we've decided to grow our own little sea dragons.'

'Our control of water is learned rather than ingrained. Growing your own won't give you your answers.'

'That's a risk we're prepared to take,' he said, and pointed the gun at my face.

'No,' my mother screamed, even as the roof was torn apart and a silver and gold dragon dropped like a stone toward us. His scaled hide gleamed like polished jewels in the bright light, his talons thick and deadly looking as claws widened then snapped shut, reminding me of the jaws of a crocodile grabbing for food. Never in my life have I seen a more beautiful sight.

Marsten spun and raised the gun. But he was too late. Trae's swoop had brought him close enough to lash out with one wickedly clawed foot. As he snatched the scientist up, the gun went off, skimming his jeweled hide, leaving a slash of blood.

Blood that was joined by a thick spurt as one of Trae's claws slashed deep into Marsten's middle, gutting him.

Trae trumpeted – a harsh, ugly sound – then his wings pumped, blasting me with air and dust as he rose skyward through the roof.

'The loch,' I screamed after him, hoping he could hear me. Hoping he'd listen. 'She waits.'

He disappeared. I slumped back, feeling an odd weariness slithering through me, making my limbs seem heavy and yet my head light.

I licked my lips and tried to concentrate. It wasn't finished yet. There were still others to be taken care of if we dragons were to have any freedom. I shifted position, and allowed my wounded leg to fall into the water. Loch water wasn't seawater, and it didn't have the same sort of healing power, but the freezing water would slow the bleeding, and the ancient energy caught within the loch *would* begin to heal the wound. Just not as fast as the sea.

'Mom,' I said, flicking my fingers through the water, letting the whirlpool of power go. 'We need to call the loch and finish this.'

'I can't,' she sobbed, splashing to a halt by my side and groping quickly for my hand. 'God, I should kill you for taking such a stupid risk.'

'I'm okay, Mom, really.' I hesitated, then said, 'I need to erase their fingerprints on this place. I need to call the loch.'

'Do what you wish. This place has no soul left for me now. It is your inheritance. Yours to do with what you wish.'

What I wished was for every bit of the scientists to be erased from this place. I wanted no memory of them left in the rooms or the cold stone walls. No trace of them remaining anywhere on the grounds.

Mom's fingers wrapped around mine in the pool, and a tremor seemed to slice the dark waters. A tremor that was all excitement, all need. The loch wanted this as much as I did. With my mom's grip somehow giving me strength, I took a deep, shuddery breath, then called.

Energy touched the air, raced across the water, across my senses. It was a rich, warm sensation, one of welcoming and of healing, and it flooded through my body, through muscles and bone and spirit, energizing and renewing. Giving me the strength I needed to fight on. To survive.

My mother sucked in a deep breath, and suddenly seemed more alive. Color warmed her pale features and her frail body suddenly seemed to have strength. She might not be able to call the magic anymore, but she was still a sea dragon, and she could still feel it.

'Come to me,' I said softly. 'By the Gods of sea and air and lake, I command thee to come to me.'

The concrete underneath us shuddered, as if the very ground was trying to answer my call.

'Come to me,' I repeated, 'and cleanse this place of the evil that has taken it. Let no room or person go unnoticed.'

As I spoke, thunder rumbled. It was a long, dark sound that went on and on, as if the very skies vibrated with fury.

'Take it all,' I whispered. 'Cleanse it all. I want nothing of them left in this place. Nothing at all.'

There was a thick, long roar, a thunderous sound that seemed to surround us, a sound that was a combination of air and water and the very earth itself. The walls around us shook, as if in fear of its fury.

Mom smiled and squeezed my hand. 'She comes. She answered.'

I had no time to reply, because the fierce dark waters rushed into our cell and swept us away to the safety of the loch.

Chapter Fifteen

That's where my mother died.

In the arms of the loch, surrounded by its power, filled with its welcome and joy. I held her gently, keeping her body close to the shore, fighting the gentle but insistent tug of the water.

Dawn was coming – the music of it was growing – but the time was not yet right to release her to the water's embrace.

The loch had been quiet for a good hour now, the fury of water and air and earth that I'd unleashed fading quickly once the last traces of those who had invaded our ancestral lands had been washed away. Several bodies had drifted past my sheltered position, guided on by the gentle currents down toward the castle. In the last hour, boats had come out to collect them, while others searched for survivors. No boats came near me. The loch saw to that.

Awareness tingled across my skin, and the warmth that always came with Trae's presence flooded my senses.

'There's cops and emergency services crawling all over your mom's place,' he said, sitting down beside me. His clothes were bloody and mud-splattered, and he smelled of smoke and fire. 'And the rumors have already started about what was really going on up there.'

'Well, there's no hiding the pens, no matter how much damage the water did.' I pressed my body against his, needing the contact, needing the strength and warmth of his touch. 'How are the kids?'

He smiled. 'Little Carli's going to be a heartbreaker when she's older. And Jace is far too wise for his years.'

'Yeah, I noticed.' I watched the water swirl past a nearby outcrop of rock, then asked, 'So are they happy to be free? Anxious to get home?'

'The boys are. I don't really think Carli remembers all that much about her family. I left them eating pizza, drinking Coke, and watching TV.'

'And with strict orders not to answer the phone or open the door, I hope.'

'I don't think you have to worry about that. Jace has them well under control.'

'He's a good kid.'

'Yeah.' He slipped an arm around my shoulders and pulled me closer. 'How's your leg?'

The wildness was back in his bright eyes, fiercer than before. Only this time, it didn't seem like a wildness that couldn't be tamed. This time, it was the wildness of a man who had been fighting for what was his.

My heart did this happy little dance, but the rest of me was simply too tired to join in.

'The leg is sore, but survivable.' The cold of the water had taken the vast majority of pain from it, and the magic that still spun around us had begun the healing process. But it would be a few days yet before I could put any real weight on it.

Dawn began flanking the dark edges of the sky, sending small flags of pink and yellow breaking across the blackness. The energy in the air was growing, tingling across my senses, dancing across the water.

The loch tugged more fiercely at my mother's legs, wanting an ending. Wanting a new beginning.

Tears stung my eyes. I blinked them away and watched the sky, listening to the growing music of dawn, waiting for the moment when the energy peaked. Trae was a silent, watchful presence by my side, warming me in ways I couldn't even begin to describe.

As the slivers of color truly began to flood the darkness, and the warmth of the coming day broke the chill of night, the dance of energy sharpened, burning across my skin, sparkling across the top of the water.

It was time.

I took a breath and briefly closed my eyes, seeking the strength to do this, to let her go when all I really wanted to do was grab and hold her and beg her not to leave me, too. But of course, it was all too late for that. She was gone in body if not yet spirit, and to bind her to this earth now would be nothing short of selfishness. Especially given everything she'd already suffered.

Trae squeezed my shoulder, as if sensing my reluctance. I gave him a quick smile, took another deep breath, then said softly, 'The Gods of loch and sea, I call on thee.'

The water began to swirl around my feet, around my mother's body, tugging at us both. Wanting us both, but for different reasons.

'And the Gods of air and land, I call on thee.'

Mist formed across the surrounding hills, spreading vaporous fingers down their flanks, reaching quickly toward the water. The air felt suddenly cooler, thicker, the energy of dawn stronger. Every breath was filled with the power of it, until it felt like my whole body was vibrating to its music. Tiny sparks danced across my skin, leapt off into the water, and skipped across the waves.

'Guide your daughter on her final journey,' I said, still holding on to my mother, not letting her go just yet. 'Help her find the peace and happiness in the forever lands that she could not find here.'

The fingers of mist drew close, creeping past my legs, wrapping around my mother's body. Her body began to glow with a cold blue light, and the vapor around her began to twirl and dance, the movement almost joyous. Then the blue light broke free, streaming upward, into the mist and beyond, reaching for the forever plains and my dad.

With her spirit free, the mist and the light retreated. As the magic of dawn began to fade, the dark water tugged even more fiercely on my mother's body.

'Take her to where our ancestors lie,' I whispered, as I released her. 'Hide her well.'

There was a splash of water, and she was gone. I closed my eyes, battling the ache, fiercely fighting the grief that welled up my throat. There was time enough for that later. Right now, there was me, and there was Trae, and the magic that still danced across the dark water. Still danced through me.

'God, I'm sorry—' he said softly.

'Don't,' I cut in. 'It's what she wanted.'

'But you've lost—'

'Don't,' I repeated, then rose unsteadily, balancing precariously on one leg. 'We need to go farther into the water.'

He raised his eyebrows, but rose. 'It's freezing in that lake.'

'What if I promise to keep you warm?'

A smile played across his lush lips. 'Tempting, but let's face it, the cold will still play havoc with the better parts of me.'

'The loch won't affect you like that. Trust me,' I said softly.

He studied me for a moment, blue eyes serious despite the smile teasing his lips. 'Why is this so important?'

'Because it's a tradition in sea dragon families.' I hesitated, knowing the importance of what I was asking, and hoping like hell I hadn't misread everything I'd been feeling and seeing in him. 'When one sea dragon dies, we celebrate his or her life by creating another.'

'Ah.' He touched my cheek lightly, then ran his fingers down to my lips. My body quivered under his touch, desire spreading like wildfire. 'I see.'

'Do you?' I asked, my gaze searching his intently. 'This *will* create life between us, and that child will bind us more than any words ever could. Is the thief ready for that sort of responsibility? Ready for me to be a permanent part of your life?'

'The thief was a goner the minute the woman with wild-looking hair decided to play chicken in the middle of an Oregon highway.'

He smiled, and there in his eyes was all the emotion I could ever want. Love, desire, need. It was right there, a fierceness shining in the brightness of his eyes. And the ache in my heart eased a little, because while I might have lost my parents, I'd gained something else. A lover, a companion, a friend. A man who would be with me, stand by me, no matter what happened, for the rest of my life.

'You couldn't escape me now, even if you wanted to,' he added, then leaned forward and kissed me. 'You complete me, Destiny. There's no other place I want to be, and nothing else I'd rather do than walk into that water with you and celebrate your mother's life. I just wish it wasn't so fucking cold.'

I laughed, gloriously, deliriously happy for the first time in years and years, and threw my hands around his neck. 'God, I'm so glad you said that, because I've been in love with you for what seems like forever. I was just too chicken to say anything.'

He kissed me, soft and slow and oh-so gloriously, and then I helped him strip. When he was finally naked, we walked into the deeper water. It was cold, but I didn't care, and he didn't seem to, either.

He pulled me close. I melted against him, wrapped my arms around his neck, and kissed him again, hard and fierce, until my head was spinning and I wasn't sure whether it was lack of air or sheer happiness.

After that, his touch and his lips seemed to be everywhere, fueled by urgency and yet filled with passion. I let my fingers roam, giving them the freedom of his glorious body, touching and tasting and teasing, even as he touched and teased. The deep-down ache blossomed and grew, becoming such a sweet agony that I groaned, arching my back, pressing into his touch, wanting him as fiercely as I'd wanted anything in my life.

Finally, he slid deep inside and it felt so good, so right, I could only groan. I wrapped my legs around him, holding him tight against me, wanting every bit of him. He wrapped his arms around me and leaned forward, kissing my nose gently.

'This is how I'll always remember you,' he said softly, his eyes the blue of the rising day, bright with the wildness and need. 'With the dark waters at your back, the heat of passion in your face, and the power of the dawn shining in your eyes.'

'Not dawn,' I whispered, 'the loch. And she is getting frustrated that you won't get down to business.'

'Sweetheart, she's not the only one. But teasing is good for the soul.'

'Not my soul.'

He laughed, a sound that curled joyously around us, filling the air with sheer happiness.

He began to move – not urgently, not desperately, but slowly, passionately. And I answered in kind, kissing him deeply, my arms tightening against his neck, as if I never, ever meant to let him go.

'Look at me,' he ordered, after a while.

I opened my eyes, looked into his. And again I felt like I was falling deep into those wild pools of blue, slipping deep under the surface, captured and secured, never to be free from his grip again. And I couldn't have been happier.

He began to move, sliding in and out, and the feel of him penetrated every fiber, enveloping me in a heat that was so basic, and yet so very pure. His hands were on my hips, supporting my butt, holding me steady as he rocked deep, his touch seeming to brand my skin as his thrusts gradually became more and more urgent, until passion and desire and need became a wildfire that burned through every part of me.

'Come with me, sweetheart.'

His words were hoarse, urgent, his breath hot as it whispered past my cheek. His powerful body stroked fast and deep, driving me insane with need. I tightened my legs around him, urging him deeper still, wanting, needing, every inch of him. He groaned, and thrust harder, and it felt so good I cried out in pleasure. Then the sweet pressure broke, and I was drowning, shuddering, under the force of a glorious release.

'Oh God, yes!'

He came with me, his roar echoing across the silence, making the dark waters shimmer and dance at the glory of it all as his body slammed mine so hard waves rolled away from our bodies and went racing across the loch.

For several seconds, we remained locked in each other's embrace. Our breathing was ragged and despite the chill of the water, sweat pooled where our flesh still met. Then he sighed, and kissed my neck.

'So do you think it'll be a boy or a girl?' he asked, amusement crinkling the corners of his bright eyes. 'And will they take after their mother or their father?'

'I don't know, and I don't care.'

He kissed my nose, and gave me a smile that was happiness itself. 'Well, there's one thing I *do* care about. I'm just about to have my nuts frozen off, so if we want to have more than one child, we had better be getting out of this water.'

I sighed softly. 'I'd love to move right into bed, but we have kids to look after first.'

His smile faded. 'It's not going to be easy to find all their parents. Especially little Carli's.'

'It's not even going to be easy to get them out of Scotland. Not with the remaining scientists still sniffing around.'

He kissed my nose, then splashed out of the water with me still in his arms. 'Let me worry about all that. Right now, we need to get dressed, then get back and see if the vultures have left us any pizza.'

Epilogue

In the end, getting the kids out of Scotland wasn't the problem I thought it would be. I'd forgotten that Trae was a thief by trade, and any thief who could get a will-o'-the-wisp to steal a ring wasn't going to find it all that troublesome to get help transporting stolen kids back to their country of birth.

Nor was it hard to find most of their parents. Jace and Cooper had both been snatched when they were older, and knew their home addresses. Their reunion with their parents had been a joyful thing, and just as many tears had flowed down my cheeks as theirs – especially when it came time to say good-bye.

Tate and Marco were both several years younger, but they'd also been captured more recently. Armed with their surnames and the descriptions of their cliques and the surrounding lands, Trae and his friends had tracked down their families pretty quickly.

Sanat was tougher. The littlest of the boys, he'd come into the cells only six months after Carli, and he really couldn't remember all that much about his family. We had their names, of course, but that wasn't a whole lot of help when it was a common surname. And all he could recall about where he lived was a bell. A shiny silver bell that had rung out every dusk.

It took us a month to find his home – a tiny cliff-top village. His clique was not connected to any of the thirteen major ones. He'd been the only son in a family of fourteen, and the party had gone on for days.

Which left us with little Carli, who couldn't remember anything except her mom's pretty smile and long brown hair, and her dad's blue eyes and bad singing voice.

Then one of Trae's friends came through with a list of missing air dragons – how, I have no idea, when all the cliques seemed determined not to help out more than necessary – and there she was. Carli Symmonds, whose small clique owned a two-thousand-acre ranch over near Wolf Creek in Montana.

We stayed there for a week, and leaving her was probably one of the hardest things I've ever had to do. In so many ways, that little girl had kept me sane in a place of madness, just as she and all the kids had kept me going once I was out. If Egan had been my rock and my strength, then the kids had been my sanity.

I'd miss them all – which is why I made them promise to write to me. And why I told their parents to contact me if there were ever any problems.

Which left us with one task – returning the ring.

And I just had to hope that the two-month delay in finally getting the ring back to his father hadn't affected Trae's sister in any way.

I looked out the car's side window, seeing nothing but the shadows of dusk and huge redwood trunks. We'd taken the fastest and quickest route to get his clique's base in Stewarts Point from his home in San Francisco, and had been driving for nearly two and half hours. Now, we were finally on clique lands. And better yet, I could smell the sea.

'Is your mother still planning a meet and greet with the rest of your family?' It was a question I'd probably asked before, but I swear the pregnancy was sapping brain cells, because my memory just wasn't up to scratch lately. And if it was *this* bad now, how bad was it going to be when I neared full term?

He snorted softly. 'She's planned a whole damn party, and invited every relation she could think of. Some of them I don't even remember.'

I glanced at him. In the growing dusky light of the oncoming evening, his hair gleamed with slivers of sunlight, and gold speckled his unshaven chin.

It was a look I was seeing a whole lot more of lately, simply because I loved it. And, gorgeous man that he was, he was willing to indulge my fantasies.

'I thought you told her we didn't want anything big?'

His smile touched his eyes, crinkling the corners and easing the tension that had been gaining ground since we entered clique grounds.

'Oh, I did, but when she gets something in her mind, there's no persuading her otherwise.' He glanced at me, blue eyes bright. 'You know she thinks it's twins. A boy born of water and a girl born of sun. Her words, not mine.'

I touched my stomach, and the barely there bulge. 'If she's right, you'll be doing your fair share of diaper changing.'

'Love to.'

I snorted softly. We'd see how positive he was when actually faced with the task.

We came out of the trees and into the fading remnants of the day. The rugged coastline curved away to our left and the surge of the sea was high, the waves riding high up the cliffs. A weapon I could call if things went wrong with Trae's dad.

We swept up a slight incline and, at the top, the heart of the clique became evident. The buildings were a mix of wood and stone structures and, in many ways, the whole place reminded me of an ancient walled village. It even had a wall, in the form of a post and wire fence that separated the housing area from the rest of the valley.

The main house was a two-story stone affair that was big and formidable looking. The houses that clustered closest to it were also stone, but as the ring of houses moved farther away, they became a mix of wood and stone, and then finally just wood. The outer ring looked just like houses you'd see in any suburban city.

'This is more feudal than what I expected,' I said, after a moment.

'Yeah, the Jamieson clique is one of the originals.' His voice was dry. 'If my father had his way, there'd *only* be originals. He can't abide having the line diluted.'

'So he's not going to be happy about you further diluting the precious bloodline by mating with a half-breed sea dragon?'

'Not at all.' His voice was decidedly cheery, although the look he gave me was full of concern. 'If you're at all worried about him, you can stay in the car. Or go see Mom.'

'No, I want to meet the bastard who made your and Egan's lives such a living hell.'

He nodded, and drove into the nearest parking space. He helped me out of the car, then, with an arm around my waist, guided me into the cavernous stone entranceway. The huge wood and iron doors were open and led into a room that could have easily stepped out of the medieval era. Stone walls, huge tapestries, and heavy wooden furniture that looked worn with time and living.

Our footsteps echoed as we crossed the room, but no one came running out to see or greet us.

'He does know we're coming?' I whispered, studying the growing shadows uneasily.

'Yeah, but he's making a big deal of it,' Trae said, his voice filling the silence with contempt.

'This isn't exactly what I'd call a big deal,' I muttered. 'I think it's more the cold shoulder the unwanted relatives get.'

'Oh, it's that, too.'

The set of doors at the far end of the room began to open as we approached them. The next room was warmer, but it was almost as empty. Almost. A red carpet led the eye down the length of the room to the steps and the huge gilded throne that dominated the top of them. On it sat a man.

A small, frail man with golden hair that was thick with gray and golden eyes that held a malicious glint.

'And Egan couldn't beat this?' I whispered, as we walked toward him.

'What you see is the result of the ring being gone too long.' His voice was clipped, and there was tension in the arm that held me so protectively. 'My father in his prime was a danger-ous man to cross.'

I stared into his father's golden eyes and saw the anger and hatred hiding there. He was still a dangerous man, even if the shell was failing.

We stopped in front of him. His gaze skimmed Trae, his expression one of cold contempt, then he looked at me. A long, lingering look that slipped down my body and made me want a shower to wash away the feel of it.

'What news do you have of my sister?' Trae snapped, his voice full of ice and his grip on my waist tightening a fraction more.

'What news do you have of the ring?' the old man said, his voice a mocking echo of Trae's.

'We have it.'

'Then give it to me.'

Trae glanced at me briefly, then said, 'Do you think I would be foolish enough to bring it into this place, without first getting the information I need?' He snorted softly. 'If you taught me one thing, Father, it's not to trust your fucking promises.'

The old man laughed. It was a cold, cruel sound. 'Ah, if only my real son had half your balls, he would have made a grand king.'

Trae's hands retreated into a fist and dug slightly into my side. But he didn't give in to the anger I could feel in him, and simply said, 'And if you'd had half the honor and courage that Egan had, this clique could have been a great one.'

The old man lurched forward in the seat. Trae released me and stepped forward, his body slightly in front of mine. I began moving my fingers, feeling the magic of the dusk swirl around me, fireflies of energy only I could feel.

'Give me the ring,' the old man said, voice soft and all the more deadly because of it, 'or I'll fry that pretty little thing by your side to cinders.'

'If I see even a spark, I'll drown the lot of you,' I said, keeping slightly behind Trae regardless of my threat. I wasn't a fool, and he could protect me from fire, as Egan once had.

'Drown?' The old man laughed again. 'Lady, we're a long way from the cliffs and the sea here. As threats go, that's pretty empty.'

'Not if you bother looking out the windows, old man,' Trae said quietly.

The old man's gaze darted sideways, and his mouth dropped. Because the sea had answered my call, and she was rushing over the cliffs and down into their valley home in ever-increasing waves.

'Give me what you promised,' Trae said.

'She's a *sea* dragon?' He sat back in his chair, annoyance and a surprising touch of humor in his expression. For one brief moment, he oddly reminded me of Egan. 'I didn't think any of them were left.'

'More than you might think,' I said, 'and that water is almost here. You might want to hurry up and give us the information, before people start drowning.'

They wouldn't, of course. I hadn't called *that* much water. It just looked like it from the vantage points of the smaller windows – a point we'd counted on when we'd first planned this.

'She's been moving around a bit, but she's currently in Fallon, Nevada. Staying in the Econo Lodge, I believe.' He reached into his pocket and pulled out a phone. 'You can call them and confirm, if you'd like.'

Trae grabbed the phone. 'I will. What's the number?'

The old man gave it to him, then glanced at me. 'Where's the ring, little sea dragon?'

As Trae dialed the number, I raised an eyebrow and flicked two fingers outward, letting some of the seawater recede back to the cliffs while continuing to call the main arm.

It began trickling through the doorways and across the stone floor, pooling around Trae's and my feet, a whirlpool of silvery blue that began to rise up our legs without ever touching us.

Trae spoke into the phone for several seconds, then hung up and handed the phone back to his father. 'She's there,' he said, glancing at me. 'Give him the ring.'

I flicked the rest of my fingers outward. The whirlpool surged upward and water splashed. Silver glittered in the middle of the spout – silver with ruby red eyes and a heart as cold as the man who had worn it for so long.

Trae caught the ring and the water splashed down, soaking the carpet but not our feet.

'The ring,' Trae said, and handed it to him.

He snatched it from Trae's fingers like a man stranded in the desert for too long might snatch at a glass of water.

He slid it over his fingers and leaned back in the throne with a sigh. Trae shook his head and looked at me. 'Come on, let's get out of here.'

We were almost out the door when the old man said, 'I want you off these lands within the hour.'

Trae didn't say anything, just kept on walking.

I held my tongue until we were out of the old stone building, then said, 'He's dying, isn't he?'

Trae smiled. 'Yes. The ring has been gone for too long. It won't help him now.'

'So Egan got his wish in the end.'

'Yes. The bastard we call father will soon be dead.'

I splashed through a puddle of seawater, then asked, 'But with Egan gone, who will take over the clique? One of the other full-blood brothers?'

'I don't know and I don't care. I have my own life and my own family to worry about.' He stopped at the car and opened the passenger door. 'And the sooner we can get away from the grip of Mom and the relatives, the sooner we can get on with said life.'

I laughed and threw my arms around his neck. 'After all the trouble your mom has gone to, you can at least give her a couple of hours.'

'Three hours tops, then,' he said, his arms going around my waist and pulling me closer.

'And then?' I murmured, my lips brushing his.

'And then,' he said, a contented smile on his lips and love and happiness shining in his bright eyes. 'We go find my sister, check that she's okay, and head on back to that big old house of mine and start making it habitable for the twins.'

'That sounds like a damn fine plan,' I said, and kissed him.

Passion flares. Danger Ignites. And . . .

MERCY BURNS

Half dragon, half woman, can she save her friend's soul – without losing her heart?

Mercy Wilson is a reporter in the San Francisco Bay Area, but she's also more – and less – than human. Half woman, half air dragon, she's a 'draman' – unable to shift shape but still able to unleash fiery energy. Now something will put her powers to the test.

Mercy's friend Rainey has enlisted her help to solve her sister's murder. Then a horrible accident claims Rainey's life, leaving Mercy only five days to find the killer. If Mercy fails, according to dragon law, Rainey's soul will be doomed to roam the earth for eternity. But how can Mercy help when she herself is a target? With nowhere else to turn, she must join forces with a sexy stranger – the mysterious man they call 'muerte', or death itself, who's as irresistible as he is treacherous. But can even Death keep Mercy alive for long enough to find her answers?

978-0-7499-5307-2

Coming soon from Piatkus, an explosive new series that's packed with everything you could want: a feisty heroine, witches, vampires, werewolves, demons, angels of death, suspense and a whole lot of sexy action . . .

DARKNESS UNBOUND

Born from a lab-enhanced clone mother and an Aedh father, Risa Jones can not only talk to the souls of the dying and the dead, but she can see reapers and walk the grey fields that divide this world from the next. They are skills she rarely uses, however. But when her mother asks her to help the parents of a little girl locked in a coma, she reluctantly agrees. What she discovers terrifies her: someone has ripped the girl's soul from her flesh.

As it turns out, a creature consuming the souls of the innocent – and not so innocent – is the least of her problems. Because someone wants to rip open the gates that divide hell from earth, and Risa is a key component in their plans. And the only person standing between her and disaster is a reaper who isn't exactly on her side.

978-0-7499-5491-8

Do you love fiction with a supernatural twist?

Want the chance to hear news about your favourite authors (and the chance to win free books)?

Keri Arthur

S. G. Browne

P.C. Cast

Christine Feehan

Jacquelyn Frank

Larissa Ione

Sherrilyn Kenyon

Jackie Kessler

Jayne Ann Krentz and Jayne Castle

Martin Millar

Kat Richardson

J.R. Ward

David Wellington

Then visit the Piatkus website and blog
www.piatkus.co.uk | www.piatkusbooks.net

And follow us on Facebook and Twitter
www.facebook.com/piatkusfiction | www.twitter.com/piatkusbooks

piatkus